FUEL TO THE FLAME

Bishop Smoky Mountain Thrillers
Book 2

LAUREN STREET

STERLING & STONE

Prologue

August 5, 2023
Glorietta, Nebraska:

EARL WATSON HAS to sit on Edna's suitcase to get it closed before he can load it into the minivan. Weeding the garden will just have to wait until he gets home from vacation.

Madill, Oklahoma:

Veronica Langley is packing her sexy new black negligee made of lace *and nothing else.* She's sure Jody's going to pop the question as soon as they get back from vacation.

Des Moines, Iowa:

Roger Heywood slams the door to his brand new 2023 Mecredes-Benz sedan in the salesman's face. If this hundred and twenty-five thousand dollar electric car doesn't make six hundred miles on a charge while he's on vacation, he will come back here and shove the car keys down the salesman's throat.

THREE TOURISTS ON VACATION.

BUT EARL ISN'T EVER GOING to weed that garden, Veronica will never see that engagement ring, and Roger won't be shoving car keys down anybody's throat.

They are all vacationing in the Great Smoky Mountains National Park in Tennessee. Within a week, all three of them will be murdered there.

Chapter One

SHE SHOOK her head fiercely to dislodge the tattered, gauzy remnants of sleep so she could focus. That's when she sensed his presence, maybe even smelled him—a sickly sweet aroma like decay.

He's here! In the house!

A clap of thunder rumbled, brutally loud, and she jumped, uttered a little peep of a scream. She scooted to the edge of the bed and stared out her bedroom window where writhing lightning torched the night sky behind the silver worms of rain squiggling down the glass.

How could she possibly have drifted off now? Dropped her guard like that, tonight of all nights?

With her heart banging against the walls of her chest, she struggled to look at every square inch of the room at the same time. Was he actually here maybe even in the bedroom? She began to tremble so violently she was afraid the bedsprings would squeak from the movement. She had to be quiet.

As her eyes darted from the empty doorway to the shadowed dressing table, she heard a sound —

. . .

3

Rap, rap, rap!

Rileigh Bishop almost jumped out of her skin. Someone was rapping their knuckles on her car window. A large woman in a flowered dress and a big hat.

Rileigh reluctantly clicked off the audio book she'd been listening to — it was just getting to the exciting part! — and rolled down her window.

"Can you help me?" the woman pleaded. "Me and Earl is lost."

How could you possibly get lost in Black Bear Forge, Tennessee?

But there were two kinds of lost— the kind where people don't know where they are and the kind where people know where they are, but they can't find where they want to go. This lady was obviously suffering from the affliction of Lost Number Two.

"What is it you're looking for?"

"I'm Edna Watson and that there's my husband, Earl."

The woman gestured to a bespectacled man driving a mini-van with — yep — Nebraska plates. He was wearing a Nebraska Cornhuskers ball cap. Rileigh would bet her pension, which she didn't have anymore because, well, just because, that the man had driven fifteen miles an hour all the way from Knoxville.

"We want to see that building that has a hundred-foot-tall King Kong climbing it. My sister Laverne seen it when she was here. There is such a place, right?"

Rileigh just nodded. The King Kong wasn't quite a hundred feet tall, but a gigantic ape clutching an airplane climbing up the Empire State Building undoubtedly looked that tall to sister Laverne from Nebraska.

"She said it was in Dollywood."

"No, it's in Pigeon Forge, before you get to Dollywood. You'll see it."

A building with King Kong clinging to the side was hard to miss.

"Is there a sign? I'd hate to drive right by it."

"Trust me, you won't. It's right after the Hall of Magic building that's upside down."

"Upside down?"

"The roof is stuck into the ground and the light posts are hanging from the porch floor. If you get to the Alcatraz replica building, or the scale model of the Titanic, or the buildings where you walk in the door through a bear's mouth or through a shark's jaws, you've gone too far."

"How do you get there from here?"

"Don't you have a maps app on your phone?"

The woman bristled. "Don't start with the maps app! My boy Larry says all I got to do is type the address on this little screen and a map will appear and take me right to it. Well, no it don't! The onliest thing it shows is a map with a little red dot with where I am. But I know where I am. I want to see where I'm going."

Rileigh started to explain, then stopped herself.

"I'll make it simple. Just stay on this street." Rileigh pointed down the block. "Going south. The street will turn into a road leading out of town. It's small, it winds and twists, but stay on it, don't turn off anywhere. In about fifteen miles, it will dead end into the highway through Pigeon Forge. You'll see the Hollywood Wax Museum from the intersection."

"Hollywood Wax Museum?"

"That's the building King Kong is climbing."

"Is it worth seeing?"

Nothing in Pigeon Forge was worth seeing. Well, except that little funnel cake shop on Cat Gut Creek that made peach funnel cakes as big a supreme pizza, with fresh peaches and strawberries and whipped cream on top. It took Rileigh, her mother and her Aunt Daisy together to eat a whole one.

Aunt Daisy.

An image flashed through Rileigh's mind like a comet — crazed eyes and a maniacal smile — and then it was gone. Rileigh struggled to refocus and shrugged.

"It's your nickel." Actually, admission to the museum was more like thirty bucks a head. "It's a wax museum, so you can have your picture made sitting on a park bench with Forrest Gump, or singing onstage with Dolly Parton."

"Oh, I'd like that!" The woman turned back to her husband with a scowl. "You think you can stay on this road?"

Her raucous voice reminded Rileigh of blue jays fighting. She leaned in Rileigh's window.

"That man could complicate a one-car funeral. Took the whole weekend just to get here. Here it is Monday already and we ain't seen a thing yet. We'll be lucky if we find Gatlinburg before tomorrow morning."

Then she smiled sweetly. "We're on vacation, you know."

No. Really?

Rileigh didn't say that, of course. It was rude and unkind. If these people were entertained by a Dolly Parton made out of wax, it was, indeed, their nickel. Rileigh just wished they'd go spend it somewhere else.

She watched the woman lumber back to the minivan. The springs on the vehicle sank a little when she got in, then Earl turned the vehicle around in the parking lot and pulled out onto the street *going north*.

Honking the horn on Aunt Daisy's old Honda, Rileigh waved her arms, tried to get his attention to tell him he was going the wrong way, but he drove merrily down the street, got to the corner *and turned off on a side street*.

They might not make it to Gatlinburg before tomorrow after all.

The door to the Souvenirs! Souvenirs! Souvenirs! Store suddenly opened and a family with two little kids emerged. The little boy wore a coon-skin cap made of some furry synthetic material that had never warmed the backside of a live raccoon, and the little girl clutched a bag of "genuine Smoky Mountain salt water taffy". Rileigh loved that taffy. She ate so much of it when she was a kid her dentist predicted she'd have caps on every tooth in her mouth before she was old enough to vote. So her mother switched her to sugarless gum.

Settling back in the seat, Rileigh took out her phone. It was still awkward, to use her left hand with the black brace that extended from the middle of her forearm to her fingers to keep the still-healing bones in her wrist immobile. Her whole hand had been in a cast for two months following the eight-hour surgery required to put it back together after Aunt Daisy had smashed it with a sledge hammer.

Rileigh had been just about helpless when she came home from the hospital four months ago. Her left hand was in a cast, and the index finger on her right hand had been broken and was in a splint— separate incidents. Her mother Lily looked after her, helped her do the really arduous tasks like washing her long, chestnut hair — she'd been tempted to get it cut in a pixie to make the process easier. Taking a shower was suddenly damn near impossible thanks to the boxing glove on her hand. Coming in a close second was getting dressed. Of course, the cast wouldn't fit through the sleeves of anything she owned, so she'd taken to dressing in surgical scrubs, which would fit over anything — and which hung on her skinny frame like an oversized raincoat on a hanger.

And that, of course, gave her an excuse to stay home, not go out or see anybody— which suited her just fine. Because she had more healing to do than just the bones in her hand re-knitting. Daisy's nightmare attack had come within seconds of costing Rileigh her life. The sight of the old woman coming at her with the chainsaw raised above her head, a strand of drool inching down her chin and a maniacal look of smiling lunacy stamped on her features, still haunted the dark passageways of Rileigh's mind. She'd been plagued with debilitating rounds of PTSD. She'd had those when she'd come home from Afghanistan too, but this was different, worse in the most painful of ways, because she hadn't been fighting for her life with some anonymous enemy. She had almost been murdered by the old lady who used to braid her hair when she was a little girl and always helped her find the prize egg every Easter.

Rileigh tapped the Audio Books Galore app on her phone. It sent her to the book title, *The Last Safe Place*. It had been one of those 99-cents books and that mattered because she blew through audio books like Sherman through Atlanta. There wasn't a whole lot else to do while you were on a stakeout. You had to keep your eyes—

The door of the store opened again and Rileigh tensed, but this time it was an old man with a cane, chewing on a block of peanutbutter fudge, gumming it actually, which was fine because that stuff would *melt in your mouth.*

Before the door closed behind him, Rileigh caught a glimpse of the woman she was being paid to watch behind the counter. June Anderson was an attractive woman in her mid-thirties who might or might not be running around on her husband. Thomas Anderson had paid Rileigh's employer, The Good GI's — Gatlinburg Investigations—

to run a surveillance on her and Rileigh had snagged the assignment, her first since going back to work.

So far, it had been boring as hell.

She hoped it would stay that way.

Chapter Two

YARMOUTH COUNTY TENNESSEE Sheriff Mitchell Webster pulled his cruiser up to one of the two gasoline pumps in the lot of the Quik Stop convenience store on the edge of Black Bear Forge and got out. He took the handle from the pump, selected the kind of gasoline, unscrewed the gas cap and began to pump gas, looking up at the sky as he did. It was overcast, which meant the meteor shower watchers were likely to be disappointed tonight. But it could clear. No way to know.

Storms could pop up in the mountains in a matter of minutes. Rain like you'd best get out into the yard and start building an ark, but then it would clear to blue sky and puffy white clouds in less than an hour.

A minivan pulled up beside the sheriff's cruiser and the passenger window rolled down.

"I need help!" said the woman inside, who didn't appear to be in any immediate danger.

"Help for what?"

"We're lost. Again."

She cast a scathing glance at the driver, an older man

who wore what Mitch suspected was a permanent look of patient forbearance on his face and a baseball cap with Nebraska Cornhuskers emblazoned on the front. The woman wore no hat, but bore the marks of one recently taken off. Her hair was mashed flat in a circle around the top of her head.

"Where do you want to go?"

"Well, I woulda told you we wanted to see that King Kong climbing up a building, but that ship done sailed for me. If that lady with the brace on her arm hadn't told us there really was such a thing, I'd suspect my sister just made it up."

"Lady with a brace?"

"Yeah, she was parked outside the Souvenirs! Souvenirs! Souvenirs! shop. She had Tennessee plates and just, you know, looked like she was local, so we asked her how to find it. She was real nice."

Mitch smiled. "Brown hair, green eyes?"

"You know her?"

"Yeah."

"See!" she said triumphantly to Earl. "This here is a small town after all! I told Earl it was, that all these mountains was just like Glorietta, just ordinary people, but when we got here and seen the crowds, we thought maybe we'd come to the wrong mountains."

"Most of the people you've seen are here on vacation. Like you must be."

"We haven't had a vacation in—"

And she was off to the races. After a long, detailed description of how the roof leaked in that motel room at Niagara Falls, she paused to draw a breath and Mitch saw his chance.

"What did you come here to see and how can I help you find it?"

"Like I said, we ain't looking anymore. Them narrow winding roads made me car sick. Earl had to pull over and I upchucked my breakfast pancakes on a flat rock."

Thanks for that visual.

"I'm wore out. We just want to go back to the motel room outside Knoxville. Earl needs to rest, too. He got hurt last year in a fire— he's a retired fire fighter, you know— and after that he never did quite get his strength back. So I told him, I said, 'Earl, you got to retire now so we can travel like you been promising me we'd do for thirty years.' So he retired about six months ago and we been—"

"A motel in Knoxville, you say. Is it on the Interstate?"

Earl spoke for the first time. "It's right off I-40, a Motel 6."

"Tom Bodette leaves the light on for you," Edna added.

"It's easy to get to the road leading to the interstate from here." Mitch gave the directions to the dithered woman and the exhausted man. But if Rileigh had already given them directions, there wasn't much hope they wouldn't get lost again.

"You got that Earl?" the woman asked.

"Yes, dear."

The sarcasm blew right by Edna.

"I need to pee before we get on the road."

All the spaces in front of the store were taken, so Earl drove the minivan to the edge of the parking lot in front of the store. Signs protruded from the building on both sides — Ladies on the right, Men on the left.

Edna got out and headed right. Earl headed left. Mitch caught Earl's eye for a moment, just a passing thing, and cast him a commiserating look. They connected for that instant and Earl nodded his thanks for Mitch's help. A tiny

12

frozen moment in time before Mitch went inside to pay for his fuel.

Mitch considered Sundeep Singh, the owner of the store, a friend. They had a mutual love of the Pittsburgh Pirates baseball team and Mitch wondered if Sundeep was as disappointed as Mitch was with the team's performance this year.

He stepped into the cool interior of the store and was greeted by the mouth-watering aroma of the hot dogs, brats and burgers Sundeep's wife cooked in the small kitchen. Making his way through a small crowd of sunburned tourists to the back of the store, he got a soft drink out of the cooler and selected a bag of peanuts from the rack, then got in line at the register.

"How about them Bucs?" he said when it was his turn, setting the soft drink and peanuts down. Sundeep smiled ruefully and shook his head.

"Last week, they couldn't have beat the Little Sisters of the Poor."

As Sundeep added the purchase to his gasoline, Mitch tore open the bag of peanuts and poured a handful into his palm.

"You see Bednar against the Padres? Bases loaded, bottom of the ninth, and he was throwing heat a hundred miles an hour."

"They say that new pitcher they drafted can hit a hundred and three and—"

Sundeep trailed off as he stared out the windows behind Mitch and a grimace of horror suddenly took over his face. Mitch turned around to see what Sundeep was looking at and only caught a glimpse of the flaming figure before the screaming started.

It was shrieking, a sound of tortured agony that rose to a screech and stayed there. Mitch dropped the handful of peanuts, shoved two teenagers out of his way, and ran toward the front door as what appeared to be a man on fire staggered and fell in the parking lot.

What happened after that was a blur in Mitch's mind. It seemed to take forever, but it was over in seconds. The shrieking cut off abruptly as the man collapsed in a burning heap on the asphalt. The handful of people in the parking lot were backing away in horror.

Mitch shoved open the heavy glass door and started toward the ball of flames, knowing the man was beyond anybody's help, when another scream, higher pitched and hysterical, came from the other side of the parking lot. Edna was running way faster than she ought to be able to run, her arms flung wide, toward the man in flames, screaming, "Earl! Earl!"

Mitch pivoted and ran to intercept Edna before she got to her flaming husband. He barely made it in time to grab her before she threw herself on his burning body and gathered him into her arms. It was like tackling a charging rhino. Screaming, she fought him, clawed at him, struggled to get away with the strength of a druggie on meth.

"Earl! Earl baby!"

"Edna, no!"

Sundeep appeared out of nowhere with the fire blanket from his kitchen. He threw it over the charred-black body at the center of a ball of fire and folded it around Earl, smothering the flames.

Mitch let go of Edna when he was sure the flames had been extinguished, and she ran to where Earl lay, smoke coming out from under the edges of the blanket, the stench of cooked flesh, burning hair and gasoline, was overwhelming.

"Earl!" she wailed. She dropped to her knees beside him, tilted her head back and uttered a cry, a wild Jurassic sound that trailed off into something like a howl. Then she began sobbing hysterically. The bystanders crept slowly toward the burning man. Several had their phones out, videoing the carnage.

"What the——?" Sundeep said from beside Mitch.

Mitch didn't respond. He grabbed the mic attached to a strap on his shoulder, pressed the button and spoke urgently into it as he retraced Earl's route across the parking lot to the side of the building where the men's restroom was located.

"This is Unit One. Code 8, repeat Code 8 at the Quik Stop Convenience Store on Bent Stump Road." He was requesting immediate backup. "I have a 10-52, dispatch Code 2, 10-45D."

That was telling the dispatcher to dispatch an ambulance, urgent but not emergency, because the patient was deceased.

"I also have a 951, dispatch Code 3." He wanted a fire marshal on the scene *ASAP.* The last request would be forwarded to Gatlinburg, the nearest location big enough for a fire department with a fire marshal.

"Roger that," said the dispatcher, who then repeated the message.

Mitch followed the sidewalk toward the men's room door. A puddle of flaming gasoline lay just outside it. Above the door was metal scaffolding. Sundeep had been repainting the building. A ladder led from the scaffolding to the ground near the back of the building. Mitch walked to the corner of the building, careful to disturb nothing as he peered around the corner. Behind the building was a gravel parking lot. It was empty.

Mitch returned to the still-smoldering figure under the fire blanket and his grieving wife as the first wailing cry of an ambulance sliced through the humid night air.

"What just happened here?" Sundeep asked, sounding a lot steadier than Mitch felt.

Mitch glanced toward the left side of the building. He spoke slowly to keep his own voice from shaking.

"If I had to guess right now, I'd say somebody doused Earl in gasoline — maybe threw it on him, maybe poured it on him from scaffolding above the men's room door — then struck a match."

"But why?" It was as much a plea as a question.

Other sirens joined the first from all directions in a symphony of alarm and horror.

"I've got absolutely no idea." He shifted his gaze from the dead man covered in a fire blanket to Sundeep's chocolate brown eyes. "But I *will* find out."

Chapter Three

RILEIGH ADJUSTED the earbuds in her ears. She was almost finished with the book and she'd soon be looking for another one. During the two weeks she'd been shadowing June Anderson, she had listened to seven books. She always picked big books. That was the first thing she looked at on the list of books— how long was it? There were certain authors you could count on to deliver door-stop books. One of them was Stephen King, and she'd just finished listening to *Billy Sommers* and *The Fairytale*. She had long ago consumed the *Game of Thrones* series and *The Outlander* series, and she had dabbled a bit in Brian Sanderson's fantasy novels.

She hadn't listened to *The Lord of the Rings* books on audio, though. She had binge read the whole three-book series over a long weekend the day after it was assigned when she was in college. Every. Single. Word. Since then, she had read the series sixteen times. Well, at least sixteen times. She had made a mark in the back of *Return of the King* whenever she finished it and she had three sets of five marks and one lone mark before the book cover fell off.

Rileigh tapped the audio book app, and the book began to play where it had left off.

THE SOUND she heard was the creak of the second stair tread. Someone was coming upstairs!

She grabbed the telephone on the nightstand beside the bed, wrestled the receiver off the cradle with shaking hands and put it to her ear. No dial tone. She stifled a small sob and felt around for her iPhone. She located it—whimpering now—picked it up and then fumbled it in her shaking hands. It fell into her rumpled sheets and she dug around frantically trying to find it in the dark. Wanting to scream but knowing she couldn't.

Run!

No, hide!

Which?

RILEIGH'S PHONE jangled in her hand, cutting off the audio book mid-sentence. She jumped She didn't recognize the number. She sat very still staring at it as the phone rang again. The area code was Texas. Which was a considerable land mass, and whoever was calling could have been anywhere in the two hundred and fifty thousand plus square miles of it.

The phone rang again, and still she hesitated. Crank callers get their jollies by upsetting the person they've called. All you had to do was ignore them and you took all the fun out of their stupid prank, then they'd hang up. No actor stays on stage after the audience has left. The most reasonable, rational thing to do — if the calls bothered her so much — was to block the number. Easy peasy. But she didn't block the number, she merely sat staring at it as the phone rang again.

She had been getting calls from this number for two months. They started when she still had a boxing glove on her left hand and it was awkward to hold the phone in her right hand with the boxing glove on it.

She remembered the first time she'd gotten the call. She had been sitting on the silent porch swing on her front porch, actually relaxed for a change, staring at the fireflies blinking on and off in the black velvet night. She'd felt good, and that was something, because in the two months since her aunt had tried to kill her, she hadn't had very many good days. Then the phone had rung. She didn't know the number, probably a telemarketer. She decided she'd enjoy taking one of them on, getting into a shouting match with some AI drone that existed only in the bowels of a laptop in Bangladesh.

"Hello."

Silence.

"Hello!"

More silence, but it wasn't empty silence, the sound of a broken connection or no connection at all. It was the silence of someone holding a phone but saying nothing.

"Hey, douche bag, what do you want?"

Nothing. Just full silence, silence that seemed to be jammed with meaning. Why, it could—

She immediately disconnected the call, her heart pounding. What was wrong with her? How could she still be fixated on her missing sister after thirty years. Three decades was a little long to leave the light on in the window.

No. It was just a wrong number, that's all. And she had written it off. A few days later, the same number called again. She recognized the number this time, the mysterious somebody somewhere in Texas who wouldn't talk.

"Hello."

Silence.

But Rileigh could swear she could hear breathing. That was nuts. You couldn't hear breathing on a cell phone, and certainly not one that didn't have particularly good reception. She was not hearing breathing. Except she was. She spoke one more time, but got no reply so she hung up.

After that, when the number called, Rileigh merely punched the green button. She said nothing. So the call was silence on her end and a matching silence on the other end. Eventually, she saw that as a sick game she didn't want to play, so she would refuse every call from that number. But she never blocked the number, couldn't bring herself to block the number, because you never knew who might be out there reaching out.

The phone rang again, then her voice mail kicked in. "Hi, this is Rileigh. Leave me a message and I'll call you back."

No message. Just silence.

As usual.

About a year after her sister's murder, Rileigh received a postcard. No writing, just a smiley face on the back. She'd gotten a new postcard every year since, each time from a different place. The last postcard Rileigh had gotten had been postmarked Venezuela. But this call wasn't coming from Venezuela. It was coming from Texas.

Which was more or less between Tennessee and Venezue—

Stop it!

She ground her teeth. This was sick and sad, and she was masochistic to keep answering the phone, to keep fulfilling some sicko's fantasies. She should just block the number. Stop the calls and move on.

But she didn't.

Jillian was not out there somewhere. She was dead. Aunt Daisy had confessed to killing her.

When Rileigh was six years old she had gone into Jillian's bedroom on the night before her big sister's wedding. But instead of tucking a school picture and a note that said, "Please don't forget me" into Jillian's suitcase, Rileigh had walked into a murder scene. Blood everywhere, and a severed tongue neatly placed almost reverently on a pristine white pillow

Nobody had believed her then and she had nobody she cared to convince now— but she hadn't imagined it. She had seen the scene where her sister had been murdered.

Which meant that her sister was dead, gone.

So why wouldn't Rileigh block the calls from?

She didn't have a reason. She just *couldn't.*

Rileigh gritted her teeth and forcefully willed the images out of her mind. She absolutely would not allow herself to conjure up fantasies of her sister sitting on a beach in Venezuela, sipping a Mai Tai, getting a tan. The woman in the fantasy she absolutely refused to allow entrance into her brain has blonde hair the color of butter, a thick mane of it and when she tosses her head just right, it surrounds her head like a halo. Like the halo around her head the day she picked Rileigh up off the floor of the coat closet. Blonde hair and blue eyes and a face like an angel. And the woman sitting there, sipping the Mai Tai, reaches for her cell phone, picks it up and punches "favorites." The first name on the list of favorites, is "Rileigh." She pauses, looks at it, then touches it with the tip of a finger.

Rileigh wouldn't allow herself to picture the woman listening to the distant ringing on her phone. Wouldn't allow herself to imagine the clicking in the receiver, wouldn't conjure up her own face, sitting here in her aunt's car in front of the Souvenirs! Souvenirs! Souvenirs! store, doing surveillance on a woman who either was or was not screwing around on her husband. But she did conjure up her own face, and when she did she saw the ridiculous look of hope on it. She saw herself say, "Hello," in the expectant voice of somebody who absolutely can't wait for the reply.

The woman sipping the mai tai listens to the voice say hello. Again and again. But she says nothing. She just listens to the voice and when the line disconnects, the woman punches the red button, puts the phone down, sniffs, and reaches up to wipe the tears under her blue eyes.

Well, if that's the fantasy you're not having, I'd like to see the one you are having.

Rileigh literally shook her head to fling out the images, picked up a quarter from the tray beside the console and tried to walk it across the knuckles of the fingers on her left hand. She'd been able to do that before — she skipped over the memories of the agonizing pain, and concentrated on manipulating the quarter. You had to get it just right, lift your finger up just so to make the coin fall all the way over onto the top of the knuckle next to it.

She wasn't that coordinated yet, though. She tried half a dozen times and dropped the coin every time. Someday, with sufficient physical therapy, she would again have total mobility in the crushed hand. Now, she consoled herself with moving the quarter across the knuckles of her right hand, hopped gaily from the top of one to—

The door to the store opened and June Anderson stepped out. Rileigh looked at her watch. Where had the day gone? Time had just evaporated. But that was better than dragging through a stakeout, checking your watch every ten minutes to see if it was time to leave. June turned back to the door and locked it, then headed out to her car in the parking lot, got in and drove away.

And that was like the last bell of the day in elementary school, signaling that Rileigh could go home.

Chapter Four

RILEIGH TURNED into the driveway leading to her house and performed the tactical driving maneuver necessary to make it up the steep incline without flying over the big lump of rock at the top and into the fence around the front yard. It took considerable skill, particularly when she had to do it one-handed.

As soon as the house came into view, her eyes searched the front porch, looking in the rocking chairs and at the porch swing, seeking out the image of the woman who wouldn't be there. Aunt Daisy.

She hated herself for being unable to control the urge to look for her in all the places she should be, places she wasn't and never would be again. Aunt Daisy was in the North Tennessee Psychiatric Hospital's criminally insane unit and she would remain there for the rest of her life. She had killed Tina Montgomery, tried to kill Rileigh, and had confessed to killing Rileigh's older sister, Jillian, thirty years ago. She'd also told them where they could dig up the body. But when they dug up the floor in the workroom, there was no sign there'd ever been a body there.

So the question remained, hung around Rileigh like a swarm of gnats. Was her sister dead? Had Aunt Daisy killed her as she said she had done, but buried her body somewhere else and then as dementia warped and twisted her brain, she forgot where?

Right. You commit murder, but forget where you left the body. Like not being able to find your sunglasses or your car keys.

Pulling the car to a stop in front of the fence, Rileigh tried to shake off the miasma of feelings that now flowed over her, into her and out of her, every time she came home.

It had not always been like that. She loved her home. She loved the mountains rising up all around it, the smell of cedar and pine trees, and air so clean and fresh it might have been scrubbed with lye soap and hung out on the line to dry in the sunshine.

That house had been her refuge more than a decade ago when she returned home after two tours in Iraq and Afghanistan, depressed and almost suicidal. That house had been the balm her soul needed. She had rested there, and the mountains had restored her. She had been whole again when she left to go to the Tennessee State Police Academy. Whole when she went to work as a patrol officer for the Memphis, Tennessee, Police Department.

And when that world came crashing down on her head almost a year ago, she had come back home again, praying that the healing force that had made her whole before would do so again. She had started to heal, felt confident enough in her own stability to take a job as a detective for the Good GIs Detective Agency in Gatlinburg.

Then the world fell apart again. (Third time's the charm?) She'd been helping the new sheriff in town figure out who'd killed Tina Montgomery and had pushed her aunt off the cliff of sanity down into the crazy abyss below.

Daisy had tried to kill Rileigh with a chainsaw and very nearly succeeded. She did succeed in smashing Rileigh's left hand with a sledgehammer. Four months later, Rileigh still had a brace on her arm to immobilize her left wrist.

Now she was clawing her way back out of a very dark place. But the darkness was not some distant spot out on the flat. It was right here in her own home. Her refuge now conjured up its own horrific images to haunt her.

Like the image of Aunt Daisy, sitting in the rocker next to the porch swing in the evenings, knitting. What passed for knitting for Aunt Daisy merely required tangling yarn into indiscernible lumps, but the activity had made her happy. She was happy most of the time now, Rileigh's mother reported after visits with her sister. Apparently Daisy had decided that the other women in her ward in the mental hospital were her sisters, all named for flowers. So the bouquet was together again in Daisy's mind, and all was right with her world.

Oh, how Rileigh yearned for everything to be right in her own world. She ached to be free of the ghosts. Jillian. Aunt Daisy. And a little boy lying in a puddle of blood on a Memphis sidewalk.

She parked her car, which had belonged to Aunt Daisy. But Daisy had gotten one of the Houlihan boys to cut the brake lines on Rileigh's car and she'd crashed it into a tree, so it was a fair trade.

As soon as she turned off the engine, her mother materialized on the front porch. Rileigh had been so deep in thought — no, so busy throwing herself a pity party — that she hadn't heard the porch screen door bang shut behind her.

Mama was beaming. She was still a beautiful woman

even at 72 and she always kept herself up, wore makeup, fixed her hair and dressed like she was on her way to her job at the Great Smoky Mountains National park office instead of staying home and not seeing a soul all day.

"You look like the cat that swallowed the canary," Rileigh said as she opened the front gate and went up the stone pathway to the front porch.

"Maybe I did!" her mother said, then she giggled. Actually giggled. That was odd. Only a half bubble off plumb, but still not quite right.

"So give, what's up?"

"I'll tell you all about it at dinner. I've got a big pot of pinto beans on the stove, been cooking since I got up this morning. And I'm gonna make cornbread." Then, without missing a beat, she added. "Would you go out to the garage and get the chainsaw for me?"

Rileigh almost choked.

"Get you *what?*"

"The chainsaw, sweetie. I've decided to cut down that rose bush." She pointed to the big flowering bush by the front gate. "Rhett doesn't like roses."

The whole thing was such a non sequitur that Rileigh didn't know whether to wind her watch or take third base. She could only stammer, "Who's Rhett?"

"I'll tell you all about it at supper. Now, off you go." She made shooing motions with her hands. "Bring me the saw."

Rileigh backed down the porch steps in something approaching shock, heading around the side of the house toward the garage. Then she stopped and stood there long enough for her mother to forget she'd told Rileigh to go get the chainsaw so she could cut down a rosebush. Like Rileigh was going to hand a 72-year-old woman a chainsaw! — *Here ya go, Mama. Try not to cut your leg off with it.*

Rileigh had only been in the garage once since the night her aunt tried to kill her there. And that time, Georgia had forced her to go. Had literally dragged her into the garage, because that's where the foldable lawn chairs were stored, and Georgia was absolutely determined to drag Rileigh kicking and screaming out of her funk.

Her method of extracting Rileigh from her self-imposed prison was to haul Rileigh along with her and the kids to Clingman's Dome to see the meteor shower. It wasn't the big one, the Perseid Meteor shower that occurs every year in July and August. A meteor shower is visible from anywhere on earth, of course. But in cities, bright lights and pollution mess with the view. So tourists from nearby Knoxville, Nashville, Chattanooga, even as far away as Atlanta, flock to the mountains to see it, where the air's so clear and the sky so black it looks like you could pick the falling stars out of the sky like blackberries off a bush.

This year, there had been smaller meteor showers all spring and that night's was predicted to be a particularly big one. It had been a typically chaotic, totally miserable time with five undisciplined children, a nerve-grating, annoying, make-you-want-to-pull-your-hair-out experience.

It had been just the medicine Rileigh needed.

Chapter Five

"*I AM NOT GOING.*"

"*The hell you're not.*"

"*The hell I am!*"

Georgia changes tactics. Instead of bullying Rileigh into accompanying her and all five children to Clingman's Dome, she resorts to emotional blackmail.

"*What happened to 'I'll help you any way I can?' I'm asking for help. So help!*"

Rileigh had promised she would do anything she could to help her best friend after Georgia kicked her cheating husband out of the house. Raising five children alone was a daunting task and Rileigh really wanted to help her out. Just not like this.

"*I can't. I wouldn't be any help with this thing on my arm.*" *The thing was a black brace, the last of the various casts that'd been used to keep her shattered hand in place so the bones could heal.*

"*You've got one good hand. Together we have three hands and alone I only have two. Come on!*"

Rileigh knows that Georgia is asking for Rileigh's benefit, not Georgia's. In truth, having Rileigh along will likely end up with Georgia managing six kids instead of five. But Rileigh also knows that there is no excuse big and bad enough to get her out of this. Only a death certificate, a recent one, would be sufficient.

"Okay, fine. But when you discover I'm more trouble than I'm worth, you'll be sorry you dragged me into this."

Georgia only smiles.

The drive to Clingman's Dome is a preview of coming attractions. The kids scream at each other and fight the whole way, with Georgia launching ineffective, "you boys behave," and "stop hitting your brother," and threats of "I'll pull over," which even the three-year-old knows is a bluff because the winding mountain road between Rileigh's house and Clingman's Dome offers nowhere to pull over. Five-hundred-foot drop-offs or rock walls line most of the way up the mountain.

Clingman's Dome is the highest spot in Tennessee and on the Appalachian Trail. It's second to Mt. Mitchell as the highest peak east of the Mississippi River. As part of Great Smoky Mountains National Park, Clingmans Dome is famous for its concrete observation tower that offers a majestic view of the Smokies in all directions. On a clear day you can see a hundred miles, into seven states. The mountain stands prominently above the surrounding terrain, rising nearly five thousand feet from base to summit.

As soon as they turn off onto the seven-mile Clingman's Dome Road, the are-we-there-yets begin. Liam is eleven years old. Both he and Conner, nine, are old enough to read the signs. They know we're not there yet, but they lead the communal whine anyway and Rileigh knows it is a deliberate effort to weaponize their younger siblings against the common enemy— authority. Not just Georgia, but anybody "in charge." It's just what kids do. It's in their DNA and controls them on a chromosomal level.

Just past Newfound Gap, they turn into the Forney Ridge Parking Area. It's about three hundred fifty feet below the summit. A steep, half-mile paved trail spirals up from the parking lot to the forty-five foot circular observation tower at the top of the mountain. There's also a small visitor information center and park store staffed by the

Great Smoky Mountains Association, garbage cans, and benches —
lots of benches— on the sides of the path.

And, of course, vault toilet restrooms, the waterless kind. The
kids make a bee line to the toilets, leaving Georgia behind yelling,
"Liam, make sure Mason gets his pants all the way down before he
pees," and "Eli and Conner— no fighting, I'm warning you."

Georgia takes Mayella into the ladies' bathroom, providing
Rileigh a few blessed moments of peace during which she frantically
tries to think of some way to get out of this. Fake a broken ankle, no,
just sprained. But if Georgia didn't buy the ruse she'd be pissed that
Rileigh came up with it, and if she did believe the ruse, she'd have to
take Rileigh and five disappointed children back home — a car ride
which would approximate one of Dante's Seven Levels of Hell.

Though the summit of Clingman's Dome provided a panoramic
view of the whole mountain range, it's possible to look up and see
the sky clearly, with no obstructing trees, from anywhere along the
whole half mile of paved walkway. That's why Clingman's Dome
is the ideal spot to watch a meteor shower. The half mile of trail
will hold thousands of tourists during the Perseid meteor shower
later in the summer, but Rileigh is surprised to see a sizable crowd
assembling for the smaller version that'll be visible as soon as it gets
dark.

The first kerfuffle of the evening involves Mason, whose zipper
gets caught in his underwear when he goes to the bathroom. The child
collapses in a total meltdown, dragging two of his three older brothers
down into the depths of tantrum-dom with him.

"It's Eli's fault. He pulled on it and—" Mason begins.

"I did not!" Eli responds.

"Did too."

"Did not. Liam was the one yanking on it."

"I was not!"

"Was, too."

"Was not!"

Mayella begins to scream at that point and Georgia cuts the argument short by dispatching Liam to the car to bring back the bananas she forgot.

They haven't made it a single foot out onto the half mile ramp and already Rileigh's nerves are shot.

"Having fun yet?" Georgia prods.

Rileigh considers punching her in the face.

The instant Liam returns with the sack of bananas, Rileigh challenges him and Eli to race each other up the ramp to the next set of benches. Once they have gone bounding off through the gathering crowd, Rileigh takes Conner by one hand and Mason by the other and tells them that if they let go of her hand, she will pick them up and toss them over the concrete sidewall of the trail. The children must sense Rileigh's close-to-the-breaking-point desperation. They shoot looks at their mother, who merely makes a gesture of something falling off a high place and splatting on the ground, and the two little boys fall immediately into line. Georgia shoves the next banana into Mayella's mouth before she has time to consider whether or not to start screaming, then takes her hand, and the little six-person army sets out for the observation deck.

By the time it's dark enough to actually see anything, the Stump family plus Rileigh, has staked out a claim on a bench near the summit, setting the lawn chairs around it and parking the two smallest children there. After Georgia drags Eli down off the concrete wall he's walking along, Mayella sees her first falling star and squeals, "I seed one. I seed one."

The whole crowd grows hushed.

The sky lights up.

The children are spellbound.

Rileigh is beginning to uncoil and relax.

That's when the crazy man who'd been standing against the wall out of the flow of human traffic begins to shout.

"That there's the fire of God, falling down out of the sky to strike down the unrighteous," he calls out with the kind of creepy urgency you associate with lunatics and serial killers.

The children ignore him.

He's a big man, at least six feet four. His arms and the back of his neck are covered in thick black hair and you can see his chest hair sticking out of the neck of his tee shirt. It certainly must form a single thick rug from his chest up his neck, but you can't tell because his mostly gray beard is huge, hangs down his chest halfway to his belt buckle, spreading out over his considerable belly. Black hair liberally sprinkled with gray sticks out from under a floppy gray/green fisherman's hat. He's wearing bib overalls with a white tee shirt underneath. Both are clean, though, even look like they've been ironed. His eyes are black coals buried under a heavy black unibrow.

As the meteorites continue to flash across the sky, the big man becomes more and more agitated. At first he just paces back and forth, up and down the enclosed concrete walkway, talking to himself, mumbling gibberish interspersed with phrases like "wrath of God" and "spawn of Satan" and "Armageddon, when the four horsemen of the apocalypse will ride."

In his heedless pacing, he manages to bump into Mason and knock him off his feet. The little boy lets out a howl like he'd just stuck his leg in a woodchipper. His mother and Rileigh know the boy is a drama king, and are unsurprised by the outburst. The man, however, instantly leaps forward and sets Mason back on his feet and then begins to yell at him.

"You got to stop sniveling and get tough, boy, if you're gonna survive what's coming." Pointing a finger toward the display of light in the sky, he says, "God's done had his fill of the evil of this world. God's going to rain fire down out of heaven just like that right there. Fire that will set the whole world ablaze." He takes Mason by the shoulders. "Are you listenin' to me son, are you prepared to be burned alive?"

Mason's face is white, his eyes huge. He is utterly terrified.

Rileigh takes two steps, grabs the man's wrist from behind with her one functional hand and twists his arm up behind his back in a movement that is almost too quick to follow. Pushing it higher up his back, she forces the man to bend at the waist in an effort to relieve the pressure.

"Now you listen to me," she says into his hairy ear. The intensity of the words more than make up for the lack of volume. "If you touch that child again, if you come anywhere near him, I will break your arm." She shoves hard on his bent arm, pushes it higher and higher up his back until he can't suppress a grunt of pain. "If that doesn't impress you, I will shove the business end of my nine millimeter Glock up your left nostril and blow your brains out the top of your head." She gives that a beat or two to soak in, then says. "Now, go. Walk away now. Or get carried away later."

She pushes the pinned arm up his back one final time, then sticks her foot out and shoves him. The big man trips over her foot and crashes to the pavement.

Gathering Mason to her side, Rileigh turns her back on the man and pilots Mason to the bench on the other side of the walkway where Georgia and the other four children have been watching in gap-jawed amazement. When she sees the looks on their faces, she's suddenly embarrassed.

"That's not nearly as impressive as it looked. He's big but—"

"Yeah like he's got twelve inches and a hundred pounds on you."

"He's big and clumsy, slow, too, with lousy reflexes, and I surprised him." She gestures toward the sky and tells the children. "That up there is what we came here to see and — look! That one is huge."

The kids reengage with the meteor shower and Georgia gives Rileigh an are-you-okay look over their heads. Rileigh gives her a thumbs up with her trembling right hand. Then she pastes a smile on her face like applying a bandage to a wound.

Thank God the man didn't call her bluff.

As she stands with her best friend and five little kids, watching the comets streak across the velvet black sky, Rileigh realizes that she is back. She didn't see it happen, wasn't aware of the shift until it was complete and she was safely on the other side. She no longer feels

34

empty deep down in her gut. Aunt Daisy's attempt to kill her had done fundamental, foundational damage to her soul and she had dug an emotional hole, crawled in and pulled the dirt in after her.

But her best friend, Georgia, had used a little kid's plastic shovel to dig her out.

Rileigh takes in a deep breath of the pine scented night air and is glad to be alive.

Chapter Six

ANGUS PARK BACKED away from the skinny woman who had moves like Chuck Norris. Who was she? He'd find out. You needed to find out about people like her, dangerous people, folks so far outside the will of God they probably didn't even have a celestial area code.

He burped out a laugh at the idea. Celestial area code. That was a good one. He'd tell Sarah about that one when he got home.

Then the good humor drained out of him as his mind returned to the portends of the future falling out of the sky all around. God was announcing the end of the world, and wasn't nothing humorous about that. God was warning the righteous, telling them to get their lives right, just like He'd warned people in Noah's day to confess their sins and turn from their wickedness.

Them people didn't listen, and they all died. Angus didn't think the people here would listen either, even as they watched God's wrath fall in flaming arrows out of the sky. If they didn't, they'd all die too.

That's all he'd been trying to tell that little boy. He was

just trying to warn him, get him to understand that the end of all things was upon them. It was time now for everybody to pick a side. Either you was on God's side or you wasn't. The almighty king of the universe didn't hold with folks who wanted to sit on the fence.

Angus stepped back out of the way of a young woman pushing a stroller with a crying baby past him and on up the walkway. He leaned back against the concrete railing and folded his arms across his chest. When he did, he felt the scars. Big gray raised welts on his arm, they wasn't like normal skin. When it got cold in the wintertime, they turned a sick bluish-white color, he supposed because there was no flow of blood through scars.

They'd started out bright red. When he'd put the white hot poker out of the fireplace to the tender skin of his arm to mark the end of the world coming, he had never considered that it had take so long. But to God, a human lifetime is so short it flashes by almost too quick for God to notice.

Angus had thought the world would end immediately when the fire began to fall from heaven. His grandfather had said so. Angus never imagined he would be scarred from the wounds because he knew the world would come to an end before his body had time to heal. He'd been wrong about that part, but he'd been just a kid then, a scared kid who was certain he had only a few days left to live.

Angus sits spellbound, staring up at the night sky. He is so frightened he might wet his pants. Maybe he already has wet his pants. He doesn't know, doesn't care. All that matters is the words his grandfather is speaking in the thunderous voice like must have belonged to the likes of Moses or Jeremiah or Isaiah.

"Look to the skies my children, look and see your doom raining down on your head."

Angus looks up into the velvet darkness and sees the flaming arrows, tries to imagine them being launched from the celestial bows of the Angel Gabriel or Michael. Tries to see beyond the black sky into the fiery glow of heaven itself, where the angels are standing in mighty rows, armed for battle with shining swords and crowns of gold and diamonds.

"God will wipe the unrighteous off the face of the earth. He will cleanse the world of all iniquity and evil. He will purge the rot from the human race in one mighty cataclysmic fire that will consume all but his own children. God's children can stand unafraid in the flames that are to come. Not so much as a single hair on their heads will be singed."

Grandfather continued to speak as the fire fell from the sky, and Angus sat huddled up against his older sister, Sarah, so frightened he knows he must be trembling. But Sarah holds him so tight he doesn't move.

Until their Aunt Fiona died last Christmas, the two of them spent summers with her in Memphis, where the city lights made it almost impossible to see the stars at all. Neither of them has ever seen anything like the flaming arrows from heaven. Grandfather warned his congregation every Sunday about the dangers of sin and the rewards of living a righteous life. And Angus has paid attention, didn't drift off to sleep during the sermons like his little sisters, or cut up and be disrespectful like his older brothers, who tore tiny pieces of paper off the pages in the hymnals, wadded them up into spitballs and launched them from the back of the church at their friends. Sometimes they missed, hit one of the elders. Once they hit Sister Hermoine and she jumped — likely woke her up — and cried out.

Grandfather had stopped the sermon, stopped right in mid-sentence and demanded that Caleb, Amos and Stephen come forward. The boys filed out of the back pew and walked down the center aisle with their heads down, like condemned men marching to the gallows.

38

Grandfather had sent Amos outside to get a limb off the willow tree, and he made the three boys lean over and grab their ankles. Then he beat them with the limb, right there in front of the whole congregation, brought it down on their legs and butts and backs until the three of them— all teenagers— were on their knees begging for mercy.

Angus had never had the desire to be disobedient like his brothers. The fear of the Lord was in him — had always been within him — and he would no more have dared to defy God than he'd have dared to take a swan dive off Tucker Ridge. Because he believed with all his heart and soul that God was watching him every second of every day and would smite him down if he committed some grievous sin.

Grandfather had brought the family out into the yard that evening and preached a sermon about the retribution of God right there under the stars, pointing out the falling fire as evidence that God was, indeed, preparing them for the fire that was to come.

After the flaming arrows faded, as dawn turned the sky from black to dark blue and began sliding through blue to pale yellow, the flaming arrows stopped falling. The family went into the house to try to sleep for a little while, but Angus couldn't sleep, couldn't close his eyes without envisioning the fiery end of the world. Grandpa had said God would know the righteous from the unrighteous, would be able to separate the sheep from the goats, but Amos wanted to be sure, was terrified that he'd slip through the cracks, that God would overlook him when he was pulling the righteous out of the world before the destruction. What if he just didn't realize Angus had been good?

Angus couldn't take that chance. He had to come up with a way, a sign to God, a mark that would set him apart from the unrighteous so when the day of Judgement came, he would be selected for the narrow path to Glory.

While the rest of the family was settling in to get some sleep, Angus got out of the bed he shared with three brothers and went into the great room of the house his grandfather had built with his bare hands. He had cut down the trees, stripped off all the limbs, fitted them together with mud to seal the seams. There was always a fire in the hearth. The glowing embers were never allowed to burn out.

Angus steps in his bare feet up onto the hearth stones, takes the poker and puts the end of it in the bed of red, glowing coals. He leaves it there, wondering idly if what he intends to do will hurt and trying to prepare himself for the pain.

When the poker is hot enough, he pulls it out of the glowing coals, rolls up the sleeve on his left arm, takes a deep breath and touches the end of the poker to the bare skin of his forearm. The pain is staggering, overwhelming, so intense the sensation eats up the whole world and the poker falls out of his limp fingers as the world goes dark. He doesn't pass out completely, hangs onto consciousness with his fingernails as the agony in his arm pulses up it to his shoulder and neck. He gasps for air, staring down at the hideous black crater in his arm while the stench of burning flesh wells up into his face and makes him want to puke.

He staggers to the water bucket, takes out a dipper full and pours it over the burn, gritting his teeth to keep from crying out. Then he goes to the outhouse behind the house and dry heaves until black spots appear before his eyes.

As soon as the sun comes up, the family wakes and the day of chores begins. He wears a long-sleeved shirt to hide the burn, manages somehow to do his jobs without complaint.

That night, fire rains out of heaven again. Grandfather gathers the family in the back yard to watch again. And when the family is asleep in their beds later, Angus sneaks out to the fireplace and burns another hole in his arm.

After four days, Angus is barely able to move his arm. The pain is almost unbearable, and he lives every second in nauseating dread of the ritual he has begun and must continue — he will make a mark every time the fires fall. The mark will identify him when the world ends as one of the chosen.

The fifth night, Angus's older sister Sarah catches himself burning his arm.

"What are you doing?" she cries, her voice so loud it surely must wake up the whole house.

"Shhhh, Sarah. Noooo!" he whispers. "Don't tell anybody. I have to do this. The mark is for God, so he will know I am righteous. Please, don't tell."

Sarah won't listen. She calls out for his parents, and when they come bleary-eyed into the room, she demands that Angus show them what he has done. The whole family is as horrified, and uncomprehending as Sarah.

Everybody except Grandfather.

They all spin around Angus in a dizzying dance of concern as his mother gets water to clean the wounds. The first one from four days ago is filled with infection and pus, and the others are in various stages of infection too. His sisters tear strips of sheets to make bandages and Angus sits as still as he can while they minister to him.

At one point, the pain of his mother cleaning the infection from the wounds is finally too much, and he leans his head back, crying out in agony. He continues to scream until his voice is gone. He has squeezed his eyes shut as he screamed, and when he opens them, he sees his grandfather's face. The old man is standing in the shadows, just outside of the glow of the lamps and candles family members have lit and set all around Angus.

The old man grabs hold of Angus's gaze with his coal-black eyes. And he nods his head. A small gesture, barely a nod at all, but Angus sees it, knows that his grandfather approves of what he has done.

Sarah sees it, too. Angus notices that she has stopped ripping up the sheet and is looking at him, then at his grandfather, then back at Angus. The look on her face is unreadable, but from that moment forward, his older sister becomes Angus's protector. She watches over him, stands between him and danger, protects him from bullies at school and the other boys in the family. Her attitude is making some kind of statement. Even as a boy he knows that.

But he never quite figures out what it is, is never able to put it

*together in his head what connection Sarah has made to the God
marks on his body.*

ANGUS MASSAGED THE SCARS — there were five, pale, like
cigarette burn marks, only bigger, the size of a quarter.
Those scars, those God marks, had started to burn again
for the first time in more than six decades. As soon as the
fire began to fall from heaven about a week ago, the marks
came back to life.

He knew that the world saw the fire in the sky as a
natural thing, meteors falling into the earth's atmosphere
from outer space. He'd learned that in school the year after
that first meteor shower, the one his grandfather said was
fire from God. He didn't believe it, knew there was more
going on than a simple natural phenomena.

But when the world didn't end, as his grandfather had
said it would, when the meteor showers came every year,
year after year, and the world was not destroyed, he came
to understand that his grandfather had been a superstitious
old man rather than a prophet of God.

About a week ago, he was awakened in the middle of
the night by the pain of it. He had gone to the window and
looked out, saw the "meteor shower" and realized his
grandfather had been right after all. God was giving Angus
Park a heads-up by setting fire to his arm all over again.
God was warning him that the end was nigh, that God
would separate the righteous from the unrighteous before
He destroyed the world with fire.

The pain kept him awake now, day and night. He was
dizzy from lack of sleep. He watched the fire fall and knew
the earth was in its last days. The really big meteor shower
was predicted to occur on August 11.

Angus Park knew it would be the end of the world.

Chapter Seven

MITCH COULDN'T FIGURE out how word got out so fast about the burning tourist, but the crowds of lookie-lous and rubberneckers showed up almost before the ambulance. Gratefully, Deputies Tony Hadley and Billy Crawford had been close by when he'd called in for backup, so they'd gotten to the scene in minutes. They were at least able to cordon the crime scene off with yellow police tape before the crowds appeared.

Mitch used Edna's cell phone to contact her daughter, who lived in Louisville, Kentucky, a five-hour drive away. The woman had taken the news of her father's "sudden death"— that's all Mitch told her— surprisingly well and asked to speak to her mother, but at that time Edna wasn't in any shape to talk to anyone, so Mitch had said he'd have Edna call her when she felt up to it.

At some point while he was dealing with crowd control, helping the forensics guys from Gatlinburg do their jobs, and fending off the attempts by various news media to drag him aside for an exclusive interview, he noticed that

Edna had gone silent. She'd worn herself out, going from hysteria to something approaching catatonia.

She sat down on the bench in front of the store, holding Earl's Nebraska Cornhuskers cap clutched in her clinched fists so tight that Mitch worried that her fingers would cramp from the effort. She rocked back and forth, looking out with a thousand yard stare at nothing at all.

He'd figured the paramedics would take her to the hospital, but she refused transport, said she was not going to leave Earl, who still lay where he had fallen, and would remain there until the forensics team allowed the body to be removed. Her emotional condition was so fragile it wasn't a good idea to push. So Mitch arranged for a nurse from the elder care unit of Brandeis Hospital to accompany Edna when they took Earl away to the Knoxville morgue, and to remain with her until her daughter arrived from Louisville to collect her.

Mitch took a moment to gather himself, then went to the bench and sat down beside her.

"Mrs. Watson, Edna, my name's Mitch Webster, I'm the sheriff of Yarmouth county." He didn't say "acting sheriff." He'd done that when he first took over for the sheriff he'd replaced so that the man could have double knee replacement surgery. He always made sure people understood that he was just a doorstop, that the real sheriff would return soon and fix whatever it was they though Mitch had screwed up.

But he'd stopped inserting "acting" into his own description of himself when he began to investigate the murder of Tina Montgomery several months ago. It was hard enough to get locals to open up to an outsider. It didn't make sense to rub their noses in just how foreign he was by identifying himself as temporary.

"Do you remember talking to me earlier?" he asked her.

She didn't look at him, but appeared to have heard him.

"You's the one we stopped to ask for directions. You was parked at the gas pumps."

"Yes, that was me. Do you feel up to answering some questions for me?"

She turned to him then, turned *on* him.

"I'll answer your questions if you'll answer mine. *Why?* Why did some monster throw gasoline on my Earl and ... and—"

She couldn't make herself say the words, just left the sentence dangling.

"I don't know, but it's my job to find out. I need your help to do that."

"What help can I be? I ain't got no idea what happened. I just went to the bathroom and when I come out, I heard this awful screaming and I seen Earl stagger around the corner of the building. He was on fire."

She said the heart-rending words without any of the hysteria she'd exhibited earlier. The emotion was drained out of them. Her speech was flat and lifeless.

"Did you see anybody, notice anybody near him?"

"No. I didn't see nothing but Earl burning."

She reached out her chubby hand and grabbed Mitch's. "You know he was a firefighter, right? He was the fire chief of the Oneida County Volunteer Fire Department for almost twenty years. He got hurt a little over a year ago in a fire, and I talked him into retiring so we could travel, like he always promised me we would. I didn't tell him at the time — because if I had, he'd have bowed his neck and gotten all stubborn on me — but I didn't want him to retire so we could travel. I wanted him to retire because I was scared to death he was gonna get killed. I was terrified he was going to die in a fire."

She took a shaky breath and her control cracked.

"So we go on vacation to the mountains, more than a thousand miles from home and the dangers of being a fire fighter. And what happens? Fire kills him. Fire!"

She froze, as if the full import of it had only just now occurred to her.

"Dear Holy God, my Earl burned to death. He *burned* to death!"

She began to sob again, big tears rolling down her fat cheeks and dripping off her jowls. Mitch put his arm around her shoulders and drew her to him, and she continued to cry, her whole body shaking with sobs. She cried long and hard, and gradually the sounds grew softer, like an exhausted child who's awakened from a bad dream and isn't quite sure yet what's real and what isn't.

"He hadn't ought to have died like that," she whispered. "It ain't fair, him spending his whole live saving people from fire. It ain't right that fire killed him. It just ain't right."

Mitch pictured the man's face, the look of long-suffering patience he wore, and knew that Earl Watson had been a good man.

Edna was right. He didn't deserve to die like that.

Chapter Eight

RILEIGH DIALED the number for the Good GI's detective agency and suffered in silence through the nauseatingly cheery receptionist's little speech.

"Hi, we're the Good GI's. If there are bad guys in your life, we're on it."

"Hi Stephanie, can I talk to Walt?"

"Sure, Rileigh. How are you?"

"I'm good."

It was like listening to fingernails on blackboard to have a conversation with Stephanie Papadopoulis. Her high-pitched nasal voice wasn't the affectation that every third teenage girl had adopted in the past few years. Stephanie's was real, which should elicit at least a modicum of sympathy since she was stuck sounding like Minnie Mouse on helium, but Rileigh just couldn't pull it off.

"If Wally's there, I really need to speak to him quick. My cell is just about out of juice."

Stephanie put her on hold, which was almost as annoying as talking to her. It was schmaltzy, insipid, elevator music with some lounge lizard singing Some Enchanted Evening.

"Yo Rileigh, what can I do for you?"

"You can give me another job. I finished the surveillance of June Anderson today. She's clean. Or she's meeting some guy while her husband's on the couch snoring or watching a baseball game. But she doesn't have a honey I can find during her work hours."

"File an official report."

"I will, I will."

It was maddening, but it was the nature of the work. A client hires a detective agency to see if his spouse is being unfaithful, he wants a report. He's paying big bucks, a couple hundred dollars an hour, and figures he should get a blow-by-blow of the detective watching paint dry.

Still, it was part of the job.

"As soon as I get the report, and not a moment sooner, I will have another job for you."

"I'll send you the report tonight."

"Then tomorrow you can take a look into a couple of cases of insurance fraud."

Whenever an insurance claim is filed on a property that the fire marshal has ruled an arson fire, the insurance company investigates to see if the claim is legit — with their own team of highly skilled investigators. But before they go to the expense of a full-bore investigation, they hire outside help to take a preliminary look, to see if something smells hinky.

"Two fires?"

"One is a residence in Gatlinburg belonging to Mrs. Lettie Jarvis. The other's a house outside Pigeon Forge belonging to one Wyman Perry."

Rileigh picked up on something in his tone when he mentioned about the second fire.

"What do you think?"

"I don't have an opinion about the Nettie Jarvis residence, but Wyman Perry? I think it's somewhere between likely he did it and hell yes, he did it. But that's just me. I don't like the guy."

That was an insight. Wally was a good guy to work for. He was tough, fair, and if you totally screwed something up, he would tell you to your face, ream your ass out, and then put you back to work. He didn't hold it against you.

But he was a private guy, too. They'd spent a considerable amount of time together when she first took the job. He wanted to hang out with her on stakeouts, watch her tail a suspect, things like that. Wanted to be sure she was good at the job and not just screwing off and making shit up for a report.

In the time they'd spent together, he'd never had much to say about himself. He didn't talk about his family. But unless the photo of a pretty woman and three cute kids on his desk was in the frame when he bought it, he must be married. He also never talked about any other cases his agency was working on or had worked on in the past. Client confidentiality was tattooed on his soul.

If you don't talk about work, or about your family, conversation tends to grind to a what-the-weather's-doing halt.

The fact that Wally didn't like the guy the insurance company was hiring his company to investigate was a little window into Wally's soul.

"Why is that? You got anything to go on but gut instinct? Any reason to believe the dude's trying to bilk the insurance company out of a payment?"

"You don't miss much, do you? No, I don't have any reason to believe the guy's a crook. I just hope he is."

Before Rileigh could demand an explanation, he provided one voluntarily.

"He lived down the street from us when we first moved to Gatlinburg. And he had a dog, a little bitty one, the kind my wife calls a "loaf of bread dog." That little dog barked non-stop from sundown to sunup. Note the sequence. Sundown to sunup. It was a quiet as the tomb of the unknown soldier in the daytime, but as soon as the sun went down that dog would start to yap. And it was yap-yap-yap-yap-yap-yap-yap for hours. I called after three or four days of no sleep, complained politely. His response was, if I didn't like the sound of his dog barking, I could stick my fingers in my ears. The guy was ready to come punch my lights out. And that would not have been a good thing because a couple of days later I saw him for the first time, and he was the size of a sumo wrestler on steroids. Funniest looking thing you ever saw, this gigantic man walking a dog smaller than his foot, up and down the twenty yards of flat sidewalk in the neighborhood. We've moved since then, but I talked to the people who bought our house, and they moved out after six months because they couldn't stand the dog barking. It would be delicious karma to nail this dude for something."

"I'll see what I can do. Is there anything I need to know about him other than he has a yappy little dog?"

"Nope. Well, that and he's an asshole."

Rileigh took down the relevant information, and began to make a file on Wyman Albert Perry, a fat man with a yappy dog who might or might not be trying to bilk his insurance company out of a couple hundred grand, and another on Mrs. Nettie Jarvis.

She went from that file to the one about June Anderson, and began to work on the detailed report the Good GIs would deliver to the client, listing in excruciating detail all the things his yes-she-was-faithful wife hadn't done during the time Rileigh was watching her.

She stopped typing in mid-sentence when she remembered the bananas.

"Mama, I'm going over to Georgia's," she called out on her way to her car. "I'll be home for supper."

The grocery sack bag of bananas had been sitting on the back seat all day. She'd picked up the big rack of them at Save-a-Lot before she'd driven to June Anderson's house and followed her to work. When she opened the car door, the banana stink assaulted her. She'd gotten used to it sitting in the car all day, as the banana stink permeated the interior. It might smell like bananas for weeks now.

The bananas were, of course, to shove into Mayella Stump's little mouth to stop her screaming, or to keep her from screaming in the first place. A world-class howler, Mayella could go vocal chord to vocal chord with the whole Mormon Tabernacle Choir. If there were an Olympic screaming competition, that little girl would bring home the gold.

As she drove from her house to Carter's Mill Road, she opened all the windows on the Honda to allow the fresh air to wash some of the tropical stench out of the vehicle. The windows invited in a fresh breeze scented with cedar trees and pine needles and clear water bubbling down the mountain side. Okay, water had no smell, but it always seemed to Rileigh that it was something she could smell if she concentrated, and she was sure she could pick out individual wildflowers from the bouquet of aromas that defined the Smoky Mountains.

She rounded the final bend before the double-wide trailer house that was squashed up against a rock wall and affixed there with a satellite dish stick pin.

What was that?

Oh, no.

Rileigh groaned out loud. Parked out front of the trailer, amid the debris of half a dozen broken riding toys, was Chigger Stump's pickup truck. Chigger was in danger of having been convicted of a murder he didn't commit four months ago. That would have been a shame, but Rileigh couldn't help believing that he ought to suffer some kind of punishment for the crime he *did* commit— adultery.

Chigger had gotten involved with a nineteen-year-old waitress named Tina Montgomery, as in, *horizontally involved*. The girl had gotten pregnant — as if the five children Chigger already had with Georgia didn't spread his genetic signature wide enough.

Tina had threatened to tell Georgia about their affair. They had argued about it at their secret rendezvous spot out by the grass hut on Ian McGinnis's land. Ian had been there and heard the argument. So had Aunt Daisy. After Chigger drove away from the woods, Aunt Daisy had attacked Tina with a butcher knife, gutted her, and cut out her tongue.

Chigger would have gone down for that crime if Aunt Daisy hadn't tried to kill Rileigh next. As it was, he was off the hook. For murder. He sure as shit wasn't off the hook for cheating on Georgia! Or for getting a teenager pregnant. Or for being an all-around contemptible asshole.

Georgia had kicked the bum out, of course. Told him she wanted a divorce.

So why was his truck parked in front of Georgia's trailer?

Chapter Nine

MAYELLA'S SIGNATURE wail assaulted Rileigh as she got out
of her car. She made it as far as the front porch of the
trailer when the door opened and Georgia greeted her
with a smile pinned on her face that looked like she'd
learned how to smile from a manual. Before Rileigh could
say anything, Georgia snatched the bag out of her hands.

"Bananas. Thank God! If I'd had to go through
another banana-less afternoon," Rileigh opened her
mouth to unload on Georgia, when Georgia turned aside,
handed the banana sack to Liam, and told him, "Go give
these to daddy."

Then she pushed the little boy out of the doorway,
stepped through it onto the porch, and closed the door
firmly behind her.

"We need to talk," Georgia said, and headed down the
rickety steps to the yard, then turned and went around the
end of the trailer, starting up into the woods.

"Hold on a minute!" Rileigh cried. she didn't ask
where Georgia was going because she already knew. She
was making her way to the "waterfall." The water running

down the mountainside spread out into the creek bed about fifty yards behind Georgia's trailer. And before it spread out, the water dropped off a ledge and fell about three feet. Rileigh had named it the first time she saw it and the name stuck. It was the Notmuchuva Waterfall.

Georgia came here sometimes for a bit of solitude from the blender of raising-five-children life, and she marched to the spot like Rommel through North Africa before turning to face Rileigh.

"I know what you're going to say," Georgia said.

"Did you take that lowlife back?"

"Chigger and I have worked out—"

"Simple yes or no question. Did you invite Chigger Stump back into your life?"

There was a beat of silence during which Rileigh watched Georgia straighten her spine and square her shoulders.

She knew that look. That's what Georgia always did when the two of them were about to do something for which they would get into enormous trouble, but they'd decided the juice — whatever it was — was worth the squeeze and went full steam ahead.

"Yes, I did. Chigger and I are—"

"Yeah, right. Are what? Married again? How'd that work out for you the first time?"

"Rileigh, please, don't."

"Don't what? Tell you what a son-of-a-bitch-worthless-piece-of-shit your husband was when he screwed around on you and got Tina Montgomery pregnant—"

"Stop!"

What Georgia lacked in volume she made up for in determination. She looked at her watch. "Okay, you've got five minutes to tell me all the reasons why I shouldn't take Chigger back. Have at it. Give it your best shot. Go!"

Rileigh said nothing, just looked at Georgia.

"Your clock's running," Georgia said. "I know you have a shit ton of things to say, so you had better get after it."

"Why?"

"Because if you don't, your time's—"

"Not why should I get after it, why'd you take him back?"

"Because I love him."

For Georgia, it really was that simple. She loved the man, and she would probably have forgiven him anything. That kind of devotion warranted somebody a whole lot better than Chigger.

"You don't get it," Georgia went on. 'You never have. You could have had any boy in high school—"

"Have you been smoking crack? If you will recall, I was the one of the two of us who did NOT go to the senior prom."

"You could have, though. You could have had your pick of them all. Every boy in school was drooling over you—"

"What alternate universe are you talking about? Because the high school I lived through in this universe did not have Rileigh Bishop at the top of the popularity tree."

"They were afraid of you."

"Who was afraid of me?"

"The boys. They were intimidated by you, how in charge and in control you always seemed. They were afraid to ask you out."

"Exactly when was it you created this little delusional rewrite of my teenage history?"

"Aw, come on Rileigh. You know it's true. Then you went off to join the military and if you want a sure-fire way to keep the boys away, learn how to beat the shit out of them in a fight."

"I did not." Then she righted her ship. "This isn't about me, Georgia. it's about you, about–"

"The little chubby girl who giggled all the time, had pimples on her back so bad she couldn't wear a strapless formal to the prom, and who actually managed to grab the brass ring."

"Brass ring?"

"Chigger."

"Chigger's more like a toilet bowl ring than a brass one."

"He was funny and good looking, had that carefree way about him. He could have had any of the girls in our class, but he picked me. *Me.*"

Rileigh and Georgia had never discussed how Georgia ended up married to Chigger Stump. Rileigh had been in the military when it happened. All she knew about what was going on at home was what her mother or Aunt Daisy wrote in their letters. Then there was the summer when Georgia just went dark. She didn't answer her phone, or when she did, she couldn't talk for long. She stopped texting — just little text abbreviations.

Rileigh had had no idea what was going on until it was too late.

"You do know I was pregnant with Liam when we got married, right?" Georgia said.

She didn't know, but she'd figured as much.

"Chigger wasn't the first boy. You were already gone, seeing the world, and I was here in Black Bear Forge Tennessee. I was with a lot of boys."

Georgia? Rileigh was dumbstruck.

But then she wasn't. It made sense in the clunking sort of way a combination lock makes when all the tumblers line up properly. Georgia had been sexually abused by Rileigh's scum of the earth father. And one of the classic acting-out behaviors of sexually abused girls was promiscuity.

If Georgia slept around, it was J.R. Bishop's fault.

"But Chigger loved me." She held up her hand, "No, he really did. He still does."

"And you trust him? You think he's seen the error of his ways and he's reformed. That he'll keep his pants zipped from now on?"

"Do I trust him?" She turned to Rileigh and the raw honesty on her face was fierce. "I chose to trust him. I get to decide that. Me, Georgia McGinnis. And what choice do I have?"

"What choice do you have? You can–"

"I have five children, Rileigh. Five. If Chigger and I can't make a go of it, I'll have to raise them by myself."

Which sounded infinitely preferable to staying with a man who slept around, but she didn't say that.

"I will never find 'somebody else,' that mythical man out there you are meant to be with. Not fifteen pounds overweight with five children."

It was more like twenty-five pounds, and she was right.

"What I choose to believe is that Chigger loves me and that whole murder thing, it scared the bejesus out of him, realizing how close he came to getting blamed and going to prison. I believe he loves me and I know he loves the kids. He swears he will never do it again.I believe him because it's all I've got."

Georgia was reaching out for approval Rileigh absolutely could not grant. But she would grant the reality of the situation.

Georgia had painted herself into a corner with all those children, her options were limited, and she saw Chigger as the best of a bunch of not-good choices.

Rileigh's shoulders slumped. "Fine. Ok. Whatever."

She would not allow the behavior of a man who couldn't keep his pants zipped to come between her and the best friend she'd ever had.

"I don't like it, but the choice is not mine to make. It's yours. And I'll hang in there with you through whatever shit storm comes along."

Because it would be a shit storm, Rileigh was sure of that. Chigger Stump was pond scum and pond scum would never be anything other than what it was — a greenish, stinky slime that floated on the top of stagnant water. Let pond scum into your life, and eventually it had make you sick.

Mayella began to scream again and Chigger opened the back door of the trailer.

"I got to go to work. You need to come see to Mayella." There was a pause. "Please."

Georgia beamed her approval at him.

Rileigh just shook her head. You could teach a two-year-old to say please and thank you. It ought to be a minimum requirement for civil interaction, not a feat of such relational prowess that it deserved beaming approval.

She and Georgia walked back to the house. Rileigh heard Chigger's truck start up out front. Mayella was still screaming.

"I need to be getting home—"

"Not yet. I got something to show you."

So into the belly of the pandemonium beast they marched. Georgia paused to peel a banana and handed it to Mayella to silence her, then she sent the boys to the play-room, which was the breakfast nook with all the furniture removed and replaced by toys.

Once the children were at least momentarily occupied, Georgia grabbed her laptop off the kitchen table and took it and Rileigh to her bedroom at the back of the house.

"You gotta see this. It was posted to Facebook, and I got no idea how come it showed up on my feed." She was opening the laptop as she spoke, then closed it again. "It's bad, I mean really gross. If you'd rather not see it I was just wondering if you maybe knew something about it."

"Go on, show me. How could I possibly say no after a buildup like that?"

Georgia was right. It was gross. Horrifying was a better word. It had been posted under the username "God's Spark" and it began as a shot in the shadow of a lighted building, so it was hard to tell what was going on until the fire started. Then it was way too clear what was happening.

A man was on fire, burning. There was no sound to accompany the video, so it was unclear if the man had said — screamed— anything. The flames that burst instantly all around him should have made the trademark *whumph* sound, but there was nothing. The face was only visible for an instant before the man was engulfed in flames and began to writhe in agony, knocking the Nebraska Cornhuskers ball cap off his head.

"That man," Rileigh gasped. "I think I met him. Earlier today. He and his wife pulled up beside my car at Souvenirs! to ask me for directions."

"Seriously? *That* guy?"

"I think so. The video didn't give much of a view of his face, but the guy I remember was wearing a Nebraska Cornhuskers cap. How many tourists have you ever seen here in a Nebraska Cornhuskers cap? It's the same guy, has to be which means, he's dead now.'"

She stopped, then whispered softly, "I want to know why."

Chapter Ten

RILEIGH FELT the room around her fade, the sounds of the boys fighting over a toy in the playroom down the hall from Georgia's bedroom were muted.

It wasn't a full-bore flashback like the ones that had roared through her life like psychos on souped-up Harleys when she came home after two tours in Iraq, followed by two more in Afghanistan. In those flashbacks, the whole world around her vanished between one heartbeat and the next.

They always started the same way. Suddenly, she'd have grit in her teeth, then she'd feel a scorching sun beating down on her, hear the screaming of the wounded and smell the stench of war — smoke, blood and burning flesh.

This flashback is almost transparent. It is a fuzzy overlay on reality, like a double-exposed photograph. But it's no snapshot. It's a video, playing out in the air in front of her.

And not a silent movie, either.

. . .

SHE WATCHES it happen but there's nothing she can do to stop it. Even if she could have shot the kid — and it was just a kid, maybe eleven or twelve years old — it wouldn't have prevented him from throwing the IED under the Humvee in line in front of her.

There is time to glance at Robinson, the soldier in the cab beside her, time to watch horror, terror, and rage register on his face before the world goes mad.

Rileigh hits the brakes, but the ATC, Armored Troop Carrier, she's driving is traveling too fast to stop before the explosion rips apart the Humvee in front of her.

The force of the explosion lifts the Humvee into the air three or four feet off the ground, as pieces of it fly out in every direction.

Thunk. Thunk-Thunk.

Shrapnel attacks the front end of the ATC. She and Robinson throw themselves sideways onto the seat as debris blows out the windshield and pieces tear into the top of the seats where they'd been sitting moments before.

Robinson makes a grunting sound and goes limp. Rileigh doesn't lift her head, just turns her face so she can watch his eyes go blank and blood gush out of the gory wound in his back where a shard of metal the size and shape of a meat cleaver has ripped him open.

The sound of the explosion has deafened her so all she can hear is a terrible buzzing, ringing sound in her head. She smells smoke, reaches back to the door handle, pops the door open, and rolls out of the vehicle onto the ground. Scrambling away on all-fours from two vehicles, both now burning, she catches sight of Dogpatch running away from the wreck of the Humvee.

Dogpatch is a funny young man from some little nothing town in Georgia that's almost as small as Black Bear Forge. Their accents spoke instantly to each other, and they were friends before they'd even been introduced.

Dogpatch is a pothead who has been high just about every minute of his government-sponsored vacation to the beautiful tour bus desti-

nation paradise in Afghanistan. High and hungry. His constant, raging case of the munchies sent him through camp every night when they were on patrol, mooching anything edible, from candy bars to sticks of beef jerky, which he shoved whole into his mouth, then chewed frantically to keep from choking to death or drowning in his own spit.

When his mouth wasn't jammed with food, he talked non-stop about the girl back home he was planning to marry as soon as his tour was over, and described in weed-induced detail the pig farm he was going to build on the field his father was using now to grow premium marijuana — the good shit that sold for five hundred dollars an ounce.

Lying on her belly, tears washing the dirt from her cheeks, she watches Dogpatch's flaming form run off across the sand. He is a human torch, identifiable only because he'd tumbled out the left front door of the burning Humvee and he'd been driving.

He is charred completely black, must be dead, has to be dead, but he keeps running, trailing a high-pitched scream behind him like the tail on a comet. How can he keep going?

She wants to run after him, to tackle him, to stop him, but she can't move. She just lies there watching the horror until he finally stumbles, falls face forward into the sand, and lies there motionless, the stench of burning flesh and hair wafting her way on the hot wind.

As soon as Rileigh is discharged, she goes to see Dogpatch's girlfriend in Georgia. Lies to her, tells her the love of her life had died from a sniper's bullet to the brain.

Never knew what hit him.

"RILEIGH, EARTH TO RILEIGH." It was Georgia's voice, and the transparent images of horror melted and ran down out of Rileigh's vision like watercolors.

"I need to call Mitch."

Georgia lifted an eyebrow at the reference, as if there

were some significance to Rileigh calling the sheriff by his first name. It didn't mean anything, of course.

When she pulled out her cell phone and went to Mitch's name in "favorites," the eyebrow went up again, but Georgia demonstrated the good judgement not to say what she was clearly thinking.

Mitch answered on the first ring, not with "hello," but with "I was just about to call you."

"You were? What for?"

"There was an incident today involving some tourists, a couple named–"

"Earl and Edna. From Nebraska. I met them. They asked me how to find the Hollywood Wax Museum." She paused for a beat. "I know about the 'incident.' There's a video posted to Facebook–"

"I've seen it. I'd like to talk to you about it, and about the couple. Would you mind if I dropped by–"

"Tonight? Sure. You're welcome to come to supper, too. Mama's serving pinto beans and cornbread."

"Thanks, I probably can't make supper. But we do need to talk."

"I'll be home all evening."

Rileigh disconnected the call and Georgia hopped to her feet.

"What are you just sitting there for? Go home! I'd tell you to fix your hair, but your hair always looks good." Pause. "A little makeup wouldn't hurt, though. And some tight jeans that show your ass."

"It's not like that, Georgia."

"Riiiiight."

"Besides, none of my jeans fit tight anymore."

"Skinnier than a pair of skinny jeans — oh, how I wish! You come by here tomorrow morning first thing. Promise?"

"What for?"

"For a piece of pineapple upside down cake that will still be warm when you get here. A biiiig piece."

Chapter Eleven

RILEIGH PULLED her car up in front of the fence around her mother's house for the second time today and as soon as she cleared the driveway lump, she saw immediately that the rose bush that'd been beside the front porch when she left earlier was now gone. Nothing left but a stump.

Holy shit. Did her mother actually go out to the garage and get the chainsaw, crank it up and cut the bush down? She'd asked Rileigh to bring her the saw before she left, and when Rileigh didn't, she assumed her mother would forget all about needing to cut the bush down because "Rhett don't like roses."

Who was Rhett?

She got out of the car and hurried up the stone walkway to the porch, veering off to the side to examine the stump of the rose bush. As she was examining it, the screen door on the porch squawked its signature wail and her mother came outside.

"Mama did you did you use the chainsaw to cut down this bush?"

Mama gave her a withering look.

"I sure as Jackson didn't gnaw it down with my teeth!"

"But–but how?"

She couldn't imagine her mother having the strength to lift the chainsaw, much less carry it all the way here from the garage. And crank it? That took some muscle.

But Aunt Daisy hadn't had any trouble cranking it.

The image of her demented aunt's face as she advanced toward Rileigh, holding the rumbling chainsaw out in front of her, flashed through Rileigh's mind momentarily, then it was gone.

"Why?" she managed to cough out. "Why'd you cut it down?"

It had been a fixture in the front yard for as long as Rileigh could remember. She didn't remember when it had been planted, but she recalled its presence beside the porch as a sort of touchstone through her whole childhood.

Question: how long can a rose bush live? She was tempted to consult Siri for an answer to the question but stifled the urge. This one had been here for at least twenty -five years, it was part of the family, and Mama had chopped it down today because—

"I done told you why. Don't you never listen? Maybe it's you needs a hearing aide instead of me."

"Humor me. Why did you cut it down?"

As she spoke, Rileigh climbed the porch steps and moved to her traditional spot on the porch swing. But Mama got there first and plopped down in the middle of it.

That was odd, too. Family positions on furnishings are as sacred as the throne of the Dalai Lama. If you sat in a particular chair in the living room, it was deemed your chair. The unspoken agreement was inviolate. The porch swing was Rileigh's. It was where she parked her butt every time she came home. Mama's chair was the rocker on the right side of the coffee table. The other chair, the one Aunt Daisy always sat in, had been removed.

And Rileigh needed to pull it back out again because Mitch had said he'd be coming over tonight.

First things first.

"I cut the rose bush down because Rhett don't like it. I done told you that."

"Ah, but what you didn't tell me is, who the hell is Rhett?"

"Oh, you know who Rhett Butler is, child." She leaned toward Rileigh, who was still standing because it felt so damned awkward to sit in the wrong place.

Surely she wasn't delusional enough to decide the character out of Gone with The Wind had suddenly appeared on the doorstep and she'd invited him in for tea.

"No, Mama, I'm having trouble with that one. Remind me."

"Rhett Butler is that dashing young man who came by here about two weeks ago. Just came marching up on the porch like Sherman through Atlanta. I was sitting here reading a book."

Rileigh imagined her Mama was thinking of "Gone With the Wind", but she didn't ask. She was stuck on the "reading a book" part, because Mama didn't read books. The occasional magazine, right, but not books. The Holy Bible that sat prominently on the coffee table inside in the parlor was as pristine as the day they'd bought it. Nobody read that book.

Well, okay, Mama had a Bible in her room and sometimes Rileigh had seen her read it. Though, as she thought about it, Mama must have read it sometime because she had a maddening habit of quoting just the right Scripture to put you in your place, a skill she'd honed to a fine art over the years.

"Reading? Reading what?"

"The Sonnets of Shakespeare, if you must know."

Rileigh almost choked.

"And you got a copy of Shakespeare's Sonnets where?"

"Don't be silly child. I ordered it from Amazon." Mama shifted gears and Rileigh was so far behind her train of thought now she wouldn't likely ever catch up. "Now, are you going to sit out here with me for a spell before supper or not? Cause I'm getting a crick in my neck looking up at you."

Rileigh collapsed into the lone rocker, trying to regain her composure.

"Rhett cain't come to supper tonight, though. I asked, but he said he didn't like pinto beans. Said they give him gas and if he ate too many, they'd give him the squirts, too."

Rhett Butler with diarrhea just would not fit anywhere in Rileigh's head.

"So is he coming to dinner anytime soon, this Rhett fellow? Or should I call him Mr. Butler? Wouldn't want to insult him."

"Oh, you can't insult Rhett. He just laughs at everything you say. His belly jiggle reminds me of Santa Claus."

"Santa Claus?" Her mother was dating an invisible man named Rhett Butler who looked like Santa Claus. Sure. Why not?

"And I don't know when he's likely to come to supper. He went into the hospital a couple of days ago, getting neck replacement surgery."

"Neck replacement surgery?"

"Stop repeating everything I say. You sound like a parrot. Now, do you want some supper or not? I got the batter made for cornbread, but didn't want to put it in the oven until you got here. Cold cornbread will stop you up."

Either feast or famine in the Bishop house — diarrhea or constipation. That's just how they rolled.

"Can we go back to the rose bush. How did you cut it down?"

"You don't look good, Rileigh. You sure you was up to going back to work? I done told you I cut it down with the chainsaw. If you ask me about it again, I'm gonna really start worrying about you."

Yeah, that's me, Crazy Rileigh. Just haul me away to Saint Somebody's Home for the Bewildered. Lock me up and throw away the key.

"I'm fine Mama, just hungry."

It didn't seem to Rileigh that she'd been hungry since the last time there was a Republican in the White house, but she needed to change the subject to something more palatable than the bowel habits of imaginary people.

"I'll go put the cornbread on, then. Beans has been cooking all day. I put a whole pound of bacon in them, so they ought to taste real fine."

A pound of bacon. In pinto beans. And who knew what key ingredient she might have left out of the cornbread. Or what she might have added that didn't belong. Eating Mama's cooking was becoming an adventure. Thank God Mitch had declined her offer to come to supper.

She went back into the house and was starting a load of wash when her mother called out.

"The law's here? What have you done?"

Rileigh set down the bottle of detergent and went to the front room, where her mother stood just inside the screen door as Sheriff Mitchell Webster pulled his cruiser up beside Aunt Daisy's car.

"I can distract him," her mother offered. "You can cut

out the back door and up the path into the mountains. I'll say I haven't seen you all day."

"I haven't done anything illegal, Mama. The sheriff just wants to talk to me about a case he's working on."

"And you ain't a suspect? You sure? Them law officers can be pretty shifty when they want to be."

What the sheriff could possibly have done to give her that impression was lost on Rileigh.

"He's fine, Mama. I'm sure."

"Good," her mother said and heaved a sigh of relief. "I'll go tell Rhett it's safe. He's hiding in the broom closet."

Chapter Twelve

Mitch maneuvered his cruiser up the obstacle course of Rileigh Bishop's driveway and was inordinately proud of himself for making the maneuver look easy. He'd moved to the mountains to take the deputy sheriff position after the first of the year and had been spared by the mild winter — thank you, Jesus!— from having to drive in the snow and ice. It was still months before the possibility of a winter storm, but even in the heat of summer he had already started to dread slipping and sliding on frozen narrow mountain roads.

Rileigh's driveway wasn't the steepest incline in Yarmouth County, but it was close. And with ice on it.

As soon as his cruiser cleared the rock hump at the top of the drive, the house came into view and he noticed two things. Rileigh was dragging a rocking chair out the front door of the house and onto the porch, and the rose bush that'd been blooming the last time he visited was no longer there.

. . .

"WELL, come on up here and sit yourself down, Sheriff," called Lily Bishop as soon as he got out of his cruiser. "We haven't seen you around here in a right smart while."

Mitch had spent considerable time at Rileigh's after she was attacked by her aunt. He came by to offer a helping hand to get her settled when she returned from the hospital With her left hand and forearm encased in a monstrous cast and her right index finger in a splint, Rileigh was pretty much immobilized.

But it had become clear quickly that Rileigh was not in an emotional space where she relished company. And their relationship had not progressed beyond that designation before Rileigh was attacked.

So Mitch had backed off. Stopped dropping by, gave her some space. He'd heard that she'd gone back to work for the Good GIs private investigation service in Gatlinburg, waved to her on the street in town once or twice, and was working his way around to coming up with an excuse to pay her a visit. But the dead tourist wasn't what he would have preferred to talk about.

He walked up the stone sidewalk toward the front porch and was mildly shocked at Rileigh's appearance. She'd been thin — he'd thought of it as slender and willowy when he first met her, but she had lost weight since then, and now had a sort of haunted, concentration camp survivor look about her.

But then she smiled at him, and he relaxed. Clearly, she hadn't yet recovered physically from the ordeal four months ago, but she appeared to be her old self in all other respects.

"Long time no see, stranger," she said.

Her words warmed him, and he grabbed hold of his emotions. He needed to talk to her about the tourist who'd been murdered — that was all. That's why he'd come here. He certainly didn't need to get out ahead of his headlights.

"I see you've progressed beyond the boxing glove."

She held up her arm with its black brace, waved it around. "I'm supposed to get this off sometime next week and it can't happen soon enough for me."

"That thing's been driving her crazy," Lily said. "She can't get it wet so when she takes a shower, I have to get in there with her to wash her–"

"How about you get the sheriff a glass of tea?" Rileigh was embarrassed, but trying not to show it. Mitch took the handoff and ran toward the goal line.

"I would love a glass of tea, if it's not too much trouble."

Lily beamed.

"It's no trouble at all. I'll fetch it right up." Lily paused. "You do like sweet tea, right?"

Actually, Mitch didn't like tea at all, but he had learned quick that there really was no unsweet tea option in the mountains.

"Absolutely."

Lily turned and went into the house to get the tea and Mitch stepped up on the porch.

"What happened to the rose bush? There was a rose bush beside the railing, wasn't there?"

"Yup. It was there alright, had been there my whole life, for as long as I can remember anyway. But Mama cut it down today."

"Why? I thought it was beautiful. Made the whole porch smell like roses."

He walked up the porch steps. Rileigh gestured, and he sat down in the rocking chair she'd been dragging out onto the porch when he arrived. He thought there once were three chairs on the porch, then realized that one of them had likely belonged to Rileigh's Aunt Daisy, and he understood why she'd gotten rid of it.

"She cut it down. With the chainsaw. Because—"

"Your mother used a chainsaw?"

They both stumbled over a briefly awkward moment that followed mentioning the saw that Daisy had used to try to kill Rileigh.

"She said she did. But I never would have dreamed she was that strong."

"What did she do with it—the rose bush? That thing was huge, had sharp thorns all over it? How did she move it?"

"I don't know. Maybe she got one of the Houlihan boys to give her a hand." She didn't say, *Like Aunt Daisy got one of them to cut the brake lines on my car.*

"As for what she did with it?" Rileigh shrugged. "No idea."

"You still haven't told me why she cut it down."

"She cut it down because—"

The screen door squawked as Lily pushed it open with her hip and came out onto the porch carrying a tray with three glasses of ice tea and a saucer with a piece of cornbread on it.

Lily set the tray down on the coffee table in front of the swing and handed Mitch a glass. Then she picked up the saucer holding the piece of cornbread and shoved it at him.

"I made cornbread for supper tonight and thought maybe you'd like a piece."

Rileigh was still standing and she took a step so she was behind her mother as she made gestures at Mitch. She shook her head, violently, mouthed 'don't eat it!'

"You think I don't know you're back there making faces behind my back?" Lily snapped without turning around. "Remember the last time you stuck your tongue out at me, young lady. I washed your mouth out with soap!"

Rileigh rolled her eyes.

"Now go on, eat you some cornbread. I put a pat of butter on it, that Irish butter they have at Save-a-Lot."

Mitch set his glass of tea down on the table and picked up the cornbread with his fingers and took a big bite. He almost choked. It had so much garlic in it his eyes watered. Somehow he managed to chew the bite and swallow it, grabbed his glass of tea and gulped it down to wash the taste out of his mouth.

"That was uh not like any cornbread I ever had before."

Lily smiled broadly.

"You want some pinto beans to go with it? I got some, still warm in the pot."

Rileigh who shook her head definitively.

"That's very kind of you Mrs. Bishop–"

"It's Lily. The only *Mrs. Bishop* I know is my mother-in-law and she's been dead for forty years." Lily laughed gaily.

"I wish I could take you up on your kind offer but I've already had supper. Can I have a raincheck?"

"Why sure you can, son. I don't make it real often, though. Rhett don't like pinto beans."

"Rhett?"

Rileigh rolled her eyes again.

"Rhett Butler."

"*The* Rhett Butler?"

Lily nodded and then giggled like a teenager.

"He's my beau. We're courtin'."

Mitch kept his face immobile.

Rileigh sat down in the chair opposite Mitch. "Mama,

would you mind giving us some time? We need to talk privately about a case Mitch is working on."

"It ain't that fella who burned up, is it?" Lily asked.

How could she possibly have heard of that?

Rileigh saved Mitch from replying.

"It's an ongoing investigation, Mama, and Mitch can't talk about it with anybody who's not officially involved in the case."

Lily picked up her own glass of tea off the tray. "I'll leave you two alone, then." She gestured toward the one-bite-out-of-it piece of cornbread. "You finish that one and I'll bring you another."

She turned and went back into the house, closed the front door firmly behind her. Rileigh picked up the piece of cornbread off the plate and threw it as far as she could out into the yard.

"Your mother has, uh, *changed*," he sputtered.

"I'm not sure she's changed that much. It's just you didn't notice before, with Aunt Daisy taking centerstage in the crazy-as-a-bedbug lunacy show."

He forced a smile.

"Well, at least she's entertaining."

That was absolutely the wrong thing to say. He realized he'd stepped in it when Rileigh's face closed up tight as a bank vault.

"You wouldn't think so if you were the one who had to clean up the mess of rotted food she stored in the oven instead of the refrigerator. Or walk along behind her from room to room, putting out the candles she lights and sets everywhere. If I'm not careful, she's going to set the house on fire."

The remark brought them both back to the reason Mitch had come. He launched into what he'd come to talk to her about, but their easy camaraderie had vanished.

Chapter Thirteen

ENTERTAINING? A crazy woman with dementia is entertaining? Rileigh hadn't remembered the sheriff as insensitive. She recalled he'd been kind, mostly, but wrapped way too tight.

Mitch set his glass down on the table and became all business.

"I was at the Quik Stop late this afternoon when a tourist couple pulled up beside my cruiser and asked for directions. Which I gave them, but they went the opposite direction and turned right. I'm not surprised they got lost."

"Edna told me she talked to you."

"She did?"

"She said they pulled up in the parking lot of Souvenirs! Souvenirs! Souvenirs! beside your car because you had Tennessee plates and you 'looked local.'"

"I wonder how I look local."

"She described the woman with a brace on her arm, and I knew it was you. I'm hoping you can give me some information about them. I didn't talk to them long and then after Edna wasn't lucid enough to be helpful."

"I'm lucid, but I'm afraid I'm not going to be helpful either. I only exchanged a few words with Edna. She wanted to know how to find the building with King Kong climbing up the side, said her sister — what was her name? — Lavern had seen it and told her about it."

"What else did she say about her sister?"

"Just that she'd seen King Kong. Edna and Earl, his name was Earl. They wanted to see it, too."

Rileigh thought about the man who'd been driving the mini-van.

"I doubt that Earl actually wanted to see the thing," she said. "He didn't look to me like he wanted to be here at all. He was just humoring Edna."

"Copy that."

"And that's all I know. I told them the back way into Pigeon Forge that avoids most okay, some of the traffic. The only way you could avoid the traffic on a Monday in Pigeon Forge is in a helicopter."

"They tried to follow your instructions, from what Edna told me, but they got lost."

"All they had to do was stay on that road and not turn off it."

"Your basic, winding-around-tight-turns-and-steep inclines mountain road, right? I've never been on it, but Edna said it made her carsick."

"I can see that."

"She didn't mention anything else? That she was meeting anybody here, or maybe somebody from back home?"

"Nope. Like I said, we didn't talk but a few minutes. She told me they were on vacation, didn't even say where they were from, but the minivan had Nebraska plates."

"He was a retired firefighter, Earl was. Did she mention that?"

"No, she didn't tell me that part. She just said he was so dithered he could complicate a one-car funeral."

Mitch smiled at that, and Rileigh couldn't help smiling back.

"So there was nobody with them when you talked to them?"

"No."

"Did you see anybody oh, suspicious-looking around them, who might have heard your directions and followed them."

"Not another soul on the street."

He paused, considering, and she hauled out her own list of questions and started asking.

"So, what happened? All I know about it was the video that was posted to Facebook. Georgia showed it to me. I can't say I recognized Earl. There was just a brief image of his face before the flames. But I recognized his hat when it fell off."

"I don't know for sure what happened. I went into the store and was talking to Sundeep while Edna and Earl went to the bathrooms. Suddenly, Earl staggered out from around the north side of the building, where the men's restroom is. He was a ball of fire."

"How could he have caught fire in just a few minutes like that?"

"Gasoline."

"He spilled gasoline on himself?"

"No, I believe somebody poured gasoline over him and set him on fire."

Rileigh sucked in a breath. "You don't think it was accidental."

"Hard to soak somebody in gasoline accidentally."

"But who?"

"That's what I'm trying to figure out. There is metal

79

scaffolding on the right side of Sundeep's building. He's having it repainted. Maybe somebody was waiting on the scaffolding in the dark above the door, had some kind of container of gasoline and when Earl walked out of the restroom, they dumped the gasoline on him and struck a match."

"Why on earth would somebody do a thing like that?"

"That's what I'm trying to figure out."

"Kids? Teenagers?"

But Rileigh didn't really believe that. The local teenagers were as wild and crazy as teenagers everywhere, but it takes a special kind of insanity to do a thing like that. A viciousness. A raging anger. This was a small town and the teenagers as far as she knew, hadn't been infected yet with that kind of madness.

"Edna told me he was a retired firefighter, the fire chief of the volunteer fire department of the little town where they were from in Nebraska. A wide spot in the road called Glorietta. She told me he'd been injured on the job recently. I'm wondering if he was hurt, was he the only one who got hurt? Or were other members of the fire department hurt too? Maybe killed? I have a call in to the police chief there, but I had to leave a message because the department was closed."

"Oh, I'm sure they roll up the sidewalks in Glorietta as soon as the sun goes down." She paused. "So you think somebody from his home town came here to kill him, maybe? That doesn't make sense."

"You're right, it doesn't. But it also doesn't make sense that he met somebody after they got here and pissed that somebody off bad enough to commit murder. Earl didn't strike me as that kind of fellow."

Rileigh nodded in agreement.

"Which leaves random act of violence," Mitch continued. "Was Earl Watson the victim of being in the wrong place at the wrong time?"

"The one millionth customer. Cross the line and collect your plaque and certificate."

"Maybe. You said you saw the video? It was posted from one of those computers in the Gatlinburg Public Library."

"Swell. There's a whole bank of them on one wall with free wifi for the tourists. Wifi is really spotty here in the mountains. One cabin's wifi is clear and the cabin a hundred yards up the creek can't get a single bar. That's why the library's open 24-7. It's not so literary types can check out a copy of War and Peace when they can't sleep."

"Whoever it was logged in with the username God's Spark. Does that mean anything to you?"

Rileigh shook her head.

"I'm going to the library in the morning to talk to the librarian who was on duty at the time, ask her—"

"Him. Adrian's Carter's a man. He's run the library for forty years."

"Ask Mr. Carter if he noticed anything suspicious about any of the tourists who came in that night."

"Have you looked around, lately? Mardi Gras crowds don't look as weird as some of the people who come here."

"How about we watch the video again together, see if we can spot something important?"

Rileigh wanted to watch that horrific video about as much as she wanted poison ivy on her ass, but she nodded agreement. Maybe the two of them could spot something in the video they'd missed individually.

Because Earl hadn't deserved what he got.

Chapter Fourteen

RILEIGH INVITED Mitch into the house and they took her laptop into the kitchen and set it there in good light. It wasn't a big image, but it was certainly better than trying to make out images on an iPhone.

She shooed Mama out of the room.

"You don't want to see this Mama. Trust me, you don't."

Then Rileigh sat down and clicked on the video file.

They watched the whole video through three times without commenting on it. It didn't even last a minute, and the first part was hard to see.

In the darkness, somebody was moving, but it was impossible to tell what the movement was. Then suddenly Earl was standing there, only a few feet away from the camera, and he burst into flames.

"If your theory is correct and somebody was waiting on top of the scaffolding to pour gasoline on Earl's head, who took the video?"

"Good question."

"No way could somebody pour the gasoline and light a

match, and then get down off the scaffolding in time to capture what happened on video."

"Right. Either there were two people involved or…"

"Or?"

"Or somebody clocked Earl over the head with something, knocked him down, then poured gasoline on him."

"It's possible. They poured gas on him, he staggered to his feet, they started filming and then tossed a match on him."

"Play it again from the top."

Mitch did.

"It looks to me like the focus isn't so much on Earl, but on the flames themselves. Do you see here, where whoever was taking the video zoomed in, but not on Earl's face? They were focused on the flames shooting up off his head."

"You think it's about the fire, not Earl?"

"Could be?"

"I'm not buying that. Somebody intentionally poured gasoline on Earl and set him on fire. I need to find out who would possibly have a motive to do a thing like that."

"It would have to be somebody from his hometown. But why would somebody drive a thousand miles to murder Earl while he's on vacation?"

"Maybe they figured they wouldn't get caught that way. The list of possible suspects in Glorietta, Nebraska, would be smaller than the one here."

Rileigh didn't think so. That didn't smell right to her.

"Was there a crowd at the crime scene?"

Stupid question. Of course there was a crowd. News of the burned tourist had spread across Yarmouth County like a fire of its own.

"It was the biggest circus in town."

"Did anybody post any videos from that?"

"A few. Have you seen them?"

Rileigh hadn't, so they watched them. Half a dozen and they all were shot from various spots outside the yellow police tape that had been strung all the way around the building. There was nothing much to see in the posted videos. There was no fire to record, and the blanket-draped corpse was nothing more than a lump under a fire blanket.

"If it's somebody who's got some kind of sick thing going for fire, he'd be out there in the crowd," Mitch said.

"So he set the fire, took the video, went to the library to post it, then back to the scene of the fire to be a Lookie Lou? In Gatlinburg traffic? Not a chance."

"Mullins said he probably was at the library when he posted it, but he didn't *have to be*. I don't know about those things, but Mullins is a geek. He said whoever posted it would have to use one of those public computers at least once. But after that first time, if he knew how he could hack the library's Wi-Fi router and clone one of the computers' MAC addresses, then he could post from anywhere."

"If you say so."

"I've got Sundeep collecting all the surveillance footage from the camera in his parking lot, but he warned me not to hope for much. The camera isn't a very good one and the images aren't usually clear. But I'm assuming I can make out cars on it."

"Looking for one with Nebraska plates?"

"Or one where nobody gets out to shop, just sits in the parking lot."

"Like I sit when I'm doing surveillance."

"Yeah, like that."

"Well, the Nebraska plates might be a place to start, but there are tourists here from all over the country.

Coming into town with the usual herd of Away-From-Here's who are just coming for the meteor shower."

Rileigh lowered the lid of her laptop, glad to remove the images of mayhem from her mother's kitchen.

"So tomorrow you're going to go looking for somebody who might have had a motive to kill Earl Watson."

Mitch nodded.

Rileigh didn't push it, but she thought that was the wrong approach. It would be a colossal waste of time, in her opinion, because she didn't believe Earl had been targeted for a reason. She believed some Looney Tune with a thing for fire had picked Earl at random from the herds of tourists in town and set him on fire just to watch him burn.

She thought the incident was about the fire.

Mitch thought it was about the fireman.

Rileigh walked him out to his cruiser. The two of them fended off an attack by Mama, who was determined waylay Mitch and force pinto beans and cornbread down his throat.

Rileigh had realized at supper tonight that she couldn't trust anything her mother prepared anymore. Whatever it was — from pinto beans to chicken casserole— it would likely not taste anything like the wonderful dinners her mother used to make years ago.

As Rileigh started up to bed, she heard her mother's voice. She stopped and tiptoed down the hallway, stood outside her mother's bedroom door.

"He wasn't looking for you. You're safe."

Either she was talking to herself, to someone on the phone, or to somebody who didn't exist. Safe money was on Door Number Three.

"Do you have the tickets yet?"

Pause.

"We'll walk to the dock after Rileigh goes to work. I've never been on a cruise before."

And she wasn't likely to be going on one anytime soon if she intended to walk to the "dock" from the house. The nearest body of water bigger than a bathtub was Douglas Lake outside Gatlinburg. It could accommodate paddle-boats just fine, but cruise ships, not so much.

"Oh, Rhett, I can't wait for you to meet my daughter. I know every mother says things like this, but I swear it's true. She is the absolute light of my life."

Rileigh felt an instant pang of guilt, for eavesdropping and for all the … call them "unkind" thoughts she'd had about her mother, who clearly was half a bubble off plumb and getting further from level every day.

But her mother loved her. Mother love was a one-of-a-kind thing, to be cherished and nurtured. She vowed on the spot to be a better daughter to the only mother she'd ever have.

"When you see how beautiful she is—"

Rileigh's heart swelled.

"—with that blonde hair and those blue eyes—"

The words struck Rileigh like a blow to the belly.

"—she'll be waiting for us in Caracas. I've missed her soooo much!"

Unable to breathe or move, Rileigh stood in the hall-way, her mother's words burning holes in her soul like drips of acid.

"Jillian calls me all the time and we talk for hours. But to see her, touch her, hold her in my arms—"

Her mother's voice was clogged by emotion, and Rileigh couldn't continue for a moment. That broke the spell of horror that had been cast over Rileigh. She ran up the stairs, fleeing her mother's voice.

She ran past Jillian's room and almost stopped, almost

went inside. It had been transformed into a sewing room when Rileigh was in high school, but if she opened the door, she wouldn't see the fabric strewn across long tables and the sewing machine in the corner. She would see Jillian's room as it had been the night she vanished, a smiley face on the wall above her bed and blood everywhere.

She ran to her own room down the hall, went inside, closed the door behind her, and leaned against it panting. Crying silently, not making a sound. Big fat tears ran down her cheeks and dripped off her chin. She didn't wipe them away, just squeezed her eyes shut and tried to think of nothing, absolutely nothing at all.

Chapter Fifteen

J. P. Rutherford was the consummate used car salesman, a man almost cartoonishly lacking in self-awareness. His business occupied the middle of a brightly lit block on the southern end of Black Bear Forge beneath a sign that read — no kidding — "Honest Joe's Cheap Cars!"

They weren't *used* cars. God, no! They were *pre-owned vehicles.* 'Used' sounded crass and Joe Rutherford was *not* crass. No sir, not Honest Joe. Though his loud voice, big toothy smile, too-long hair swept back in a style last popular in about 1985, pastel suits with ties that were too-wide and too-colorful, and shiny black patent leather shoes might seem to indicate otherwise, Joe was "just folks." The Rutherford family, scattered all over Chicken Gizzard Ridge in northern Yarmouth County, were "poor but proud." He had come from "good people," he'd tell anybody who asked, had pulled himself up by his own bootstraps.

Joe had assumed the mantle of Yarmouth County mayor during the Covid lockdown, in an election with the lowest voter turnout in the county's history. Up for reelection in 2024, he was facing stiff opposition. His campaign signs, featuring the slogan "I'll do right by Yarmouth County" beneath his grinning face, were plastered to every utility pole for twenty miles in every direction.

As the chief executive officer of the county, his authority included supervision of the sheriff's department. Sheriff Jedediah T. Mumford had ignored him and had instructed Mitchell Webster, his stand-in, to do the same.

"Beneath Honest Joe Rutherford's gregarious exterior lies a limitless capacity for treachery," Mum had said the day Mitch had moved his things into the sheriff's office. "Don't trust him any farther than you can throw Mount Rushmore, and don't turn your back on him or you'll find a knife in it."

Rutherford was waiting in Mitch's office when he came in to work Tuesday, the morning after Earl Watson's death.

"Mitchell, my man," Rutherford bellowed, and jumped up from where he'd been sitting in Mitch's chair behind Mitch's desk. He pounded Mitch on the back. "Me and Maggie been meaning to have you over to the house for supper. My Maggie makes pot roast that falls off the bone and the best corn bread in Yarmouth County."

She certainly had no competition from Lily Bishop in the cornbread-making department.

"What can I do for you today, Mr. Rutherford?"

"Joe, my friends call me Joe. And we're gonna be good friends, you and me. I can tell you're my kind of people."

"Well, then, Joe, why don't you have a seat and tell me why you're here?"

"I like a man who gets right to the point. You and me are gonna get along fine, son. Just fine."

Son. From a man who couldn't have been five years older than Mitch. It had the greasy, off-putting feel of being called, "boy."

Mitch remained silent then, assuming Joe had some kind of warmup routine he performed every time he met somebody new. Best to just let him wind down on his own so he would get to the point, say what he had to say, and leave. Mitch had work to do.

Rutherford pontificated with a few more inane remarks, then finally settled in the chair in front of Mitch's desk. He didn't sit back in it, barely parked his backside on the edge, like he might need to leap up and go running off somewhere at a moment's notice.

"Okay, I'm here to talk to you about that tourist who passed on last night at the Quik Stop store."

"Earl Watson? What about him?"

"It's nothing about him personally, it's more about how we frame his death for the public."

"Frame his death? My preliminary investigation indicates that somebody poured gasoline over his head and set him on fire."

"Now see, there's the thing. You don't need to be going off half-cocked with your personal theories from a preliminary investigation. Truth of the matter is, you don't even have an official cause of death, do you. I know, 'cause I talked to the coroner in Gatlinburg this morning and he said he had not yet performed an autopsy."

"You don't need a medical degree to determine what killed Earl Watson. His body was burned to a crisp."

"That is unfortunate phrasing, sheriff. 'Burned to a crisp' is not the kind of professional terminology I expect from the law officers in my command."

Law officers in his command? Mitch didn't like where this seemed to be going.

"I apologize for the crudeness of my description. I simply meant that there is no dispute about how Earl Watson died."

Rutherford rose from the chair and walked casually to the window in Mitch's office that looked out over the town square.

"I was born and raised in Yarmouth County. So was my daddy and his daddy before him. When I was a boy, Black Bear Forge was a typical little mountain town, struggling to stay afloat from one year to the next."

He turned back toward Mitch and gestured out the window. "Now look at it. Our economy is thriving. There's not a single empty store front on Main Street. You go look at other little towns around here and see if you can say that about them. You can't. We're prosperous. And do you know why we're prosperous? One word, Mitch. One word. Tourism."

Now, he could see where this conversation was headed.

"I am well aware of the importance of tourists to the economy of this county, Mr. Mayor."

"Not just important. Tourists are our life blood. Their presence puts food on the tables of every man, woman and child in Yarmouth county. And those of us who have been given responsibility to oversee the health and well-being of our fellow citizens must always keep in mind how fragile a thing tourism is. You never know what might set people off, what might make John and Jane Tourist decide they'd rather take their dollars somewhere besides the Smoky Mountains. Sometimes it doesn't take but one little thing that gets all blown out of proportion. The papers get ahold of the story and they twist it and distort it, and all of a sudden, the folks out there on the flat decide they might rather go to the beach this year because the beach is *safer* than the mountains. Are you getting the drift of what I'm saying, son?"

Mitch got it all right.

"Mr. Mayor—"

"Joe."

"All right then, Joe. I know we have to be careful not to unduly alarm our guests. We need to do everything we can to make them glad they decided to spend their vacations with us. What I don't get is how the death of Earl Watson fits into it. What is it you would like for me to do regarding his case?"

"It's not what I want you to do. It's what I want you *not* to do. I don't want you making a big thing out of that man dying. If you let them, the press will write stories that make it seem like the mountains are full of killers and it ain't safe to bring the wife and kids to the Smokies."

Mitch started to speak, but Rutherford cut him off.

"Let me be clear. I'm not just speaking for myself. This message is coming from all of my colleagues in the surrounding area, and from folks higher up the food chain than they are."

"And that message is?"

Rutherford, turned and leaned over Mitch's desk.

"That message, son, is put a lid on this investigation and keep it there. If somebody killed the man, then find the killer. Find him fast and make this go away."

"I am devoting all the resources of the Yarmouth County Sheriff's department to solving this crime and bringing the monster who set Earl Watson on fire to justice."

"Fine. Good. Justice is great. I'm all for justice. But right now what matters more to me is that you throw somebody's ass behind bars so we can call this murder solved and move on."

Chapter Sixteen

RILEIGH DROVE past the courthouse the next morning on her way to pay a visit to Wyman Perry, one of the two people the Good GI's had been hired to investigate to determine if either of them had set fire to their own property for the insurance money.

She saw J.P. Rutherford come strutting down the wide steps leading from the old building to the sidewalk and grimaced. Rutherford had to be the most thoroughly unlikeable man she'd just about ever met. How he'd managed to become the mayor of the county was a mystery for the ages. She would bet the pension she no longer had that he wouldn't be reelected in 2024, all his self-aggrandizing posters plastered to every flat surface in the county notwithstanding.

He was a jerk, who smiled broadly at her when he saw her and waved like they were best friends.

She pretended not to notice. Then it occurred to her that maybe the mayor had come out of the courthouse because he'd been paying a visit to the sheriff. Oh, how she hoped Mitch had been spared.

Rileigh had gotten the current address for Wyman Perry from the receptionist at the Good GI's office. He was living in a room at the Mountain View Motel now. Before she went there, she took a detour to the address of his house that had burned. There was almost nothing left of it.

Returning to the motel, Rileigh parked her car and walked down the sidewalk to the doors that faced the parking lot. When she got to number 107, she knocked. She could hear sounds from inside, but no one answered, so she knocked again. The sounds suddenly quieted. Somebody had turned down a television set.

"Somebody out there?" called a voice from inside.

"Yes, I would like to talk to you, Mr. Perry."

"Well, open the door and come on in, then. It ain't like I can come open it for you."

Rileigh opened the door and stepped into the room and was immediately hit by the smell of pizza. Half a dozen empty pizza boxes were strewn across the bare furnishings in the dimly-lit room. It took Rileigh a moment to see the man sitting in the shadows across from the television set, which was on but muted.

"Mr. Perry?"

"Yeah, I'm Wyman Perry? Who are you?"

Rileigh stepped farther into the room, trying to get a look at the man she was talking to.

"Close the damned door. You're gonna let the place fill up with flies."

Rileigh turned and closed the door. When she turned back around, the man who'd spoken out of the shadows had turned on a lamp.

He was *enormous*, so fat he sat encased in a motorized wheelchair like he'd been melted and poured into it. Four hundred pounds if he was an ounce. His huge thighs and backside barely fit between the arms of the wheelchair and his bulging belly hung out over the edge of the seat. His face was — it was the Pillsbury Dough Boy. No discernible features. His nose, mouth and lips had been distorted by fat and his eyes were barely visible, just slits between his bulging cheeks and his eyebrows.

Managing not to show her surprise, Rileigh approached the man and extended her hand.

"I'm Rileigh Bishop. I'm here to talk about the fire that destroyed your home."

The man ignored her extended hand.

"It's about time you showed up. They ain't going to process my claim until I talk to you and I need the money. I got to get me another house— with a ramp." He gestured toward the door of the room. "If I want to go somewhere, I have to call the manager. Then he gets the custodian and the two of them together push on the back of the chair while I use the motor—just to get over the door sill. If there was a curb outside, I'd be stuck here."

"Were you at home when the fire started?"

"No, I was out surfing the beach! Hell yeah, I was home. It's a miracle I ain't dead." He looked down into his lap. "My baby Isabella would have saved my life if she could have."

Rileigh had not even noticed the dog. It was, indeed, about the size of a loaf of bread, but it looked thin and fragile. Clearly this was a senior dog, which meant it was probably the same dog that Wally had complained about when Perry was his neighbor years ago.

"How could he have saved your life?"

"She! Her name's Isabella. She doesn't look like a boy dog. You don't put pink bows on boy dogs."

Now that she looked carefully, she could see that the dog had a pink bow headband stretched across her ears.

"Sorry, how could she have saved your life?"

"She'd have picked my ass up, thrown me over her shoulder in a fireman carry, and hauled me outside." He curled his lip in a sarcastic snarl. "She'd have started barking. Duh."

"But she didn't start barking. Why not?"

"She can't. Got something wrong with her throat and the vet wanted to do surgery to fix it, but I wouldn't let him cut up my baby."

"So, if her barking didn't wake you up, what did?"

"Did I say I was asleep?"

"No, I just—"

"You came here to ask questions, so listen when I answer them."

Rileigh kept her mouth shut.

"I was not asleep. I was watching television in the basement and suddenly all the fire alarms upstairs started going off."

"In the basement. How did you—" she gestured toward the chair— "get out?"

"I flew out." Another sarcastic snarl. "Did your mother have any children that lived?"

Again, Rileigh remained silent.

"I drove my wheelchair out, that's how. I had the house built especially to accommodate it. The doorways and the halls are extra wide, the shower has no lip, and none of the doors have sills. The basement is a walk-out to my deck. And I have an elevator, but you're not supposed to use an elevator in a fire, remember?"

He paused.

"*Had* an elevator and wide halls and doors and no sills. Now …"

For a moment his nasty disposition was siphoned away by real sadness and she felt sorry for him.

"I can't go anywhere now. This is the only motel in town I can afford and–"

He must have caught himself and realized he was being a decent human being, because the snarl again curled his lip.

"The insurance company said they couldn't pay my claim until they investigated. You're the investigator, right? You done?"

"I have all the information I need, yes."

"Good, then get the hell out of here and go back to your office, write up a report or whatever it is you do to get the ball rolling."

He shook his head.

"They're gonna refuse to pay my claim. Mark my words, they're gonna find some loophole that frees them from liability and I'm gonna have to sue the bastards."

Rileigh turned toward the door. Before she got to it, there was a knock.

"Dammit. What's that — Avon calling?"

The door opened a crack and a young man in a red uniform and cap stuck his head inside.

"Pizza delivery," he said. "A supreme with extra everything— bacon, sausage, pepperoni, cheese and anchovies."

"Dammit. Can't you get anything right? I said no anchovies. Doesn't anybody listen anymore?"

Rileigh started toward the flustered young man in the doorway.

"Where do you think you're going?"

"My interview is finished and–"

"You ain't leaving here until you tell me whether I passed or failed your 'investigation.'"

"I can't tell you the eventual outcome of your case–"

She held up her hand to forestall the raging diatribe she could see forming on his face. "But I can tell you what my recommendation will be. I will recommend that the claim be honored."

His face froze. He'd probably been expecting some other response.

"Oh. Well, then, thank you."

There was a heartbeat pause before the big man turned his attention back to the pizza delivery guy.

"Put that pizza box on the table over there," he told the young man, who would have to place it on top of three other boxes already on the table or scoot them off onto the floor to make room for it. "Open it up. You're gonna pick off every one of them damn anchovies. Do you hear me? Every one."

Rileigh made her escape then, edging past the trapped pizza delivery boy and hurrying out of the motel room into the fresh air that didn't reek of marinara sauce. She had told Wyman Perry the truth. She would tell her boss and the Long Run Insurance Company they did not need to unleash a ravishing horde of investigating locusts on Mr. Perry, though God knows she wished they would. Any idiot could see the man could not physically have set fire to his own house. Somebody else had started that fire.

Wally was going to be disappointed when she turned in the final report, and now she could see why he would want to nail that miserable human being for something. But he was just that — miserable. Wyman Perry's life was bad enough even without karma visiting retribution on his head.

Chapter Seventeen

Rileigh did the same thing with the second suspect that she'd done with the first. Before she went to talk to a woman named Nettie Jarvis, she went to the address of the house that had burned to the ground a week ago. It was a sad site, nothing left now but a row of blackened concrete blocks that looked like rotting teeth. Though nothing stood now but the chimney, from what she could see of the remains, it had been a small frame house. Rumors said it had burned shockingly fast, suggesting that someone had helped the fire along with an accelerant.

What was left behind all around it, though trampled into the mud by the firefighters who'd tried in vain to extinguish the flames, was a garden full of flowers. All the way around the house, bent and brutalized, blossoms struggled to right themselves in the morning sunlight.

Whoever had planted those flowers had taken good care of them, which, in Rileigh's book, was always a point on anybody's scorecard. If you loved flowers, nature, wildlife — you couldn't possibly be all bad.

Rileigh's GPS directed her to a large brick house on a small piece of land just outside Dollywood, the house of Nettie's daughter. She rang the doorbell and a young woman about her own age answered.

"My name is Rileigh Bishop, and I believe the Long Run Insurance Agency notified someone living at this address — Nettie Jarvis — that they'd be sending someone to talk to her about the house that burned."

"She told me about that." The woman eyed her up and down. "I don't mind telling you, I told her not to talk to you, Mama doesn't know anything about the fire. She just woke up in the dark to the dog barking and the smoke alarms going off. She barely got out of there alive."

"Selena, dear, I can handle this," came a voice from behind the young woman. An older woman, looked slightly older than Rileigh's mother, stood behind her daughter.

The old woman came forward. "I'm Nettie Jarvis–" she cast a disparaging look at her daughter— "and I am happy to talk to anybody who might be able to figure out what happened to my house. Please come in."

The young woman turned and left the two of them standing inside the foyer. Nettie led Rileigh to a small parlor that smelled of fresh flowers and furniture polish. Before the old woman took a seat, she stopped to bury her face in the blossoms of a dozen beautiful yellow roses in a vase.

"Now, how can I help you?"

"I promise not to take up a whole lot of your time. I just have a couple of questions. Would you mind telling me about the day your house burned?"

"Not day, sweetheart, night. It was the dead of night and I was sound asleep." The old woman's voice was soft and colored with a rich southern accent— Georgia,

Alabama, or Mississippi. It gave her an almost aristocratic sound. She was small and delicate, with pure white hair in a bun at the back of her neck and small delicate hands that fidgeted in her lap when she spoke.

"In fact, if it hadn't been for Clementine—"

"Clementine?" Rileigh asked.

"My dog. She's a little miniature Schnauzer, not much bigger than a loaf of bread."

Rileigh thought about the loaf of bread dog that was so obnoxious, her boss had sold his house and moved to get away from it.

"Clementine started barking. It wasn't like her to do that. She hardly ever barked and certainly not in the middle of the night. And it wasn't an excited yapping, like some dogs do all the time, the yap-yap-yapping the makes you want to cut your ears off with a cheese grater."

Rileigh burst out laughing, and the old woman waited patiently for her to quiet.

"You and my boss have the same opinion about those dogs."

"Clementine wasn't yapping. She was full-on barking. She sleeps in a little doggie bed at the foot of my bed, and she jumped up on my bed — she's never allowed on the furniture — but she jumped up and was hopping around on the bed on top of me, barking and barking, and then the smoke alarm went off."

The woman paused. "When that young man came to install the smoke detectors in my house, he told me that I'd need to be careful about cooking things that smoked, that the detectors were so sensitive even a cigar could set them off."

She made a humph sound in her throat "Clementine woke me up long before the smoke detectors got into the act. I ought to go demand my money back." She paused. "But really I don't think Clementine woke me up because she smelled smoke. I think something else set her off."

"What else?"

The old woman shrugged.

"Everything happened so fast after that. I sat up in bed, I could smell smoke then, and I went to go see. But as soon as I opened my bedroom door, I knew I just needed to run. The whole back part of the house was full of smoke."

"Have you talked to the fire department about the cause of the fire?"

The woman went on as if she hadn't heard Rileigh, conjuring up images of that night in the air in front of her.

"I ran through the parlor and started out the front door, and then I saw ... There are picture albums on shelves in the parlor, and I thought I couldn't leave them. So I started back. I had to save them, else there'd be no record of my life, my kids growing up, birthdays and Christmases. But Clementine wouldn't let me go back. It was like she was one of those Australian shepherds. She was herding me toward the door. Got between me and the book shelves and barked like she was about to bite my leg off." Nettie sighed. "So I left."

When she was silent, Rileigh asked again if the fire department had told her how the fire started.

The woman still didn't answer her question. Just took up her narrative where she'd left off. Rileigh understood then that once she started the story, she had to go all the way through it to the end. She had to tell it all.

"I ran outside with Clementine. I got all the way to the gate in the fence and my hand was shaking and I couldn't seem to get the latch to work. It only took me a little while to get it open and I got out of the yard and turned around. But in that little amount of time, it was all ... all on fire."

Rileigh was tempted to again ask about the fire department, but she held her tongue until Nettie was done telling her story.

"So I stood there outside the front yard, with Clementine whining at my feet, and watched everything I owned in the world vanish. There's a picture window in the living room and I could see the flames in the curtains spreading to the couch and chairs and the rug on the floor. It looked like — like I was looking in a window into hell."

She began to whisper then. "The little curio cabinet where we put the figurines we got at Niagara Falls on our honeymoon. George built that cabinet from scratch out of black walnut, cut the tree down and everything. The pictures of the kids on the walls, the ones when they were little. The glass on Ellie's picture turned black. John's picture didn't have glass, so his face caught fire."

Her shoulders began to shake then, but she didn't cry out loud, kept whispering as tears ran down her cheeks.

"And the birds! I didn't think about the birds. I had two parakeets in a cage by the window beside the back door. I didn't even think about them until later. And I thought, I could have saved them. I could have run around the house and gone in the back door, they were right there." she paused. "But the firemen said no. They said that's where the fire started, in the back of the house."

There was Rileigh's opening.

"What else did the fire department tell you about the fire?"

"They said it was set. It was deliberate. Somebody did it on purpose. Can you imagine that? Setting somebody's house on fire on purpose?"

She said the firemen knew that because there had been what they called "an accelerant" used to start the fire. Gasoline.

Rileigh asked a few more questions, thanked Nettie for her time, and drove away. Rileigh had known when she got there that the fire had been deliberately set.

But what she knew when she drove away was that the arsonist wasn't Nettie Jarvis.

Chapter Eighteen

IT TOOK Mitch a few minutes to shake off the foul mood occasioned by his visit with His Honorable Asshole, as Mum had referred to the Mayor Rutherford.

Why was it that so many people like him wound up as "public servants," when the only entity in the universe they "served" was their almighty self?

Let it go, Mitch, he told himself. Let it go.

It was not to pacify the county mayor that Mitch needed to find Earl Watson's killer. And it wasn't just that it was Mitch's job, either. It felt like more than that. He'd made something of a connection to Earl, who he had known for less than fifteen minutes — from the time Edna rolled down her window and told him she needed help until a dying Earl screamed out his life and then fell over dead in the parking lot.

But there was something, when their eyes met and locked. He was sure that if he'd known the man, he'd have liked him. They'd have been friends.

Mitch was determined to find out who had killed him. And most of the investigation was likely to be "virtual."

That was the way of things though, now, and it was a tick up the ladder from a phone call.

The Glorietta chief of police of had agreed to go on a Zoom call with Mitch at nine thirty, Eastern time, which was eight-thirty in Nebraska. Mitch said a prayer for reliable wifi and went to the county's zoom channel a little after nine. Chief Charles Henderson clicked in instantly.

"Thanks so much for agreeing to talk to me Chief Henderson. As I said in my email, a resident of Glorietta was killed last night here in Tennessee and–"

"What happened? Tell it to me straight. Me and Earl, we was good friends."

That made it even harder for Mitch to say the words.

"Straight up, then. Earl Watson and his wife, Edna, stopped at a convenience store on the edge of Black Bear Forge, Tennessee — here in Yarmouth County — to ask me for directions to the interstate leading to Knoxville."

The police chief, a ruddy-faced man whose receding hair was probably carrot-colored when he was young, burped out a little laugh.

"Edna Watson couldn't pour water out a boot if the instructions was on the heel. I'm sure they've been wandering around lost most of the time they've been gone on vacation."

"After I talked to them, they went to the bathrooms on the outside of the building and I went inside to pay for my gasoline. Maybe five minutes later, I heard screaming and Earl was–" He only hesitated for a moment, had promised to tell the story straight up. "—on his knees crawling away from the sidewalk. He was on fire, completely engulfed in flames."

He saw the words hit the police chief in the belly, heard the little groan he let out, but he kept his face impassive and professional.

"There was nothing anybody could have done for him. He was obviously dead by the time I reached him."

"What happened? Why? How'd he—"

"It wasn't an accident. He'd been doused with gasoline — a lot of it — and then set on fire."

"Son of a bitch!" The man slammed his fist down on his desk and looked away for a few moments, then looked back and reengaged.

"Who? Why? A bunch of damned teenagers high on something?"

"I don't think so. I ran to the side of the building where he'd gone and there was a puddle of burning gasoline in front of the bathroom door. I don't believe a group of kids could have gotten away that fast. There's a parking lot behind the building, and I believe somebody, maybe more than one somebody but not a group, drove away before I had time to get around the building."

"What was the motive? Just some random killing?"

"That's what I'm trying to find out. It's why I called you. I wanted to get find out if there was anybody back home who'd have any motive to—"

"To kill Earl Watson? Not a chance. He was probably the best liked, most respected man in town. I know I'm biased, we have been friends since high school. But I'm telling you that Earl was … he was special."

"Edna mentioned to me that he was the county fire chief and that he got injured recently. What do you know about that?"

"I know that it was the kind of heroism you see on television. The kind you ought to see but they won't publicize, because they want everybody to think there are no good people in this country anymore. Earl went back into a burning building to get a cat. A cat! For the Conroe family. Gas leak, it was a miracle they weren't all killed. But then

Brandy, she's six, she started screaming, saying her cat was still inside. And damned if Earl didn't go running back in there to get it. He got her, but he was in bad shape when he brought her out. Smoke inhalation, and he inhaled some kind of toxic gas— they had some kind of plastic chairs that burned and…" Henderson paused for a moment. "Anyway, that was last year and Earl ain't never been the same since. Can't breathe right, and it messed with his vision too, though he didn't let on there was nothing wrong with him at all."

"So you're saying you don't know of anybody who would have anything against the man, some kind of grudge, any reason to–"

"To set him on fire and burn him alive? Hell, no!"

The police chief had to fight for control then.

"Let me tell you something about Earl Watson. This is something don't nobody else in town know. Edna has always been strange. That's all you could say about her, just always was odd. She got real reclusive. It started years ago, and she's just gotten worse and worse over time. I figured agoraphobia or something like that, but she got where she wouldn't leave the house, wouldn't let anybody come in neither, not even her kids. Earl had to do everything — go to the grocery, do all the shopping. He kept the yard neat as a pin, had a big garden with vegetables and flowers and he took care of the whole thing."

Mitch couldn't help but wonder what this had to do with Earl's death, but he trusted the other sheriff to have a reason for telling him this.

"When Earl got hurt, I picked up Edna to take her to the hospital in Lincoln. She was waiting for me outside, and when I asked could I go inside to use her bathroom before we left, she said the toilet didn't work. I thought that was odd."

He gave a little shake of his head, like he still couldn't fathom Edna's lack of hospitality. Then he continued:

"After Earl retired, his car was in the shop so I offered to give him a ride to an eye specialist in Lincoln. I went to his house and knocked on the door, but didn't nobody hear me. Edna musta had her hearing aids out and she's about deaf without them. And Earl was in the shower. So I knocked again. Nothing. Then I opened the door and stuck my head in to call out, you know like you do. And I couldn't believe what I was saw inside that house. Edna's a *hoarder*— like one of them people you see on TV, but my God. There was not a flat surface anywhere in that whole living room not piled high with junk, and you could see into the dining room and down the hall— stacks of news-papers and magazines all the way up to the ceiling, just a little aisle between the junk you'd have to turn sideways to walk down." Henderson's voice trailed off.

"I have never seen anything like it in my life. Earl's been living in *that* in that mess for twenty-five years and never said a word about it. I wasn't gonna say anything, but Earl's good at reading people. He made me swear not to tell anybody, said Edna'd be so embarrassed. He loves her and he don't want her to be embarrassed." He paused. "*Loved* her. He's gone."

The police chief was openly crying now, his voice was almost too tear-clotted to understand.

"I'm sorry. I didn't mean to go on and on like that. But you can see, can't you. You can see what a good person he was, what a fine man. Ain't nobody in the world got anything to hold against Earl Watson. That man was a saint."

Mitch ended the call and sat for awhile, looking at his blank computer screen. He had the names and phone numbers of other people to call in Glorietta about Earl, but he knew it was going to be a total waste of time. It had been a long shot anyway— somebody from home traveling a thousand miles to commit murder. Now Mitch was sure that's not what happened. Somebody from here, or some other tourist, had done the deed.

And if it was indeed a random crime, there was almost no chance in the world he'd find the killer and make him pay for what he did.

Chapter Nineteen

RILEIGH WENT from Nettie's house to the Black Bear Forge Volunteer Fire Department to talk to the fire chief. The department had already reported that the fire marshal had ruled the fires arson to Long Run Insurance Agency in Gatlinburg — that's who'd hired the Good GI's to look into the case.

Rileigh wanted an official copy of the fire marshal's reports. Just dotting her i's and crossing her t's before she turned in her own official report.

"You got a minute, Pete?" Rileigh asked as she stuck her head through the open door to the fire chief's office. Pete Brady was a big bear of a man who played Santa Claus every year at the annual Christmas parade. He had gone to high school with Rileigh, and he'd had a crush on her for years.

"If I was any better, I'd have to be twins," he said, looking up from a pile of papers on his desk and smiling. "Please tell me you've come to kidnap me and take me to a remote cabin somewhere in the woods and ravish me!"

"Uh, that'd be a negative on the kidnapping and

ravishing, but I'll buy you a cup of coffee if you'll talk to me about the fire at Nettie Jarvis's house."

"What do you say we skip the kidnapping part and I come along voluntarily for the ravishing?"

Rileigh shook her head. "Coffee offer will expire in five, four, three, two–"

"I got coffee in the break room. Let's go see if we can find a clean mug."

Ten minutes later, they were seated in the break room, where Rileigh was drinking black coffee as thick as crank case oil from a mug that said, 'I'm not insensitive, I just don't give a shit.'

"Somebody set both of those fires deliberately, you're sure of that," she asked the fire chief.

"Not a single itty bitty doubt, Sugar. The fire marshal ruled the same thing. Neither one of them fires was a sophisticated arson, though. In the Wyman house, somebody splattered gasoline all over the floor and walls in the kitchen and living room and then lit a match. You can tell that kind of thing by the scorch marks on the walls and floor. There wasn't enough house left to check for marks on the walls and floor at the Jarvis house. But we did find the gasoline can."

"Seriously? Somebody set fire to the place and then left the gasoline can?"

"I don't figure the arsonist dropped it on purpose. Musta got startled by something and boogied. But the can burned, so no chance of prints on it."

Rileigh remembered Nettie telling her that she didn't think her dog started barking at the smoke, that she thought Clementine had been awakened by something else.

"Have you met the woman who owned the house, Nettie Jarvis?"

"No, I got lucky and missed that one. The guys said she was one devastated old lady."

"That one? There have been others?"

"Yup. We've been called out four, no, five times in the past month to building fires that I think were deliberately set."

"Is that normal? Are there usually that many on-purpose fires?"

"Nope."

"Did you report it to the sheriff?"

"That new guy?" he asked dismissively. "In a manner of speaking."

"What does that mean?"

"It means I file a report on every fire run we make, so they've all been 'reported.' If you mean, did I tell anybody I thought some of the fires were arson— no, because the arson part's just my opinion. The state fire marshal hasn't ruled on all of them yet."

"Would you mind telling me where the other two fires were beside the Wyman and Jarvis houses?"

"I will tell you anything you want to know, Darlin'. You just remember how helpful I've been. The next time I make a kidnapping/ravishing offer, you might want to give it more careful consideration."

Rileigh left Pete's office half an hour later with official fire reports on three other buildings in addition to the two she'd been hired to investigate. The fire marshal was still working on the other three and had made no ruling yet in any of them.

She was off the clock now, could go home and file her report and be done with it. But the other three fires were an itch she had to scratch. One of them was an out-building behind Ian McGinnis's house. Ian was Georgia Stump's older brother, a man Rileigh had spent one whole awful afternoon believing had murdered her sister. He hadn't, but he had taken her Aunt Daisy out to the grass hut the day Tina Montgomery was murdered, giving Aunt Daisy the opportunity to kill her.

Ian was working in his wood shop when Rileigh pulled into his driveway, and she heaved a sigh of relief. The fire report said the building that had burned was an "out build-ing," and Rileigh had been terrified it was Ian's wood shop. He was a master craftsman — made furniture from oak, cherry and walnut he cut down in the woods on his prop-erty, one-of-a-kind pieces special ordered from people all over the country. Georgia had told Rileigh that her brother was so swamped by orders on his website, he would be covered up in work until Christmas.

When she got out of the car and approached the woodshed, she spotted the remains of the outbuilding that'd been torched and went to take a look at it.

"If you came to borrow my weedeater, you're an hour late and a nickel short," Ian called out when he saw her.

He put away the sander he was using on the side panel of an oak armoire and came to stand beside her as she surveyed the ruins.

"Got your tool shed, I see," Rileigh said.

"Better that than the workshop. I wasn't here when the fire started. My neighbor, Hank Pettigrew, saw the smoke and called the fire department, then he called me. By the time I got here, there was nothing left but burnt timber."

"What all did you have stored in there?"

"Mostly yard equipment — the lawn mower and the weed-eater, rakes and hoes, a wheelbarrow and some fertil-izer. Stuff like that. There was a can of gasoline, too, and maybe that was used to start the fire."

"You have any idea who could have set it?"

"My, but you're full of questions. You didn't just

happen to be driving by and saw the burned-out hulk and stopped to offer your condolences, did you?"

"I'm working a case for the Good GI's. Insurance fraud. And when I started looking into it, I saw that building fires weren't a particularly stand-out event this month in Yarmouth County."

"So it wasn't just me?"

"Four arson fires so far, if yours was arson."

"It was. The fire marshal hasn't ruled yet, but how could it not be? Buildings don't just catch on fire from spontaneous combustion. I've had two theories on who the culprit might be. But now, maybe there's a third explanation."

"What were your theories?"

"Theory Number One — there are a whole herd of teenage boys living on the other side of Buck's Point, enough to start their own street gang. They go around knocking mailboxes off poles, shooting holes in stop signs, that kind of thing. Maybe they're responsible."

"And Theory Number Two?"

"Random act of violence. This building's right up beside the road, easy to get to, easy to get away from. Some asshole got drunk and decided to burn it down."

"Wouldn't have anything to do with that group of friends of yours at the Wheaton House, the ones I got to know up close and *impersonal* — since they blindfolded me and I couldn't see them?"

Rileigh had gone looking for Ian when she was working on the Tina Montgomery case and had found him at an old estate deep back in the hollows, meeting with a dozen or more other people who kidnapped her.

Okay, maybe it was only technically kidnapping, since they merely tied her up with duct tape and put a cap over her eyes, but they didn't actually take her off the premises.

When she'd asked Ian about the group, he'd gone all mysterious on her, saying they weren't doing anything illegal … *yet.* And that because of them, there was a day coming when Rileigh would have to "pick a side."

Ian's face went hard.

"None of those people would have burned down my tool shed."

"Draw the line at kidnapping, do they? Not at arson?"

She knew as soon as she spoke the words that she shouldn't have said them.

"Nobody *kidnapped* you. You were the one sneaking around with a gun. They–"

"Look, I'm sorry, I didn't mean–"

"To go running off at the mouth about people you know nothing about? Save your apology for some time when you can deliver it personally. An opportunity that, I suspect, might not be long coming."

"What in the hell are you talking about?"

"You brought them up, I didn't. I'm just saying they didn't have anything to do with this fire. And that sooner or later, you're bound to run into them again. Between now and then, you might want to keep an open mind."

"You are being deliberately mysterious— why?"

"I'm just choosing not to tell you something that's none of your business."

Rileigh backed off. He was right, of course. Who those people were and what they were doing was none of her business. And Ian was her best friend's older brother, a man who'd kept his mouth shut about a whole lot of family secrets over the years, both his and hers.

"Fair enough. So what's you third theory?"

"Think about it Rileigh, four fires. If you've decided to burn your house down to collect the insurance money, it might be a good idea to do whatever you could do to keep your fire from standing out. You know, divert suspicion by setting some other fires. So yours isn't the only one."

Rileigh hadn't considered that possibility.

"Did you see or hear anything that would help the sheriff figure out who did this?"

"The sheriff? He's checking into who burned down my storage shed?"

"Not yet. But if there's some kind of pattern here, he might be."

"If I think of anything, I'll let you know."

Rileigh turned to go, had gotten halfway back to her aunt Daisy's car when Ian called after her.

"Does this have anything to do with that tourist who got killed yesterday?"

"Maybe," she said, and only then considered the possibility. Perhaps there was some link between the person who burned down Ian's out building— maybe Wyman Perry's, Lettie Jarvis's and Frank Smothers's business, too — and the man who burned to death last night. The connection being fire itself.

Was the arsonist some sicko who got his rocks off watching something — or some*body*— burn?

Chapter Twenty

AFTER THE SMOTHERS AUTO BODY SHOP on Half Mile Creek burned to the ground, the state fire marshal ruled the fire was arson.

Frank Smothers was the owner of the business, located between Black Bear Forge and Pigeon Forge, an eyesore where he parked dozens of dead cars to use for spare parts. It was an elephant's graveyard of Fords, Chevy's, Nissans and Toyotas, and all manner of other vehicles in such a state of decay it was impossible to tell what kind of car they might once have been.

He was breaking a whole host of county ordinances by keeping such an eyesore within a hundred feet of a main road without putting up a berm, a fence, bushes, something to hide the view. The metal fence he had installed was unpainted and had quickly rusted, turning it into as big an eyesore as the cars behind it. The fence only stretched across about a third of his property, and when Rileigh had looked into the records about his property, she found that he was being sued by several of his neighbors for various offenses, including creating a public nuisance and keeping unlicensed, unleashed dogs on the property.

She didn't know the man, but she had heard he was a loudmouthed drunk who had run off his wife and children, and now lived alone in a dilapidated trailer house behind the business.

The structure that had burned was not easily accessible from the road — it was not a building that would be easy to access undetected.

Rileigh drove out to his address and pulled off onto a bumpy lane that dead-ended in front of the ruins of the business. She sat in her car for a few moments after she turned off the engine, gathering herself. It was possible there were dangerous dogs on the property; at least several neighbors had alleged as much when they took him to court six months ago. Rileigh was a cat person, if she had to choose any pet at all. She had never felt comfortable around dogs, particularly not big dogs.

She saw no animals, or humans either for that matter, so she got out and walked with a whole lot more confidence than she felt around the picnic table that sat beside the rickety metal porch, then up to the front door of the trailer house, where she knocked on the door.

No one answered.

She knocked again, and her fist was still in the air when the door was suddenly yanked open. An ugly man in grease-covered overalls stood just inside.

"Who are you and what do you want?"

Behind him stood a huge dog of indeterminate lineage — some kind of Doberman-pit bull mix. It growled at her, baring its teeth, and it took all the courage she possessed not to turn tail and run back to her car and drive away.

"My name is Rileigh Bishop and I'd like to ask you

some questions about the fire that destroyed your business."

The man was instantly suspicious. Glancing past her at her car, he said, "You're one of *them*, the ones tryna fill up the mountains with outsiders. Bet you're there every day, all smiles, invitin' strangers here. You are, ain't ya? Every day!"

For a moment she had no idea what he was talking about. Then she she remembered the *Y'all Come* sticker Aunt Daisy had slapped on the car's bumper. Her aunt was a faithful volunteer at the Chamber of Commerce's *Y'all Come* cabin, until she got too crazy to work there.

But it was Rileigh's car now, and she needed to peel that sticker off the bumper.

"Were you at home when the fire that burned your business started?" she asked.

"Everything I owned was in that building and now it's all gone and my life has gone to shit."

"Do you know how it started or—"

"Why the hell do you want to know?"

"I'm investigating a series of arson fires that have happened in Yarmouth County recently."

"Arson. Fire that was deliberately set, right?"

"Yes, sir. Though the state fire marshal has yet to issue an official report on one of the fires, their preliminary investigation indicates that—"

"Somebody set those fires on purpose, that what you're saying?"

"Didn't the fire department notify you of their findings?"

"You think I set fire to my own business?"

There was clear menace in his tone.

"I'm not accusing you of anything, Mr. Smothers. I just—"

"'Cause if you sayin' I was the one done it, that's a pretty serious charge, arson is."

As the man's mood darkened, so did the mood of his dog. It stopped growling, which, as Rileigh understood it, was not a good thing. She'd read somewhere that when a dog growls that's a warning. It's when the dog stops warning you and prepares to make good on the threat that you're in trouble.

"Mr. Smothers, I—"

"Who sent you out here? Was it the law? You a cop?"

"No, I'm not a cop."

Saying the words caused her to mentally square her shoulders. No, she wasn't a police officer, but she had been one once and it was time to start acting like it.

"Not right now, anyway." She dangled the words out in front of her as a shield. "You're not in trouble with the law. I've been hired by—"

"If you ain't the law, you ain't got no right to be here. Get off my porch. I ain't saying another word."

At that point, she would have expected to see the door slam in her face. But Frank Smothers didn't do that. Instead he shoved it *open*, stepped aside, and allowed his dog to go through it. The dog didn't lunge at her, like she thought it would, just backed her into the corner of the porch against the railing.

"It'd be a shame if you's to come out here and I wasn't home. If I left my dog guarding my house and he thought you was here up to no good."

It was a pure reflex. Rileigh had the Glock out of its holster with her right hand and pointed at the dog in an instant.

"You call that dog off or I'll shoot it dead."

"You ain't gonna shoot my dog."

"First the dog, so he can't attack me after I shoot you."

"And you ain't gonna shoot me neither."

"Pal, you need to get your head out of your ass and come to a quick understanding of reality here. I will drop you where you stand in a heartbeat. I've killed dozens of men in Afghanistan and Iraq. The number of seconds you have to breathe in and out is a one-digit number unless you *call off this dog.*"

"I can't call him off. I didn't sic him on you. If I'd sicced him on you, he'd a tore your throat out by now."

"Five seconds, Mr. Smothers. Four, three."

Rileigh absolutely would shoot the dog if the man didn't call it off. The part about shooting him afterward had been a bluff, but the other was pure truth.

"He just knows you're scared of him and he's being a bully, like he always does." Smothers took two steps toward the dog and grabbed his collar, then started dragging him back inside.

"Come on Rex. Dammit. Back off."

The dog didn't obey, stood his ground and never stopped snarling at Rileigh, ears laid back close to his head. He would attack at the slightest provocation. She held completely still.

"Get in the house fore I take a belt to you."

Smothers had to drag the animal by force back into the house. He shoved the dog inside and slammed the door in his face, which left Smothers on the porch with Rileigh.

"You can put that gun away now," he said, and for the first time she could see that she had definitely intimidated the man. She was not about to holster her weapon though. The neighbors had complained about vicious dogs — plural. There were likely more beasts around as foul-tempered as Rex.

"Not a chance. You go back into the house. Move slow."

"Fine. But you get off my property, you hear me, and don't come back." He turned and opened the screen, then looked through the mesh at her. "And you're gonna be sorry you messed with Frank Smothers. Mark it down. You're gonna pay for pulling a gun on me. And tell whoever sent you to back off. Anybody else comes nosing around out here, I'll sic the dogs on them."

So there were more than just the one.

Smothers had to shove the dog out of the way in order to get into the house, then he shut the door behind him.

Rileigh kept her gun drawn. She wasn't able to hold it in a true two-hand grip because her left wrist was immobilized. She steadied the gun with her left hand, though. That was the best she could do. A trained adversary would have noted the brace on her arm, might have pressed an advantage. It was way easier to knock a weapon aside if it was held in only one hand.

She walked to the steps and went down them quickly, but she didn't run. Damned if she'd give that son of a bitch the satisfaction of seeing her run. She did, however, walk with purpose back to her car, holstering her gun only when she needed her right hand to open the car door.

Driving away from Frank Smother's house, she made a decision. She'd be reporting later that neither of the two cases she'd been hired to investigate were guilty of trying to defraud the insurance company with their claims.

But Frank Smothers?

Now there was a man not only capable of such an act but stupid enough to commit it. The fire marshals had yet to officially designate the fire at his business arson, but she was sure they would. Maybe Long Run Insurance agency happened to be his insurance carrier.

It was worth finding out.

Chapter Twenty-One

RILEIGH HAD LIVED in Yarmouth County her whole life, knew it and all the Smoky Mountains like her back yard. The hollow deep in the hanging valley on the far side of Clear Creek Mountain was about as isolated as it was possible to get, one of those places so remote the sun only shows up a couple of times a week.

The road leading up the mountainside was aptly named Pebble Road. It had once been gravel, but whatever the road surface had once been had mostly washed away. If the firetruck actually had come out this far, it was a miracle it ever got back down the mountainside. Rileigh wondered if perhaps she'd taken a wrong turn somewhere, because there was no place big enough to build a house.

But then she topped the rise and a small hollow opened up before her, not completely flat, but with considerable less incline than the grade getting there. In the hollow was an old house that looked like it had been there a couple hundred years. It wasn't rundown so much as just old. The paint had peeled and the wood bleached out to gray, with a gloss to it like the coat on an Arabian horse.

Beside the house was a huge garden and the obligatory chicken house. She also saw goats and a couple of head of cattle grazing in the meadow beyond. The building that had burned down, the barn, was on the other side of the garden. Nothing remained but a blackened foundation and singed grass and weeds.

The driveway wrapped around the house like her mother's driveway did. The back yard was small and there were several old outbuildings around it.

Rileigh parked her car beside the house and crossed the yard to a stone walkway leading to the back porch. She knocked politely.

What was the difference between a polite knock and a timid one? She didn't want to sound timid. Her disaster interview with Frank Smothers had let her know it was never a good idea to show fear.

Angus Park opened the door as she had her fist raised to knock a second time. He stood behind the screen staring at her.

"I remember you," he said. She recognized him, too. This was the crazy man who had almost scared Mason Stump to death during the meteor shower at Clingman's Dome.

Goody.

If she'd connected the name to the man she'd literally had a fight with that day, she never would have come here unannounced.

"Hope there are no hard feelings. It's just that you were scaring Mason."

"What'd you come all the way out here for?"

She absolutely did not want to tell him she was looking for evidence of insurance fraud. She did not want to have to fight this man. In a fair fight, absent the element of surprise she'd used to subdue him before, he could probably beat her to a bloody lump.

"Uh your barn burned down recently, didn't it? I saw the blackened foundation stones for the driveway."

"It did."

"Would you mind telling me about the fire?"

"Why do you want to know?"

"Well, there have been a rash of house fires in the past couple of months and I'm trying to find out if that's just a coincidence or if the same person is setting them all."

"We called the fire department. Wasn't no use in it, barn was long gone before they got here. But the woods is awful close up behind the barn, and I didn't want it to set the woods on fire."

Everyone was conscious of the danger of forest fires right now, in the middle of a drought. The underbrush was as crisp as cornflakes and it wouldn't take much to do a whole lot of damage.

She picked up on the "we." Was he married? Either that or he just had a mouse in his pocket?

"I see they kept it from spreading."

"*I* kept it from spreading. Drained our whole system. We better get some rain soon or I'm gonna have to start hauling water to take a bath."

He did have good hygiene, she'd give him that. Some of the people way back up in the mountains smelled like they'd never had a bath. His white tee shirt and overalls looked like they'd been ironed.

"Were you here when the fire started? Do you know how it started?"

"I wasn't home, but Sarah was. The fireman fella said the fire'd been set, that somebody used a what do you call it?"

"An accelerant," said a voice from behind him.

Rileigh thought that whoever it was would come to the

door, too and talk to her, but no conversation was forth-coming. Angus remained alone behind the screen.

"Yeah, that. He said it was probably gasoline, ruled the fire arson."

"Will your insurance cover what it'll take to re–"

"I ain't got no fire insurance on the barn! Who puts fire insurance on a barn?"

The man was right, but it was possible the building was covered under some other provision of the homeowner's plan. Though, somehow, Rileigh, couldn't put this man into the category of those prudent enough to purchase homeowner's insurance, either.

Unless he saw something suspicious about the fire that might link it to another one like it, she was wasting both their times discussing it further. Nobody commits arson on a building they don't have insured.

"You done?"

"Yes, thank you for taking the time–"

"Angus, that was rude," said the same voice from behind him that'd told him the arsonist used an accelerant.

"Well, she's gonna have to move her car, else we can't get out of the driveway."

From out of the shadows, a woman emerged. Rileigh was instantly struck by how beautiful she was. Her hair was the purest white, though not thick. It was thin and soft and curly. Rileigh would have bet that mythical pension she no longer had that the hair had been almost as cotton white when she was a child, as it was now. She had the pale blue eyes and complexion of a cotton top.

Tall and slender, she carried herself almost regally. As soon as she stepped into the light, Rileigh saw that she had a bandage on her head that covered much of the left side of her face, including her eye.

"I'm Sarah Park," she said, "Angus's sister."

When she said the sister part, Rileigh saw it instantly. The big, broad, black-haired man and the slender, pale, white-haired woman bore no resemblance whatsoever in body structure, but there was a striking family resemblance in their facial features —same nose, chin and wide mouth with full lips. In fact, it was entirely possible Angus Park was a good-looking man, but there was no way to tell under all that hair. But the sister certainly explained the starched and ironed tee-shirts and coveralls.

"We got to go. I'm taking Sarah into Gatlinburg to see Dr. Afanasev."

Rileigh had heard of him. He was a neurologist.

What begged for an explanation could not be asked — why did a brother and sister in their mid-seventies live together in what was certainly the family home? Did neither of them ever move out of their parents' house, get married, have children, travel, have a life?

"I have a brain tumor that needs tending," Sarah Park said, as matter of fact as if she'd said, *pass the salt*. Perhaps the bandage on her head and face was from recent surgery.

"I'm sorry, I'm blocking your driveway. I'll move my car." She turned and went down the steps, then remembered her own manners. "It was nice to have met you."

The proper response was some form of "me, too" but neither said a word. As Rileigh pulled away, she caught sight of the two of them in her rearview mirror and her mind took a picture of them standing side by side on the porch.

There was something off about the Parks, though Rileigh couldn't quite put her finger on it. They stood so still, side by side like that with no sense of personal space, like little kids do. And both of them had expressionless faces. Either they both had all kinda emotions boiling around in there and were holding them in check or they just didn't make the same kind of relational connections other people made.

Even standing together like that, they both struck Rileigh as very isolated, very alone, and very unhappy people.

Chapter Twenty-Two

ANGUS and one of his sisters, his older sister, Sarah, sit on the floor in the back of the pickup truck as it bumps along the winding, twisting unpaved roads to the spot just inside the front entrance to the park where the ceremony will be held. Papa didn't see his father load up his two grandchildren, probably would not have allowed it if he'd known. It doesn't make any sense that their grandfather would attend the 25th anniversary celebration of the founding of the Great Smokey Mountains National Park — given that he believes it is a blight on his beloved mountains and that it will attract hordes of people who will pollute the purity of one of God's greatest creations.

Grandpa doesn't go directly to the celebration site. He knows a back way that will lead him to a logging road in the woods on the far side of the parking lot. It's a bumpy ride, and Angus doesn't believe his grandfather has gone to all the trouble to use that route just so he can avoid the traffic. It's something else.

The ceremony has attracted a whole herd of what Grandpa would call High Muckety-Muck people. The governors will be in attendance— all three of them, from Tennessee, Virginia and North Carolina. So will just about every other elected official for five hundred miles in every direction, from the mayor of far-away Knoxville, to the mayor of Yarmouth County. They will come together today to celebrate the commissioning of the park, and to have their pictures taken while smiling and shaking hands, to be found on the front pages of more than a dozen local newspapers, in addition to the Black Bear Gazette.

The occasion is so auspicious that carpenters have been busy for two weeks, erecting bleachers to hold the crowds they believe will come. The Mucky Mucks will be seated on a raised dais in front of the bleachers.

They finally jolt to a stop and Grandpa gets out of the truck and walks around to the back, lowering the tailgate so the children can get out.

"Why are we here, Grandpa?" Sarah asks. Angus wishes he could snatch the words out of the air and stuff them back into her mouth. He knows—

The slap catches Sarah high on the left cheek and propels her backward. She flies through the air and lands hard in the dirt, sliding across the little path into the pile of leaves beside it.

Sarah doesn't cry out. She's tough. Her lip is split but she doesn't make a sound, just sits in the leaves, touching her bottom lip and looking up at her grandfather.

"Don't you never question what I'm doing, girl. Do you understand what I'm saying to you?"

"Yes sir."

"I am on a mission from Almighty God and the Devil will send out his minions to stop me, to delay me. He will turn all those he selects toward evil, even a pretty little girl." He looks up toward heaven. "But I am a servant of the most High God, creator of the universe whose will is supreme. I will not be turned aside by the servants of the Father of Lies."

Angus wants to go to his sister to help her to her feet, but she shoots him a warning look and he understands. When Grandpa gets like this, with fire in his eyes and his face contorted in a wild look, the only way to avoid his punishing hand is to vanish into the scenery so he ignores you.

Angus had tried that when he heard his grandfather calling him earlier. He should have pretended he hadn't heard, should have hidden in the woods until his grandfather gave up and went away. But he could see Grandpa already heard Sarah, and Angus didn't want her to have to suffer whatever fate their grandfather had in mind alone.

Grandpa moves stealthily through the trees to the edge of the woods, beckoning the children to follow. They can hear the mumble and rustle of a large crowd getting louder and louder as they approach the edge of the tree line. The three stop behind an oleander bush and peer out through its branches. They are behind the bleachers where the crowd has gathered, the boards straining under their weight. Grandpa points through the posts and support beams.

"You see them piles of rags there."

Both children look. Under both ends of the bleachers, at the spot where the steps go up on both ends, are rags in a pile, about a foot tall and a couple of feet wide.

"Them's soaked in gasoline." He gestures to the steps above the piles of rags. "I been soaking the wood of them steps in kerosene every night for a week. All's I got to do is light them rags and—" he makes a grand gesture with his hands—"whump! It'll all catch."

He turns to look at them, one at a time. "That part's going to be your jobs."

Sarah's eyes widen but she says nothing. Angus is terrified.

"I put them rags there last night after the carpenters went home for the evening. I'm going to need for the two of you to crawl under these bleachers— and out under the front seats. I picked you 'cause you're small and you'll fit just fine. When I signal you, you gonna light one of these and set them rags on fire. They'll catch the wooden bleachers, and the whole thing will go up in flames."

Grandpa reached into his overalls pocket and pulled out two Bic lighters. One was blue, the other yellow. He gave the blue one to Angus and the yellow one to Sarah. "Try it, make sure you can light them."

Both children thumb their lighters and flames leap up from them.

"You got to do it when I signal you, both of you at the same time."

"What's the signal?" Sarah asks and this time Grandpa doesn't punish her for asking a question.

"I'm going to interrupt their little party." He holds up what looks like a Maxwell House Coffee thermos. "Got a little surprise for the governor in here."

He smiles, but his eyes are cold.

"Gonna wait until everybody's here and the big wigs start to wagging their tongues. I'm going to expose the unrighteous, let them know that God's wrath will strike them down. I'll shout in a loud voice, 'I now call on Almighty God, creator off all things, to rain down upon you the fires of heaven.' When you hear me say that, you flick them BICs and set the rags on fire."

He leaned close. "And then you run, you run faster than you ever run in your whole life, run like the hounds of hell are nipping at you heels, because they very well might be."

Grandpa gestured toward the bleachers, and when neither of the children move, he grabs Angus by the upper arm and yanks his face up until it is only inches from his own.

"It ain't me who's telling you to perform this task. You have been commanded by Almighty God to avenge the evil that has been brought upon this place. If you fail to do what the Lord has commissioned you to do, he will bring down upon your heads all manner of suffering. You will never marry, will go to your graves barren and childless because God will not allow the disobedient to reproduce others like them."

The old man pushes the children out in front of the oleander bush, puts a hand in the middle of their backs and shoves them forward. Sarah stumbles, but Angus takes her arm and pulls her to her feet.

"Go with God, my children," Grandpa says, then he moves out of sight. Angus turns around halfway and looks to see if Grampa is *still watching them. He is. But when Angus finally gets into position next to the pile of rags, he turns again and Grampa is gone.*

Angus waits. He cannot see his sister from where he is crouched down beneath the bleachers, hovering over a pile of gasoline- soaked rags. He feels the plastic cylinder in his hands, turns it over and over. A Bic lighter. Can he?

Then the ceremony begins. The rustling of the crowd on the bandstands above him quiets and he hears the squawk of feedback on a public address system from the dais in front off the bandstands.

"Welcome to the twenty-fifth anniversary celebration of the founding of the Great Smoky Mountains National Park," says a distorted voice. There is more squawking and a screech. Someone says into the microphone, "Is this better?" and the words are clear.

There's more shuffling, then the first voice begins to speak.

"It is an honor and a privilege to be with you today to—" and he keeps droning, but Angus finds he can't concentrate on what the man is saying. He can't seem to keep his mind focused on the words. They skitter away on their own, flashing unrelated images into his mind.

He is self aware enough to recognize that his mind is trying to distract him from the reality of his situation. His grandfather has ordered him to light the gasoline soaked rags on fire. The fire will spread to the bandstands. There are people in those grandstands. People. Is Angus willing to hurt those people?

They'll run from the fire, of course. But there's going to be fire at both ends of the bleachers. Can he do that? Can he burn people? Some of them, maybe a lot of them, will die. Can he kill somebody?

And what about Sarah, down on the other end where he can't see. Does she realize what she's about to do? Can she do it?

But they have to, don't they? It wasn't a command from their grandfather. It was from Almighty God. And if they fail to do what God has commanded them to do—

No. That's not right. It can't be. God wouldn't have commanded him and his sister to kill innocent people. God isn't like that. Grandpa is wrong.

Suddenly, Angus knows two things with an absolute certainty. One, he cannot "flick the Bic" as his grandfather told him he had to do. And two, he has to get to Sarah, get her out of there.

Angus drops down onto his belly and begins to crawl frantically along the ground under the front row of the bleachers. He must make his way through a tangle of girders on the ground and it is slow going. A second man is speaking now, with a deeper voice than the first. His words are crisp and clear, almost sound like a song, but Angus can't understand the words. Finally he makes his way through the last of the supporting girders and he can see his sister far ahead. She is kneeling, hunkered over a pile of gasoline-soaked rags.

Just then, Angus hears a commotion in the crowd above him. The voice who is speaking falters and stops mid-sentence. Though Angus can't see him, he recognizes the next voice that speaks. It's Grandpa.

"Vermin! Foul polluters of the earth. The God of the Universe is disgusted by what you have done here."

Angus sees his sister hold up the yellow Bic lighter Grandpa gave to her and he struggles to crawl faster. There is a general hubbub in the bleachers above him now, people talking and feet stomping. Even if he dared to call out to her, she wouldn't hear him. The noise would drown out his voice. He only catches little pieces of the words his grandfather is saying.

"… national park breeds evil like a fly breeds maggots … destruction of God's great creation … bring down the wrath of God on your heads …"

Angus calls out to his sister as he crawls frantically across the dirt.

"Sarah, Sarah, no. Don't."

He knows he might not hear the signal, but knows it will be soon. He can hear the desperate, deranged quality in his grandfather's voice, even if he can't hear the words. He knows he is ramping himself up to the finale and he has to get to Sarah.

Angus is still a few feet away from Sarah when he hears his grandfather's voice rise above the crowd noises.

"I now call on Almighty God, creator off all things, to rain down upon you the fires of heaven."

Sarah holds her lighter above the rags and Angus flings himself at her, knocks her sideways and the yellow Bic lighter in her hand falls to the ground.

"Angus, what——?"

"No. You can't do that."

"I have to do it."

"No, you don't."

He is a year younger than Sarah but much bigger, and he grabs her arm now and throws his body away from the pile of rags, dragging her along with him. She protests, tries to get free, but Angus holds on with all his strength, dragging her back beneath the bleachers to a point where he can stand up.

He lunges to his feet, dragging Sarah upright with him, and runs toward the north edge of the bleachers. Plunging out from the shadows into the sunlight, Angus squints to see where he is and what is happening.

He sees his grandfather. His grandfather sees him. It almost seems their eyes lock.

And then …

That's when the screaming starts.

Chapter Twenty-Three

VERONICA LANGLEY STEPPED UNSTEADILY around the car parked in front of The Beer Experience entrance, cursing the driver who'd left his ride right there by the big "no-parking" signs and just walked away. She was already a couple of steps away when it occurred to her what she ought to do. Turning around was harder than she thought it would be, doing anything in three-inch heels was hard, particularly since she had been putting them away for the past hour pretty hard. Maybe she was a little more drunk than she'd thought.

Two steps back to the bright red … something. One of them foreign cars, a Nissan or a Subaru, one of those — She took out her car keys and walked slowly along beside the vehicle, scraping the biggest scratch she could in the fancy red paint job.

Teach him to leave it where it wasn't supposed to be.

He was probably one of those "star gazers" who'd come to see the meteor shower earlier tonight. She and Jody had trouble getting a room, settled for a more expensive one because those assholes had all made reservations.

Why'd they have to come here to watch meteors? You can see the sky from anywhere.

Feeling good about teaching the asshole a lesson, she turned again, held onto the car she'd just keyed for balance, and started across the street to the parking lot where she had paid twenty-five dollars to park. The foreign car dude would wish he'd paid up himself when he saw the side of his car.

Her car was at the end of the first row, the far end, by the cross street. She hated it when she had to look for where she'd left her car, it made her feel stupid, so she'd been careful tonight to remember — she was on the end, right off the sidewalk on the far side.

She stumbled a little, but righted herself. Then she stopped, right there in the driveway of the parking lot, and took off her shoes. Without having to balance on those stilettos, she could walk easier, and she didn't mind the feel of the gravel on her bare feet. She was a farm girl from Madill, Oklahoma and she'd gone barefoot in the summertime when she was a kid every day.

The door of the Beer Experience bar opened behind her. She could tell by the blast of sound that the music was still so loud in there you couldn't talk, but she hadn't gone in there to talk. She'd gone in there to get drunk and flirt. Flirt first, then get drunk.

She'd show Jody. He'd be sorry he was mean to her. She was making him pay. She had planned to go to the bar, pick up a stranger and screw his brains out. She figured Jody was back in the hotel room by now, all sorry that he'd yelled at her. She'd planned to stay out all night—that'd teach him— but the fight had started in the bar and soon both the men she'd been flirting with were nursing split lips and black eyes, so she'd just left.

They'd been fighting over her! A thrill of delight

rippled down her spine. Over Veronica Langley! Who'd have believed such a thing was possible when she was a chubby, pimple-faced teenager, hoping to God somebody, anybody would invite her to the prom?

But she'd got her shit together, moved to Oklahoma City and took a waitress job, lost weight, learned how to fix herself up. When she went home at Christmas, Jody Corcoran was all over her! Even though he wouldn't have given her the time of day when they were in high school.

They'd been going together for seven months now, and she was thinking about moving in with him. It would save a fortune on her rent, and they could use the extra money to do cool things, like going on this vacation.

She'd had to save up for three months to get enough money and it was a good thing she did. Otherwise, she wouldn't have known the truth about him until it was too late. Living with him for just the past three days on the road had been a real eye-opener. He was a pig, didn't shave unless she made him, didn't even want to shower. Gross. She'd spent many nights with him and knew he snored real loud, but he was at least clean then, brushed his teeth when he came to bed. She didn't think he'd brushed them since they left Oklahoma, didn't think he'd even brought a toothbrush.

No way was she going to live with a man like that. And now, she didn't have to.

Because she had proven to herself that she didn't need the likes of Jody Cocoran. She could get any man she wanted if she unbuttoned the top three buttons on her shirt and showed enough cleavage, shook her considerable ass just right when she walked, swaying in a provocative way.

She finally made it to her car, dropping her shoes on

the gravel. She still had her keys in her hand, so she unlocked the door and opened it.

There was a crunching sound behind her, someone approaching across the gravel. It was one of the guys who'd fought over her, come looking for her, and he'd take her home with him so she could stay out all night after all. That'd show Jody!

She turned toward the sound and planted a smile on her face as wide as Dallas—

There was the stink of … something … *fumes*… and suddenly she was soaking wet. Her hair, her clothes, all over. Staggering backward against her car, she couldn't breathe. It was *gasoline*. Someone had splashed gasoline—

She saw the spark. For an instant could see the smiling face behind the flame. And then there was the *thwump* of fire catching.

She screamed, screeched, her whole body in agony, writhing and trying to get away. She was on fire, her hair, her face. *Burning!* She ran away screaming, beating at the flames but they were everywhere. She tried to scream for help, but she couldn't make words, just sound.

Crashing into something solid, she careened off it, then she couldn't scream anymore. No sound would come. It hurt so bad. She staggered, fell, kept screaming but there was no sound. The agony was unbearable, unthinkable. She was burning, burning alive. She wanted to die, God, please let her die.

There was no air anymore, she couldn't scream, couldn't breathe, couldn't see. There was only agony. She writhed, then she couldn't move. Could only feel.

Then the mercy of darkness took her and she was no more.

Chapter Twenty-Four

RILEIGH'S CELL phone rang just as she was passing the city limits sign for Black Bear Forge. She glanced down at the screen, dreading what she might see. A number she didn't know. Except she did know it now. She knew the Texas area code, the number of the breather, and she was absolutely not going to answer if that's the number she saw.

Except she would answer. She wouldn't want to, but she would.

Thankfully, that wasn't the number she saw. It was Georgia.

It was still awkward to hold a cell phone and drive at the same time, but she managed to punch the green button, and as soon as she did, Georgia's excited voice filled the car.

"Did you hear? There's another one. Somebody else burned."

"What are you saying. Calm down and tell me."

"Chigger came home talking about it. That friend of his, Lester Massey, has a police scanner."

Not surprising. Rileigh had met the esteemed Lester

Massey and his equally esteemed brother, Ben, and they were both the kind of guys who had no life, and sat around all day listening to police calls.

"There was another tourist burned. Chigger said this one was right in Black Bear Forge, in the parking lot across from the Beer Experience Bar."

Rileigh's breath caught in her throat. Another one.

"Chigger said this one was a woman, at least that's what Lester said, just walked out into the parking lot across from the bar and bam, somebody threw gasoline all over her and set her on fire."

"Holy shit."

"I'll second that holy shit and raise you a hot damn."

"When did this happen?"

"Chigger just came in a little while ago, so it can't have been very long. Are you at home?"

"No, I'm just coming out of town. But I'll turn around. I'm going back there."

"You sure you want to do that? It'll be a zoo. That sheriff friend of yours is going to have his hands full."

"That's why I'm going."

Rileigh pulled her car into the next driveway she came to, turned around and headed back into town. She had heard the wail of sirens, but figured it was the rescue squad called out to a wreck. There were a lot of those this time of year, some tourist tried to make a hairpin turn too fast.

She never dreamed it would be … another one.

She pulled her car onto a side street when she got near Copeland Street, which was clogged with traffic and people. Pushing her way through the crowd, she tried to get closer to the actual crime scene, but the streets were packed with people, all of them talking in excited voices.

"… imagine getting gasoline thrown all over you …"

"… some tourist, I heard …"

"... heard her car just burst into flames."

"Colin is a friend of Deputy Hadley, and he just jumped up from the supper table and went running."

Rileigh shoved her way forward, squeezing between people who gave her a dirty look for getting in their way.

She finally got close enough that she could hail Tennessee Highway Patrolman Jimmie Fornham standing guard at the yellow police tape barrier that'd been stretched across the road. Jimmie would let her through.

As soon as she got beyond the tape, she saw the first of the big television station satellite trucks come lumbering up the street. The crowds parted for it like the Red Sea for Moses as it pulled right up to the yellow tape. Somebody leapt out of the passenger door. The back doors of the truck opened for a handful of people to scurry out too.

Rileigh got close enough to see the news anchor from WATE 6, Melissa Mendosa, get out of the truck, followed by a young man with a huge camera balanced on his shoulder. The crowd parted for them — which made Rileigh grind her teeth. The "celebrities" had come here to craft a story to suit whatever narrative they wanted to create. And whatever that narrative was, it absolutely would not paint a flattering, or an accurate picture of Yarmouth County.

Rileigh followed in the wake of the news crew as they wedged their way through the crowd. When they got to the inner ring of police tape, Mendosa presented a press badge to Deputy Mullins and he allowed her and the cameraman to pass. She strode around the various emergency personnel at the scene.

Rileigh saw Pete decked out in his firefighting gear, an ambulance, the local rescue squad trucks. And sheriff's department cruisers — she could see three, and figured there were more of them around somewhere. Mitch would have pulled out all the stops for this one

The local team from WHAS was actually late to the party. The ABC affiliate from Gatlinburg had a news anchor talking head standing in front of the lights they had set up. On the other side of the parking lot, the NBC affiliate was setting up lights. Mendosa was making her way toward a clump of officers in gray uniforms. One of them was bound to be Mitch.

Rileigh nodded to Mullins, ducked under the tape, and strode toward them.

Chapter Twenty-Five

MITCH WAS SMACK in the middle of the pandemonium, but unlike the eye of a hurricane, it was not calm here. There were firefighters standing around the fire truck that had been called to hose down the area. Mitch had gone head-to-head with the fire chief, Pete Something, to make him leave the crime scene alone until Forensic was able to clear it.

Deputy Jeb Rawlings had been the first officer on the scene, dispatched from only a few blocks away after a hysterical 911 call reported a fire in the parking lot of the Beer Experience bar on Copeland Street.

A small crowd had already gathered when Rawlings rolled up, and he'd called for immediate backup, then somehow he'd gotten the bystanders to back away until Deputy Mullins arrived, with Deputy Crawford on his heels.

By the time Mitch arrived, the other four officers had strung yellow police tape around an area about thirty yards by thirty yards on the far side of the parking lot. If Mitch had gotten here sooner, he would have spread the tape out another ten yards in all directions, but it was too late for that.

The likelihood that forensics would be able to find anything useful in one of the busiest parking lots in town was small, but he would have liked the opportunity to look.

What he found when he arrived was just about what he'd expected. The body had been covered with a blanket, but the stench of burned flesh and hair hung as a miasma in the air. As he walked from his cruiser to the tape, a tourist gagged and threw up on the sidewalk.

Served her right for showing up at the sideshow.

Mitch stepped to the body, lifted the blanket, and looked at the charred remains. The victim was lying behind a Range Rover about fifteen from a parked car with the door open. Her shoes were lying in front of that door. The side of the car and the ground around her had been soaked in gasoline too, and there was scorching near the door, but the rest of the car hadn't ignited, so there was no car fire to complicate things.

Deputy Rawlings approached, holding a purse, his hands protected by rubber gloves. He reached into it and pulled out the cellphone. The phone identified the victim as 25-year-old Veronica Langley of Madill, Oklahoma.

As soon as the Highway Patrol arrived to do crowd control, Mitch dispatched his officers to get whatever information they could glean from bystanders. From witness accounts, it appeared that the victim had been drinking in the bar. There had been a disturbance: the bouncer had had to break up a fight between two men. One of them had left the scene before the fire, but the other was still there, and he told deputies that they had come to blows over a dark-haired tourist, who left shortly afterward.

Rawlings turned up another tourist whose car had been parked outside the bar's entrance at that time, a mother summoned by her inebriated son because he was actually being responsible, didn't want to drive drunk. When the woman and her son got back out to her car, somebody had keyed the whole side of it. She had stayed around because of the disturbance in the parking lot, had joined the crowd of onlookers who'd rushed to get a look at the carnage.

"Sheriff Webster, I need a word with you," said a voice from behind him. Mitch turned, brushing off the reporters' questions, and saw that the man speaking to him was none other than Rutherford.

"I'll be glad to give you a full report later—"

Rutherford grabbed his upper arm and literally dragged him a few feet to the side.

"We're talking right now."

"What do you want?"

"I want you to keep your officers from grandstanding for starters."

"Grandstanding?"

"They're out there preening for the crowd and the reporters, puffed up and self important, talking about how *another tourist* has burned to death. They do not need to be making that connection between the cases."

Mitch knew that his officers had kept their mouths shut, they were more professional than that, but he didn't argue.

"Is there anything else."

"Of course, there's something else." His voice was a fierce, angry whisper. "There's a video. Have you seen it?"

Mitch had. Sundeep had shown it to him on his iPad. It had been submitted under the profile God's Spark, just like the first one, and though Mitch had yet to confirm it, he was certain he'd find that it had been posted from the Gatlinburg Public Library's bank of visitor computers.

"You have to do something about that video."

He wanted to make it clear to the mayor that there wasn't anything he could do about the video, but he let that go, too.

"There's nothing to be done. It was removed almost immediately for violating "community standards" clause of Facebook's content control."

What he didn't say was that it didn't matter what had happened to the original content. Enough viewers had seen it and made copies, then posted it to their own pages, so it had splashed up several times on YouTube and Twitter. In other words, the horse was out of the barn and there was no way to put it back in.

"Now listen to me, Sheriff Webster. We can't let this get out of hand. We have to stop it right here. You have to reassure the public that you're on top of the crimes, that you have suspects."

"I don't have any suspects."

"Bluff! Act like you know more than you do. You have to do everything you can to keep this whole thing from getting out. Hundreds of thousands of tourist dollars are at stake."

"Is that all, Mr. Mayor? I need to get back to work."

"Are we clear?"

"I understand what you want me to do."

He didn't say he would do it, but letting his honorable jackass-ness know that he'd been heard and understood seemed to pacify him.

"You keep me in the loop, do you hear?" Rutherford said. "I want to know what's going on at all times during this investigation."

Mitch nodded. Receipt of message, not an agreement to abide by its contents.

The mayor turned away. Then Mitchell saw Rileigh making her way in his direction.

He was absurdly grateful to see her.

Chapter Twenty-Six

"Excuse me, Sheriff Webster. I'm Melissa Mendosa with WATE 6 News, can you tell our viewers what you know about this case?"

The words came at him from off to his right, and when he looked that direction, a bank of bright lights flashed on and blinded him.

"Crawford," he called out. "You need to back the press up behind the yellow line."

The deputy came forward and tried to move the reporter and cameraman back out of the way, but she wasn't budging.

"Is there some reason you don't want to talk about this crime?"

Rileigh was standing beside him, and she leaned close.

"Not a good idea to piss off the state press. Make an enemy of Melissa Mendosa and you could live to regret it."

Mitch looked at the reporter and nodded to the deputy who was pushing her to the side.

"I only have a few minutes, what—?"

"Tell our viewers who happened here tonight, Sheriff."

The camera and the bright light swung Mitch's way and he was again blinded, but he looked at the reporter and concentrated on not squinting. Squinting and sweating had cost Richard Nixon the presidency in 1974.

"We have not yet notified the family so I can't release any names or details about the victim, but it appears that at about midnight, a woman was unlocking the door to her car when someone approached her from behind, splashed gasoline on her and set her on fire."

"Do you have any leads to indicate what the motive might be?"

"This is an active investigation and all I can tell you is that we are following up any lead we can find. We're investigating whether this might have been a crime of passion. There was an altercation involving the victim in the Beer Experience bar shortly before she was attacked."

"This is the second person in two days who has been murdered this way. What is the connection between the two?"

"We are investigating that angle, but I have no information at this time."

"Sheriff Webster, if there is no connection between the victims, does that mean both of these crimes were just random acts of violence?"

"It is possible, yes."

"And both of the victims were *tourists*. Is that correct?"

"Yes, we believe they are."

"Are you saying that it's possible someone is randomly targeting tourists?"

"I didn't say that."

"But it is possible, isn't it?"

Mitch paused, knowing the mayor would blow a gasket

when he heard what Mitch had said. Maybe he'd get lucky and they wouldn't broadcast that part.

"Yes ma'am, that is a possibility we're investigating. Now, if you'll excuse me."

Mitch turned and walked away from the reporter, heard her over his shoulder.

"You have just watched a WATE exclusive interview with Mitchell Webster, the sheriff of Yarmouth County. He confirmed what we have learned from earlier sources that the victim of today's murder was indeed a tourist, which brings up the possibility that this victim and the man who died yesterday under similar circumstances were targeted *because* they were tourists."

Mitch walked up to stand beside Rileigh, who told him bluntly, "I agree with you, but you're likely to regret saying that."

"Wait a minute. First you tell me I could live to regret pissing off the media and now you tell me I'm going to regret talking to her. Was there some middle ground here that I missed?"

"Oh, I don't know. Maybe talking to her but not *admitting* that it's entirely possible some nutbag out there is targeting tourists? Mayor J. P. Asshole will likely have a coronary when he sees that clip. Which, by the way, would be a fitting way to terminate his reign of ineptitude and self-aggrandizement for the past four years."

Mitch just shrugged. She was right.

"I know you didn't ask for my help, and I don't want to be pushy."

"But you've decided to be pushy anyway and help me whether I like it or not."

Officially, he should tell her to stay out of this. But he couldn't say that he wasn't feeling a little bit relieved by her presence. If there was something she could do to help them stop this lunatic sooner—

Mitch nodded. "I'm listening."

"At the very least, I can rule out what you and I both know is a lousy lead. No way was this a crime of passion. Some dude in a bar gets pissed that a pretty tourist rebuffs his advances. Maybe he punches her lights out. Or, the more violent type, maybe he shoots her, or stabs her, or strangles her. But splash gasoline on her and light a match? He happens to carry around a can of gas in his truck for just such occasions?"

"It is a line of investigation I have to pursue."

"I know, the old leave-no-stone-unturned thing. I get that. What I'm saying is I can save you some time and some manpower. I'll go over to the Beer Experience. I know the owner, Charlie Thacker. He'll talk to me, where he might not be willing to spill his guts to the law."

"The universal, *I don't want to get involved.*"

"That, mixed with liberal portions of *I used to be a moonshiner* and *I don't trust anybody with a badge.*"

"Fine. Go talk to him and see what he says."

"Done."

Rileigh turned and walked away through the crowd of emergency personnel, heading for the bar. She stopped briefly to talk to the fire chief, and when they both turned toward Mitch briefly, he wondered if he'd made a mistake in saying yes.

Then Rileigh disappeared into the crush of people.

She was right, of course. It wasn't reasonable to think that anybody would just happen to have a can of gasoline in their hip pocket which they carried around in the unlikely event that somebody pisses them off and they want to burn them alive.

Mitch turned back to the scene in time for the coroner

to lift the burnt body up onto a stretcher to take back to the coroner's office in Gatlinburg for an autopsy and a ruling on the official cause of death.

Two people burned alive in two days. There was something linking the two crimes, and he so very fervently hoped it wasn't the most logical link: that somebody had set out to torch some tourists.

Chapter Twenty-Seven

MITCH HAD BEEN EXPECTING the visit, but that was not to say he was prepared for it. When the mayor came charging into his office Thursday morning, Mitch had to grab hold of his emotions to keep from showing how very badly he did *not* want to talk to the man.

He'd come into the office before 5 a.m. to try to get a jump on the day, which he was certain was destined to be a barn burner. He hadn't finished up at the crime scene until about three o'clock and he'd gone home for a shower, shave, and fresh uniform, then took a thirty-minute nap before coming in to the office. He had cultivated the ability to nap when he was in college, and he had learned from trial and error that if he slept less than thirty minutes it wouldn't do him any good, but if he slept longer, he'd be groggy, grumpy and unable to get back into the swing of things.

The half-hour nap and several cups of coffee had fortified him, but not enough to greet the wrath of an asshole when the sun hadn't even cleared the mountain and it was still dark outside.

"What in the hell do you think you were doing, Webster?"

Rutherford steamrolled across the room to stand in front of Mitch's desk.

"Good morning, Mr. Mayor."

"Good morning, my ass. Don't you play with me, son, I will chew you up and spit you out on the side of the road. You'll be tore up worse than road kill."

"Please, have a seat, Joe, and let's talk."

"I am Mayor Rutherford to you, and you need to sit right where you are and listen to me, 'cause I don't ever say a thing twice."

Mitch said nothing, just spread his hands out wide and indicated that the mayor had the floor.

"Look at this." The mayor shoved an iPad at Mitch but didn't hand it to him. Just held it out so he could see it, then he touched the screen.

What began to roll was the WATE News, probably broadcast last night and again this morning. It was an ABC affiliate station, so no telling where it had gone from there. And would be again later this morning.

Melissa Mendota's face appeared on the screen beneath the WATE News *We're on your side!* logo. A trailer of words ran beneath the image, identifying the time of night the segment had been shot and the location, in the parking lot of the Beer Experience in Black Bear Forge.

"The sheriff's department of Yarmouth County is investigating a heinous crime this evening, which was called in to the 911 dispatcher."

Melissa stopped talking, and there was a delay that was almost long enough to be awkward before the voice-over played.

. . .

911 Dispatcher, what is the nature of your emergency.

Help. You gotta send somebody quick. Oh, dear God, dear Jesus—

What is your name, ma'am.

I can't believe—Oh my holy—

Your name.

What difference does it make who I a?. There's a woman in the parking lot on fire. Burned up. It's the most horrible—

Parking lot where?

Across from blank's Bar. She's burned to a crisp.

Melissa Mendosa reanimated then, giving a brief and mostly accurate description of what had happened last night. Then she introduced a clip of her interview with Mitch.

He grimaced at how he looked on camera — pasty-faced from the bright lights. And squinting. He'd tried so hard not to squint.

"We have not yet notified the family, so I can't release any names or details about the victim. But it appears that a woman was unlocking the door to her car when someone approached her from behind, splashed gasoline on her, and set her on fire."

"Do you have any leads to indicate what the motive might be?"

"This is an active investigation and all I can tell you is that we are following up any lead we can find. We're investigating whether this might have been a crime of passion. There was an altercation involving the victim in the Beer Experience bar shortly before she was attacked."

"This is the second person in two days who has been murdered this way. What is the connection between them?"

"We are investigating that angle, but I have no information at this time."

"Sheriff Webster, if there is no connection between the victims, does that mean both of these crimes were just random acts of violence?"

"It is possible that's the case, yes."

"And both of the victims were tourists. Is that correct?"

"It is."

"Are you saying that it's possible someone is randomly targeting tourists?"

"I didn't say that."

"But it is possible, isn't it?"

Mitch paused, "Yes ma'am, that is a possibility we're investigating."

The mayor pulled the iPad away from Mitch's face.

"A possibility we're investigating. You said that. A possibility we're investigating."

"It is a possibility we–"

"Did you not hear a word i said to you yesterday? I told you no grandstanding. Didn't I say that? No grandstanding."

"I wasn't grandstanding. I was telling her the truth."

"I instructed you not to let this get out of hand. You remember that part? I told you to reassure the public that you're on top of the crimes, that you have suspects."

"I didn't have any–"

"I told you to bluff. I told you to act like you knew more than you did. I gave you strict, specific instructions to keep this thing from blowing up. And what do you do? You give an interview to the press and say that it's possible there's some sicko out there who's jumping out of the bushes, splashing random tourists with gasoline, and lighting them on fire. A statement like that is not reassuring the public."

"I'm sorry if you don't approve of the way I handled that interview. I am more than happy to decline all future interviews and refer the press to your office so you can dispense whatever information you see fit."

You could tell the narcissist in Rutherford longed to go for that option, longed to step in front of the bright light and preen.

"I should do that very thing, but you and I both know we'd be slapped with allegations of a coverup if I instructed the sheriff to refuse to speak to the press. You have to talk to them."

He leaned back over Mitch's desk, just as he had done the last time he was in this office. but this time the gloves were definitely off. He was playing hardball and there was no veneer of civility to it.

"You are not, I repeat, not to tell the press that tourists are being targeted by a killer. Are we clear on that?"

Mitch nodded.

"Repeat it back to me so I know you understand."

That was a bridge too far. Mitch merely glared at the mayor and said, "I understand your instructions."

The mayor didn't press the point.

"Understand this part, too, son. If you say anything even remotely linking the deaths of these two people to a serial killer going after tourists, I will fire your ass. Is that clear? I will find somebody else to hold down the fort until Sheriff Mumford is cleared to return to duty, and you will be standing in the unemployment line. Are we clear on this Sheriff Webster?"

"We are clear."

The mayor said nothing else, just whirled around and marched out Mitch's door, almost knocking Rileigh Bishop off her feet in the process.

Mitch stayed where he was as Rileigh stepped into his office.

"Sounded like that went well. "

Mitch relaxed back into his seat.

"I don't know. Maybe I should have reached across my desk, grabbed the son of a bitch by the throat and choked the life out of him. What do you think?"

"Not a bad idea. I wouldn't have thought of it. I'd just have pulled out my Glock and shot the bastard."

Mitch laughed and it felt good.

"Sit down and tell me what I can do for you."

"It's not about what you can do for me, it's about what I can do for you. First off in that category is: report what you really don't want to hear, which is that the 'crime of passion' motive is a lost cause."

"Figured as much."

"I talked to Jessie Abbot. He was tending bar at The Beer Experience last night. He told me the woman — what's her name?"

"Veronica Langley?"

"Have you notified her family, yet?"

"Got in touch with her father last night. From what I could hear in the background, he took my call from a bar."

"Like father, like daughter. Anyway, Jessie told me Miss Langley spent a couple of hours in the bar. She'd flirt with one guy and then get tired of him and start trying to get a rise out of somebody else." She paused. "Pun intended. He said she was a little honey bee, flitting from one flower to the next. When it got late and the men started to get a little testy, she'd pit one against the other just to start a fight. The final two men she hooked up with were Jason Bagley and Trevor Lane. Trevor is a checker at Save-A-Lot and Jason works for the state road department. He's the guy you see standing in the sun all day rotating the Go and Stop sign to direct traffic around road construction."

"So you know both those men."

"I'd be able to pick them out of a lineup, but we're not BFFs or anything like that. What I can tell you is they're probably just a couple of good ol' boys out on the town getting drunk. They got into a fight over the girl from Oklahoma because she egged them on. They threw a couple of punches, probably fell down from the effort, and the bouncer broke up the fight. That was that. No way was there enough emotional connection for either of them to decide to murder Virginia because she dumped them. And throw gasoline on her and light a match? Not. A. Chance."

"Thanks for saving me a lot of trouble chasing down dead ends."

"I have another little tidbit, if you'd like to hear it."

"I'm listening."

"I'm working on a case for the Good GI's, investigating possible insurance fraud. The two people I was investigating are clean as far as I can tell. But when I went by the fire department to get the official state fire marshal's arson investigation findings to put in my report, the fire chief, Pete Brady, told me there had been five suspicious fires in a little over a week. He thinks they all were arson."

"*Five?* And he didn't report that to the sheriff's department."

"Well, look, he's like everybody else around here. They're stand-offish because of your lineage in Away From Here. I told him he was off base. And in truth, he did report the fires — *all* the fires, like he always does. He just didn't bother to make the connections for you."

"I need to meet this Pete Brady sometime."

"You'd like him."

Then she paused and her face actually colored a little.

"What?" he asked.

"Pete has had a crush on me since kindergarten. I haven't run into him any time in the past decade that he didn't make a pass at me."

Mitch almost said the man had good taste, but managed to choke the remark back before the words spilled out of his mouth.

Rileigh regained her composure.

"I got curious about the three other maybe-arson cases besides the two I was investigating, — because one of them was Ian, Georgia's brother— so I went out and talked to the 'victims.'"

"What'd you find out?"

"Well, Ian didn't set fire to his own tool shed just to collect the insurance money. Then there's Angus Park — his dipstick doesn't get anywhere near oil, but the fire at his place was an old barn that wasn't even insured. That was the first fire, last Monday. The last guy, though.He was definitely the kind of dude who'd do a thing like that. Tons of complaints about him from his neighbors, and he didn't look like a man so prosperous he'd pass up an opportunity to make a couple hundred thousand dollars."

"What's his name?"

"Frank Smothers. His business, Smother's Auto Body Shop, burned last Wednesday. He was immediately hostile as soon as I told him what I wanted. Then he sicced his dog on me."

"Didn't bite you, did it?"

"I had to threaten to shoot the dog to get Smothers to call him off, so you might want to look into the fire at his business. Also, Ian mentioned a theory that I didn't think of — that maybe somebody burned down something to collect the insurance money, and maybe set fire to some other places to hide his crime. I have absolutely zero evidence that Smothers did that. But if anybody would, he'd be the dude. Might want to check into his finances, where he was when the other fires were set."

Mitch got to his feet. "I'm going to Knoxville to have a talk with the medical examiner. Then I'll get right on your Mr. Smothers. As soon as I find out who threw gasoline on two tourists and then set them on fire."

"Any leads?" she asked as she walked with him to the door.

"Not a clue."

Chapter Twenty-Eight

RILEIGH LEFT the sheriff's office and went directly to Georgia's house. She needed to take Georgia to the *Y'all Come!* cabin so she could open it at 10 a.m. She should have left more time for this, because she might have to rope and hog tie Georgia to get her to actually go.

Well, it was Georgia's fault for roping Rileigh into it in the first place.

Still, she hadn't been too happy when Rileigh asked — okay, demanded that Georgia take her place today, since she had an appointment this morning in Gatlinburg to deliver her reports to the Good GI's.

"Are you kidding?" Georgia had said. "You have sufficient digits on your hand to count to five. There is a child here represented by each of those fingers. Five of them little suckers. Count them, you'll see I'm not bluffing."

"Your mother can come over and watch them for a few hours. It's not like you're going to be gone all day. Or, and I realize this is a stretch here, their father could step up to the plate."

"Chigger has to work."

Work being defined as selling drugs and hoping he doesn't get caught at it, which, in Rileigh's view, didn't qualify as actual employment.

"Your mother, then."

"She's getting too old to chase after five little kids."

"She's their grandmother. Babysitting is what grandmothers are for. Says so right there in the S'posta Book."

Georgia grimaced. The S'posta Book didn't exist, which had caused Rileigh and Georgia considerable consternation when they were little kids. There had to be a S'posta Book, didn't there, somewhere that it was all written down, all the things that were s'posta happen. Like, it was s'posta snow on Christmas Eve. You were s'posta take baths, clean your ears, wear clean clothes. And grandparents were s'posta love babysitting their grandchildren.

"Seriously, Mama's not well."

"Of course, she's not. She's seventy-seven years old, she's got shit wrong with her. Everybody that age does."

Actually, her own mother, who was admittedly only 72, had absolutely no physical disabilities. Unless you counted being as crazy as a bedbug a disability, and often in her mother's case, it was less debilitating than it was invigorating. Imagining that Rhett Butler was waiting to sweep you off your feet and take you on a cruise had her mother pumped.

"Liam's coming down with a cold. He might have a fever. I can't leave him—"

"How about we skip this part, where you tell me all the reasons you can't take my place at *Y'all Come* and I shoot down every argument, one by one. It'll save time if we just cut to the chase, and I present my ace in the hole argument."

Georgia just glared at her

"And that argument is, drum roll please — *you* volunteered *me* for the job. Without my knowledge or consent, I might add. So when I can't make it, you're more or less obligated to take my place."

That was the clincher. Georgia slumped.

"I'll call Mama." She launched a Hail Mary — "but if she's busy…"

But both of them knew her mother had absolutely nothing to do since she retired and she was likely looking for something to occupy her time.

The lone legitimate argument Georgia had floated was the fact that they had only one vehicle, Chigger's truck. Rileigh solved that problem by volunteering to pick Georgia up and take her home after her shift.

It would be good for Georgia to get out. She'd volunteered Rileigh to do the job for just that reason, back when Rileigh never left the house. Georgia spent all day corralling five children, stuck in the double-wide, seldom having conversations about anything more significant than spilled jelly.

"The trouble with talking to a three-year-old all day is that, in no time, you start to sound like a three-year-old," she'd once told Rileigh. "Eventually you began to wonder if anything you say actually makes sense."

Working a shift at *Y'all Come* would put some spring in Georgia's step and some color in her cheeks.

The *Y'all Come to Yarmouth County* cabin had been built and was operated by the Yarmouth Chamber of Commerce. It was a tiny log cabin set back down a tree-lined lane just past the *Welcome to Yarmouth County* sign on the main road leading into Black Bear Forge. It was operated by volunteers, who signed to spend a morning or afternoon giving out information to tourists, urging them to move to Yarmouth County.

Of course, the whole county knew about the place and

there was a fair amount of opposition to making that kind of offer. Normally, Rileigh would likely have lined up with the opposition, which made it problematic that Aunt Daisy had stuck that stupid *Y'all Come* sticker on her bumper.

Why would you invite more people to come to the mountains when they were too crowded already?

She'd also heard of a couple of occasions where volunteers had caught grief for giving their time there. Well, at least Georgia wouldn't have to deal with that, since according to the list on the front page of the *Y'all Come* website, Rileigh would be operating the booth this morning.

When Rileigh stopped in front of Georgia's trailer, she could hear Mayella wailing. That wasn't a good sign. Might be Georgia was out of bananas to shut the kid up with. Her mother really wouldn't survive four hours of Mayella's screaming and —

The screaming stopped abruptly. Good, they had bananas.

Rileigh didn't go in, just beeped her horn and waited in the car. When Georgia emerged from the trailer, Rileigh smiled approvingly.

"You clean up good, girlfriend," she said when Georgia slid into the passenger seat of the Honda.

"Go now," Georgia said urgently. "If the kids think they might have a chance of keeping me at home by throwing themselves under the tires of the car, they will be out here in a New York minute."

Rileigh pulled away from the trailer and turned toward Black Bear Forge.

"Seriously, Georgia, you really look nice today."

Georgia beamed. "Ok, truth bomb. I'm looking forward to seeing some real, in-the-flesh grownups having adult conversations."

"I've already had an adult conversation this morning, with the sheriff."

Georgia was instantly nosey. She had decided, with absolutely no empirical evidence, by the way, that Rileigh had something going with Mitchell Webster. Total fantasy on her part, but any mention of the man and Georgia got that you-need-a-man-in-your-life look in her eye.

"Tell me about it."

"Not a fun conversation. I showed up right after His Honorable Asshole left. He'd been in Mitch's office, reaming him out for the interview he gave to WATE 6 last night."

"I saw that interview on the news. The sheriff looked good, and I mean yummy! He's a hunk, Rileigh, admit it."

"Hunk is not a description I would have used, but whether he's good looking or not is beside the point. He's not interested in me *in that way* and I'm not interested him him. That's all, the end, so let it be written, so let it be done."

"Methinks she doth protest too much."

"Put a sock in it."

But now Rileigh couldn't stop thinking about Mitch, no matter what else they talked about.

She hoped he was making progress on the murders.

Because what if the killer stopped targeting tourists and start targeting the locals who welcomed them -- starting with the *Y'all Come* cabin volunteers?

Chapter Twenty-Nine

RILEIGH STEPPED out of the warm sunshine into the refrigerated offices of the Good GI's private investigations office and wondered why her breath wasn't coming out in little white puffs in front of her face.

They must keep the thermostat on the air-conditioning set at like fifty degrees.

When she was done with her appointment, she'd sit for a few minutes on the stone bench in front of the building to thaw out her ass.

Steeling herself for Stephanie Papadopoulos's screechy voice, she smiled a greeting and said she had an appointment with Wally.

"How are you, Rileigh?"

Screech, fingernails slowly dragged down a blackboard.

"Doing just fine, Stephanie."

"Well, so am I," she said, even though Rileigh had not added the obligatory *and how are you?* in response to Stephanie's greeting. "I've been getting out in the garden. Got some ripe tomatoes if you want some."

"Thanks Stephanie, maybe I'll stop by your place

sometime and get some." When hell freezes totally solid and polar bears have to slog across Satan's frozen tundra looking for baby seals to eat.

"Wally's in another meeting right now. If you'd like to sit down, I'll get you a cup of coffee."

"No thank—"

"How do you take it? Black, I bet. I can usually tell that about a person just from looking at them. You look like a black coffee kind of girl."

She thought about asking for coffee with a bucket of cream and a pound of sugar in it, but that would be engaging Stephanie, and she'd keep talking.

"No coffee, but thanks."

Rileigh turned and took a seat by the window looking out on a busy Gatlinburg street. There were wall-to-wall tourists as far as the eye could see. Looked like some street in New York City, with people walking five and six abreast past one souvenir shop after another.

The streets seemed even more crowded than usual — but that was probably her imagination. Or maybe the ranks of tourists swelled by those attracted to the meteor shower, which had been getting more and more spectacular every night. The biggest show was supposed to be from midnight Friday until dawn on Sunday. Maybe she ought to take Mama out to see it.

The door to Wally's office opened and a man in an Hawaiian shirt stepped out, shook Wally's hand, and headed for the door.

"Yo, Rileigh, come on in," Wally said. "Would you like some coffee? Stephanie could make—"

"No, I'm good, really. But thanks."

Stephanie was saying something as Rileigh hurried into Wally's office so they could close the door behind them and she wouldn't have to listen to the squeaking anymore.

Wally shut the door and went to his desk.

Wally Hansford was a late-thirties-ish man who was losing his hair way too young. He was taller than Rileigh, but so was most of the rest of humanity. He also had broad shoulders and a works-out-every-morning flat belly that might or might not be ripped.

His tan was just a little too perfect, probably from a tanning bed instead of the beach. He'd have been handsome except for a large nose that would have given his face a predatory appearance — if it weren't mitigated by a grin like a teenager.

"Whadda ya got for me?"

Rileigh handed him a folder that contained a printout of the report for the Long Run Insurance Agency, along with the official fire reports of the incident and the Fire Marshal's ruling.

He scanned down the report.

"So, you don't think either one of them is filing a fraudulent insurance claim."

"No, I don't. Sorry. I know you'd have loved to catch Wyman Perry in the act of doing something illegal, but it just won't fly. The man's in a wheelchair."

"Injured somehow?"

"Self-inflicted disability. He must weigh five hundred pounds and a powered wheelchair is the only way he can get around. The house that burned had been designed especially for his needs. Ramps and an elevator, wide doors, that kind of thing. He'd have no reason to burn it down. He's living in a motel room with a door sill he can't get the chair over, so he's just stuck there. He needed the house the way it was. And in his condition, if he'd tried to burn it down, he'd likely have set himself on fire."

"Burned to death like those tourists." Wally shook his head. "What an awful way to die."

She didn't tell him she'd been at both the crime scenes. He had no idea how right he was in his assessment. It was a horrible way to die.

"You know if there are any suspects in the cases?"

"I talked to the sheriff this morning and he had a handful of nothing."

"Had to be the same person both times, didn't it? Throwing gasoline on someone and setting them on fire is a pretty specific M.O. for a serial killer."

"Hope that's not the case. If there's a serial killer out there targeting tourists–"

"You'd think something like that would keep the tourists away, but I don't think anything short of Armageddon would be a deterrent."

Rileigh nodded. She could hear it in Wally's voice, his anger at the influx of gaudy people in tee shirts and shorts, clogging the streets and stores anywhere near the mountains.

If she let herself, she'd feel the same way.

"What about the other case, Mrs. Jarvis? You say here you don't think she did it either. Why not?"

"It was a you-had-to-be-there conversation. She's either the most talented actress ever born or she's genuinely devastated by the fire. She lost everything — mementos of her dead husband, pictures of her children. There is nothing in the world she could buy with the insurance money that would mean as much to her as what she lost."

"Alrighty then. I'll forward these reports along–"

"Might be we could get bonus points here."

Wally raised an eyebrow. "I'm listening."

"I found out there'd been some other fires that were suspected arson, and I took it upon myself to have a talk with the victims."

"Because?"

"Because one of them was my best friend's brother, but mostly, just insatiable curiosity."

"You know what that got the cat."

"You're telling me. One of the people I talked to set his dog on me."

"Whoa."

"I survived, but I do wonder. The guy's a one hundred percent creep. Absolutely the kind of man who'd burn down a business to collect the insurance money. And I got to wondering. Maybe he's insured by Long Run? It's worth checking out."

"It is indeed."

Rileigh gave him Frank Smothers's name and Wally wrote himself a note.

"I'll let you know what I find out," he said.

"I would be absolutely delighted to look into that man's affairs further, if the insurance company would be willing to pay us to do that."

"Duly noted."

Rileigh looked at her watch. There was time to swing by her favorite mom-and-pop taffy store before she went back to *Y'all Come* to collect Georgia.

She got up to leave, then thought of something else. "I couldn't nail the Wyman guy, but you would be interested to know about the dog."

"He still has the dog?"

"Yup. And the dog got struck by a karma lightning bolt. She can't bark anymore. Can't make a sound."

Wally let out a satisfied laugh.

"There is a God in Heaven after all."

Chapter Thirty

GEORGIA WENT into the little cabin at the end of the lane behind the *Welcome to Yarmouth County* sign, set her purse on the desk, looked around, then spontaneously spun around in a circle, squealing, "Wheeeeeee!"

The place was pin neat. Last night's volunteer had obviously been the kind who couldn't let a picture hang crooked on a nail — even the brochures on the tables were lined up perfectly and in alphabetical order.

Someone had even polished the black bear sculpture set on a formal pedestal beside the front door. Georgia remembered the grand plans for a giant black bear to sit beside the welcome sign. It had first been proposed when she was in high school — the Yarmouth County Chamber of Commerce had started talking about it that long ago. Yes, sir, it was going to be a huge black bear, a tribute to all the bears in the world, a perfect replica made in bronze.

Yeah, right.

They'd started taking donations to pay an artist to create the sculpture when Georgia was a junior. Five or six years later — Liam was still in diapers — the chamber announced its revised plan for the statute. It was still supposed to be a big statue, but bronze... well, bronze was pricey. And finding an artist who worked in bronze, that was pricey too. So they'd decided to make the bear out of fiberglass. A glass bear, what a hoot.

But then they discovered that fiberglass was pricey too.

Bottom line, nobody in the county was all excited about contributing to a statute of a bear when they'd probably see two or three of them beside the rode when they drove home tonight.

The big bronze bear on a pedestal in the *Y'all Come* cabin was what they'd finally ended up spending the collected funds on. It was the size of a medicine ball, and weighed forty or fifty pounds. She knew that part because one of her girlfriends who volunteered in the cabin regularly knocked the thing off the pedestal and it fell on her toe — crushed it.

Today the bear was shined to a polished sheen.

So...nothing to do, no feeling of I-need-to-be-cleaning-up-a-mess-somewhere-but-I'm-not. Oh, that felt delicious.

She stood very still and listened. There was no sound but the distant swish of traffic on the road beyond the lane as cars made a bee line to Pigeon Forge and Gatlinburg. But other than that, it was quiet.

Georgia giggled. Quiet. And she didn't even need a banana.

Then she sneezed. Dammit. She'd hoped getting away from the lavender rhododendron bushes that grew wild beside the back door of the trailer would stop her sneezing.

She reached into her purse and told out a bottle of allergy pills. Benadryl. It worked, although it made you sleepy. But who cared today? If she fell asleep in the desk chair, she'd wake up to the bell above the front door as soon as somebody came in.

Georgia plopped down in un ungraceful splat onto the little settee where visitors could sit and peruse all the activities they could pursue in Yarmouth County.

There were no children that she was responsible for anywhere near. It was glorious.

She felt a little guilty that she was so thrilled about it. But only a little, because she knew deep in her heart she loved her children more than life, would die for them. What she didn't often admit to herself was that they wore her out. Five of them. What had she been thinking? After the first three boys, they should have let it be. But Chigger had wanted a little girl, so they tried again. And got Mason.

Georgia had been determined to get her tubes tied and put an end to the insanity then, but before she had a chance, she was pregnant. And nine months later, out popped Mayella, who was the most adorable little girl ever.

Yeah, she was a little spoiled. Georgia could tell that Rileigh thought she ought to discipline the little girl more, make her stop screaming. But Rileigh didn't know what it meant to be a mother. She'd never loved a child that way. What difference did it make if Mayella made a little noise? She'd grow out of that phase eventually.

Besides, Georgia absolutely was not in the market to get into a battle of wills with a three-year-old. They had more stamina than you did. The kid would always win in the end.

But she did yearn for private time in the midst of the five-kids chaos. Why had she never thought before of volunteering at the *Y'all Come* cabin? She'd passed the thing about every day of her life, but never gave it any thought until Rileigh fell into such a funk and Georgia had been wracking her mind to think of some way to force her to get out of the house and re-engage with life. That's why she'd signed her up.

Now Rileigh was fine, and Georgia had wound up with the brass ring. Four glorious childless hours. Four glorious silent hours. It was *suh-weet*.

An hour later, Georgia was walking from the window on the north side of the building to the window on the south side — both were single-pane to give a unspoiled look at the beauty of nature outside — and back to the desk against the back wall. She walked to the door, that also had a single pane window, out into the empty parking lot.

There hadn't been a single tourist in the building all morning.

She should have brought something to read. She walked to the settee and settled down on it, then fluffed up the pillow and put her feet up. Picking up a magazine off the coffee table, she thumbed through it. Tennessee Life. Right. The pictures of the people and the fancy houses in the magazine certainly didn't depict the Tennessee life of anybody she knew.

Thumbing through the pages, looking at the pictures, her eyelids grew heavy. Maybe she could take a little nap, just a little—

Something smelled odd. Georgia couldn't place the smell, but it definitely didn't belong here.

She was dreaming.

No, the smell was real. She opened her eyes and saw nothing but fog all around her. Yep, she was dreaming and she needed to wake up because it wouldn't be long before—

The smell.

Smoke!

Georgia leapt to her feet and began to cough instantly. She couldn't breathe, the smoke was everywhere, all around her. All she could do was cough. She dropped back down to sit on the settee, and then found herself on her knees on the floor.

Smoke.

Something was burning.

Burning!

She was instantly completely awake and alert. It was that antihistamine she'd taken for her allergies. It had made her sleepy and her thinking foggy.

She was aware now, though. Aware that she had to get out of here. Smoke was pouring through the chinks in the grout between the logs on the back wall.

She didn't leap to her feet this time, just crawled as fast as she could to the front door. She reached up and turned the knob. It was stuck. She sat up on her knees, coughing frantically and turned the knob again, yanked it back and forth. Jammed. Something was stuck tight between the door and the jamb, so she couldn't turn the handle to open the door.

She was trapped.

A bolt of terror shot through her. Behind it trailed a wave of panic like the tail on a kite.

She stood all the way up. Yanked and yanked on the door, coughing so much she couldn't seem to get her breath between coughs.

The door wasn't opening. She staggered to the windows. They were for show, not the kind that actually opened. Looking around, she was getting dizzy, couldn't think, was clumsy, stumbling.

She had to get out. Somehow, she had to.

The next thing she knew she was face down on the floor, her cheek on the wood planking. With surprising clarity, Georgia understood that if she didn't do something in the next sixty seconds, she would die here.

Die. here.

Out … get out … *break* out… *break the glass!*

How?

Georgia got to her knees, keeping her head as close to the floor as possible for breathable air, and crawled to the pedestal where the bear statue sat. She shoved it hard with her shoulder and it wobbled. She shoved it again as hard as she could and one side of the pedestal lifted off the ground. One more shove, and the bear statue tumbled with a thud off the pedestal and onto the floor.

She rolled it like a ball along the floor to the door. Then grabbed a breath and held it, stood up, and picked up the statue, with the bear's head in one hand and the base in another. She turned with her back to the door, then spun around a little like she was hurling a discus at the glass pane.

There was a mighty crash of breaking glass. Staggering to the door, she leaned out the waist high window and tried to drag clean air into her lungs. But the infusion of oxygen ramped up the fire in the back wall and it raced out along the roof and into the walls beside it.

Had to get all the way *out.*

No shards of broken glass were stuck in the bottom of the frame, but several vicious jagged pieces stuck out on both sides. She ignored them. With her belly on the bottom of the frame, she leaned awkwardly out as far as she could and tried to drag the rest of her body along with her.

The world was spinning around her. Black spots obscured her vision. Scrambling, trying to climb the inside of the door with her bare toes, she managed to get a knee over the window ledge.

And then she was falling. She landed awkwardly on her shoulder and a bolt of pain shot through her whole body. Then the world went black.

Chapter Thirty-One

MITCH COULD SEE the smoke billowing above the treetops from half a mile away. He felt a hole open up in his stomach. He'd been out when the dispatcher had called him on his cell phone to tell him that the fire department had been called out to *Y'all Come* cabin.

Hadn't Rileigh said she was scheduled to be working there this morning?

Mitch had flipped on his lights and siren, and roared around the mountain roads, refusing to wait for slow tourists. He was a danger to himself and anybody on the road between him and the fire.

He didn't care.

What he saw when he bulldozed his way through onlookers and the other first responders grabbed his heart in an iron fist. The building was a torch, massive flames licking the bottom of black pillars of smoke. The fire department was making no effort to put out the blaze, that was a lost cause, but they trained their hoses on the woods behind the building in a desperate effort to keep the fire from spreading into the trees.

Mitch leapt out of his cruiser and rushed to where the EMTs were leaned over a woman lying motionless on the ground. Rileigh!

He stepped close enough to see. It wasn't Rileigh. It was Rileigh's best friend, Georgia.

"Is this the only victim, Jeb?" he asked Deputy Rawlings, who had approached as soon as Mitch got out of his car.

"Yes, sir. She was the only person in the building, as far as we can see."

Mitch said nothing else as relief washed over him in a warm tide.

"Pete says it's arson, at least in his opinion, and he's not often wrong about that kind of thing. He said there's no way a log structure could have caught fire so quickly without an accelerant."

"Gasoline," Mitch said. It wasn't a question, but Rawlings nodded assent.

Mitch watched the medics at work, marveling as he always did at their skill and efficiency as they talked to each other in medical-speak.

"ABC," said the young medic whose name tag merely identified him as Jenkins.

"Airway clear," said the other, an older woman with short gray hair whose name tag said she was Fairmont. "Breathing shallow and irregular. Circulation–"

She checked something Mitch couldn't see and merely nodded.

At the same time, Jenkins was easing a cervical collar around Georgia's neck and placing an oxygen mask over her mouth and nose. Fairmont inserted an IV needle into her arm, then the two of them eased her body onto a spine board and strapped her down. Mitch had been to the scene of enough emergencies to know that most of what they were doing was precautionary. She probably didn't have a broken neck or back injuries, but that was protocol.

The two medics lifted the spine board and placed it on a stretcher, then pulled together to lift the stretcher up to waist height and began pushing it toward the ambulance.

Mitch went back to his cruiser as the ambulance pulled out and tried to call Rileigh. The phone sent his call immediately to voice mail. He left her a brief message, then sent a text as well. Some people checked texts even when they weren't answering their phones.

He'd thought she was scheduled to be working at the *Y'all Come* today, but apparently she'd gotten Georgia to take her place. The text simply asked her to call him immediately, then he pulled in behind the ambulance as it raced toward the hospital in Gatlinburg.

Rileigh didn't call immediately, as he'd expected. She'd turned her phone off for some reason, but he was sure she'd call as soon as she could.

He parked beside the emergency entrance to the hospital and followed the medics into the building. It appeared to Mitch that the hospital's entire trauma team was waiting for Georgia to arrive.

He stood off the the side, allowed access by virtue of his uniform and badge, and watched. The blue-scrubs clad doctors and nurses inserted more IV lines and drew blood, and rushed out of the room with the vials. They cut her clothing away to examine her from head to toe for injuries. The medics at the scene had bandaged a cut on her arm and they removed the bandage to examine the wound. Several machines he didn't know the names of were wheeled in, and he gathered that they were doing CT scans and ultrasounds and X-rays. He wondered what they expected to find.

One doctor examined Georgia's mouth and nose and

said, "Nasal hair singed, soot around her mouth and nose, let's get her to the hyperbaric chamber."

Then they wheeled her out of the room. Mitch approached one of the doctors.

"We suspect the fire she was in was arson. Can you tell me when I can talk to her?"

"I can't tell you anything about her condition. We're putting her in a hyperbaric chamber — pure oxygen at higher than normal air pressure, to help get more oxygen into her lungs."

The doctor hurried away.

Mitch walked out of the emergency room into the sunshine.

Had the killer been targeting Rileigh, he wondered, or was he just hoping to capture any tourist who might have stopped by?

And who would he go after next?

Chapter Thirty-Two

RILEIGH GOT out of the Good GI's office as fast as she could, sat down on the warm concrete bench outside and felt the chill being drawn out of her bones.

She reached into her purse and took out her cell phone. She'd only turned it off when she went into the building to turn in her reports, and it had blown up with texts.

She started down through them.

Mama: *Would you stop by the store on the way home and get me some Eagle Brand milk and some lemons. I'm making Rhett a lemon meringue pie.*

Hope ole Rhett has the number for the poison control hotline committed to memory.

Mama: *And some pecans. I don't have any pecans either.*

Pecans were not an ingredient in any lemon meringue pie Rileigh had ever had.

Sheriff Mitchell Webster: *Call me as soon as you get this message.*

She didn't like the sound of that. Glancing down

through the other unread texts, there were two more from her mother.

One from Pete Brady. Had the fire chief finally screwed himself up to asking her for a date?

And one from Chigger.

She went to her phone screen, to Favorites and punched the icon. Mitch answered on the first ring.

"Rileigh, I wanted you to hear this from me first. There was a fire this morning at the *Y'all Come* cabin."

"Is Georgia all right?"

"She was taken to the hospital in Gatlinburg."

"Is she all right?" Rileigh demanded.

"Her injuries were not life threatening. That really is all I know."

She didn't even disconnect, just ran to her car and raced to the hospital.

When she got there the "information" desk at the front entrance provided zero information. Unless she was a relative, they couldn't release Gwenneth Stump's personal information, wouldn't even confirm that she'd been brought to their ER.

Rileigh pulled out her phone to start calling her friends in emergency services when she saw a shaggy-haired man at the end of the hall that led to the emergency entrance. Chigger!

The lack-of-information desk drone called after her as she ran toward Chigger, something about a restricted area and calling security. Rileigh ignored her.

She came up behind him and startled him. "Chigger! How's Georgia?"

He turned around. When she saw his face, she was suddenly as scared as she'd ever been in her life.

"I don't know!" He sounded close to tears, and his eyes were red. Either he'd been smoking weed, which wasn't just possible but likely, or he'd been crying. "They won't tell me anything. Just parked me in the waiting room and I– it was too small, I couldn't stay in there." Even as he spoke, he resumed pacing up and down the hall, and she had to trail along after him.

"What happened?"

"I don't know that either. All's I know is there was a fire at the *Y'all Come* cabin. I think it burned all the way to the ground. And Georgia was hurt."

"It was the cabin that was on fire. That's what you're telling me, *the cabin*, right?"

The thought that Georgia had been the victim of the maniac who was burning people alive was more than Rileigh could bear.

"Yeah, the building. They said somebody set it on fire."

And Rileigh froze in place. She knew. She was as certain as sunrise on Easter Sunday morning how the fire had started, why it had started and who had started it.

Frank Smothers had sneered at the *Y'all Come to Yarmouth County!* sticker on the back bumper. Said he bet she was there every day. All he had to do was go to the cabin's website and BAM, there was Rileigh's name as this morning's volunteer. She hadn't bothered to change it when Georgia agreed to take her place there.

Rileigh was supposed to have been the one who died this morning.

She pulled her attention back from speculating on the arsonist. There'd be time for all that later. Right now…

Chigger had walked away from her. Before she could go after him, he turned again and was coming her way. He paced, his face a study in anguish.

Rileigh didn't suddenly change her assessment of his character, but she had to acknowledge that Georgia had been right about him in one regard. Chigger did love his wife. His concern and terror for her were stamped on his features.

"How was she injured? Do you at least know that? Was she burned?"

"No, not burned. They told me they were treating her for smoke inhalation and that she'd got hurt somehow getting out of the building to get away from the fire."

Rileigh relaxed marginally. Not burned. Thank God! Whatever else she'd injured, well, Rileigh was living proof that the human body could take a whole lot of punishment and still manage to knit the pieces back together good as new. Or close to it.

There was nothing to do but wait until a doctor came to the waiting room to tell Chigger about Georgia's condition. As Chigger paced, Rileigh went back through the messages on her phone.

Pete and Chigger had both messaged her about Georgia. As she scrolled down, she found a blank message. There were no words on it. The phone number was as familiar as the Texas area code.

Not now, dammit!

Then she realized she could respond to the message with a reply. She typed the words *"Leave me the fuck alone!"*

She stared at the message but couldn't send it. Instead, she erased both the reply and the original message.

The door that led into the waiting room opened and a blue scrubs-clad man with a stethoscope dangling around his neck came out of the hallway holding a clipboard.

"I'm looking for Roger Albert St–" the obviously-a-doctor said, as if the hall were crowded with people rather than empty except for Chigger and Rileigh.

"That's me. I'm Chigger. How's my wife?"

"Your wife is a very fortunate young woman, Mr. Stump. She was overcome by smoke. There's no way to know yet if there will be any permanent damage. But right now, she's stable."

Chigger almost collapsed with relief.

"What about her other injuries?" Rileigh asked, and the doctor looked from Chigger to Rileigh before finally replying.

"She has a dislocated shoulder and a concussion. She was unconscious for more than an hour."

Rileigh knew what most people didn't — that being unconscious was not the nothing movies and television made it appear. Being unconscious was a very big deal.

"Where is she?" Chigger asked. "Can I see her?"

"Only for a minute. I'll take you to her." The doctor led Chigger through the door back into the waiting room, but Rileigh didn't follow. Georgia and Chigger needed to be alone right now.

Rileigh had other things to do. She turned to go back down the hallway and out of the building and there stood Sheriff Mitchell Webster.

"How is she?"

"She's *stable*." Rileigh stuffed her anger and continued in a controlled voice. "Thank you so much for letting me know. I appreciate it."

Mitch merely nodded his head but said nothing.

"Tell me what in the hell happened." The words rode the anger she thought she'd stuffed out into the world.

"Fire chief's sure it was arson, said logs didn't catch that fast without help. He figures somebody poured gasoline all over the back outside wall of the building and lit a match. It's miracle the fire didn't spread with the building so close to the woods. By the time it was out, the firemen had trampled up the scene, so there's no—"

"No forensic evidence, I get it. I don't need a boot print

or a tire print or an eight-by-ten glossy photograph suitable for framing to know who set this fire."

"And that is?"

"Frank Smothers. He threatened me when I went out to his place to question him about his burned business."

"You believe he thought you would be working there."

"I was supposed to be there this morning. Georgia was taking my place. Smothers burned the place trying to get at me."

"That's definitely a possibility."

"Possibility?" Rileigh was incredulous.

"Every one of my deputies said there have been an untold number of threats against the place ever since it was built. Apparently, a lot of locals don't think it's a good idea to be urging a bunch of strangers to come and live here."

"You think that's it? Somebody who's pissed about construction everywhere and jammed streets just got up this morning and thought, *You know what? I'm gonna go burn that building down.*"

"I'm just saying there are a lot of people who'd have a reason to burn that building, not just some guy you pissed off. We really won't know anything until I have a chance to talk to Georgia. Maybe she saw something."

Rileigh said nothing else. If she opened her mouth, she would eviscerate the sheriff and what was the point in that? Clearly he was terminally stupid, couldn't see the forest for the trees. She didn't need his help. She'd find evidence of what Frank Smothers did and leave it on Mitch's desk, wrapped up in Christmas paper with a bow on it.

"Right. Well, you need to go out there and chase down everyone who ever threatened to burn down the *Y'all Come* cabin. Good luck. I've got better things to do with my time."

Rileigh turned on her heel and marched down the hall, leaving the sheriff standing in the hallway in bewildered silence.

Chapter Thirty-Three

RILEIGH COULDN'T JUST SIT AROUND and do nothing as she waited to find out more about Georgia's condition. She'd go nuts if she just sat.

What she wanted to do was drive out to Frank Smothers' trailer and confront him about the fire. Wouldn't he be surprised when *she* showed up after he thought he'd killed her?

Though that might make Rileigh feel better, it was a purposeless gesture that would actually be counterproductive. No sense putting him on his guard. Surely, he thought he'd gotten away with his crime — probably crimes, plural — and she needed to wait, to gather evidence against him. And then she'd have to give that evidence to Mitch.

Thinking about the sheriff made her grind her teeth. He was so calm and collected, which she absolutely understood was the professional way to deal with the situation. She'd have behaved exactly the same if she were in his shoes. It was irrational to be angry at him for doing his job well.

But dammit, he ought to feel *something*. That was Georgia! This was personal. And the fact that he wouldn't listen to her just totally chapped her butt.

Smothers was responsible, that couldn't be more obvious, and the sheriff's *wait and see* attitude was maddening.

Well, she'd just have to do his job for him. The way to link Smothers to the fire today was to prove that he'd set his business on fire in order to collect the insurance money, and that he'd gone after Rileigh to shut her up because she was suspicious and he was afraid she'd figure it out.

The problem was that she needed legal authority to do that. She needed to see Smothers' bank records. She was certain they would reveal that his business was belly-up and he needed the money. That was first base, and she was stuck at home plate.

But there was something she could do that was a necessary thing. It wouldn't help her nail Frank Smothers to the wall, but it might help in the investigation of the torched tourists.

And she wanted to help there, despite how angry she was at Mitch. She wanted to help solve those crimes because she wanted justice for the victims. Poor Earl Watson, just a nice guy, and that girl from Oklahoma had a whole life out there in front of her.

Somebody needed to pay for that. It didn't take a rocket scientist to figure out that there was a serial killer on the lose who was using fire as his weapon. And it was no coincidence that the two previous victims were tourists. Some local was targeting tourists. He'd gotten away with it twice, no reason to believe he wouldn't do it again. As God made little green apples and stuck them on the limbs of apple trees every spring, the guy who'd killed Earl Watson and Veronica Langley would kill again.

She'd do anything she could to prevent that from happening.

There was one little thing she could do that might yield some leads — maybe not, but it was worth a shot. She could look at past issues of the newspaper. It was possible the killer had struck before, but for some reason nobody spotted it as a crime, maybe thought it was an accident. She'd look up past instances of people killed by fire, or maybe just seriously injured, search for similarities to the two tourist murders.

But when she went to the newspaper's website, the archives were "unavailable."

Fine then, she'd go to the newspaper's office,

She drove to the Black Bear Gazette, the weekly newspaper that'd been published for the residents of Yarmouth County for more than a hundred years. The newspaper was in what was now considered a quaint building in the center of black Bear Forge. It was the original location of the newspaper, founded by Elliot Haggardy, who grew up in the mountains, went to college, and then came back home to start a newspaper *for* the people of the mountains, not just about them. A newspaper that described life in Yarmouth County and provided content for the events.

Rileigh had known Mr. Haggardy, but not well. He'd died while she was in the military, and his son had taken over the newspaper. From all reports, the younger Haggardy was as dedicated a journalist as his father had been.

What would the country be like if the national media took their jobs as journalists as seriously as the Haggardy family had done? It would certainly be better off than it was now, where every media outlet had an agenda and a narrative of its own, and the facts — what had actually happened at any given event — were twisted and bent to serve those agendas.

Before she went into the Gazette building, she texted Chigger to ask him how Georgia was doing.

The bell over the door of the Gazette office tinkled gaily when Rileigh went inside. She approached the counter to speak the newspaper's receptionist— who also sold classified ads, put obituaries and yard sale ads in the paper, and likely was the photographer for all the ginormous tomatoes and lumpy potatoes that looked like Abraham Lincoln.

She was an elderly woman with shining white hair and glasses perched on top of her head. When she brought them down to her nose, you could see that they were ridiculous cat-eye frames that gave the woman a mildly-clownish look.

The nameplate said her name was Mildred Sandusky.

"Hello, Mrs. Sandusky, I'm—"

"Oh, I know who you are child. You're Lily's youngest. I know you don't remember me, but I volunteered in the library when you were in elementary school."

Rileigh wracked her brain but could not conjure up a single image of the library itself, let alone the people who'd worked there, but she smiled and bluffed.

"I didn't spend a lot of time in the library when I was in school. I wasn't exactly a stellar student."

"Nonsense. You were there all the time, checking out those old, old books. I think you might have been the only child who read those Nancy Drew Mysteries."

Rileigh definitely remembered those. She still had a whole shelf of Nancy Drew books she'd bought or had gotten for her birthday up in the attic of the house. That's where her passion for "sleuthing" had come from.

"That's right. I loved those. Thanks for reminding me of them. I've got some in the attic. I need to dust them off and read them again."

"Well, what you loved as a child might be too simplistic to enjoy as an adult, but give it a shot. Now how can I help you today. Having a yard sale?"

"No, actually, I'd just like to look through your back issues. Can you tell me how to access those online? I went to your website, but the archives were grayed out and marked unavailable."

"They're working on our computer system. They fixed what was broke, then broke three other things. That's one of the broke things they're supposed to fix. Eventually."

"You mean I can't see the older issues?"

"That's not what I said. I said they're not online. They exist in bound volumes in the attic."

"Well, then, can I go look through the bound volumes?"

"Sure can. Just warning you, if you have allergies, you're going to die up there. The dust is probably an inch thick on some of them."

"I'll survive."

Mildred led Rileigh through the back rooms of the newspapers. Her mother had worked here briefly a long time ago, and she'd talked about huge banks with slanted racks where the production staff literally "cut out" images for ads from giant books of clip art, and then pass them through an apparatus that looked like the rollers on a ringer washer to apply wax, plain old candle wax, which was used to "paste" them onto pages. Thus the origin of the term cut and paste.

Now the staff sat at computer terminals with big monitors. Ahhhh, progress.

They went up a broad staircase in the back of the building and into a huge open attic that occupied all the space above the entire building. Along the walls were huge windows that looked out over main street on the front and the alley on the back, and shelves upon shelves upon shelves of big books.

"It's almost like working in a library again," Mildred said, gesturing to the shelves.

The books were bound volumes of the actual newspapers themselves, so they were the size and shape of a newspaper. Each of the bound volumes had a date on the outside. January to June 1981, July to December 1981.

"They're all yours. Everything's here except the volumes for 1958, 1959 and the first six months of 1960." She gestured toward the far corner of the huge room. "Three years ago … no, four, it was four years ago we had a big storm and it damaged the roof badly. Water just poured in on that back corner and we didn't realize it until it was too late to do anything. Water soaked all the volumes under the leak, destroyed them, and of course there was no way to replace them. But everything else is here." She pointed to large tables set in the center of the floor. "Spread them out there. I hope you find what you're looking for."

Rileigh walked around the room slowly, looking at the dates on the newspapers. With no "search" function to find what she was looking for, she'd have to go through them all. It would take years to do that. She decided to look back ten years. Just front page stories. What she was looking for — victims of fire — would have been big news in a small town.

She picked up the big book with January to June 2013 on the spine and a cloud of dust billowed up around it. She laid it out on one of the tables and began going through the newspapers bound in it. She found nothing in it, or in the other 2013 volume. Nothing in the January to June 2014 volume either.

But in November of 2014, there was a fire at a farmhouse on Saxon Road. It started in the creosote built up in the chimney and spread to the walls. The whole family was killed.

When she finished with those volumes, she paused again to text Chigger to ask about Georgia. He still hadn't responded to her first text.

In May 2015, a man was struck by lightning while he was in a field cutting down a tree. The lightning bolt literally set the man on fire. The other loggers with him tried to put out the flames, but the man died.

On the Fourth of July in 2018, a teenager lit a firecracker with a fuse that was too short. It went off in his hand and caught his shirt on fire. He survived but was horribly injured, lost his whole left hand and was scarred all over his torso from third-degree burns.

In February of 2020, right before the whole world shut down, there was a barn dance at a farm right outside of town. The organizers used huge gas space heaters to warm the building, and a woman in a full skirt got too close to one of the heaters. Her dress caught fire. She was severely burned, but survived.

The final front page fire story was on Labor Day, last year. A man used lighter fluid to start the fire in his grill and the flames followed the fumes to his shirt and caught it on fire. This was a lucky-man story. The man took two steps and jumped into his swimming pool, extinguishing the flames. He got off light, with first- and second-degree burns on his hands, arms and chest.

And that was it. The newspaper was published weekly on Thursdays, so the issue that would have stories about the two tourists — Earl Watson on Monday and Veronica Langley on Wednesday —wouldn't be on the streets until late this afternoon. The fire at the *Y'all Come* cabin would have to wait until next week's issue.

It was dark by the time Rileigh finished. She stopped at the reception desk to thank Mrs. Sandusky, who was standing with the circulation manager, talking about the burned tourists.

When Rileigh stepped up to the counter, Mrs. Sandusky was saying, "—like that man who caught fire and burned up during the ceremony."

"Excuse me," Rileigh said. "I don't mean to interrupt, but I heard you mention some man who burned during–"

"Oh, that was years ago. I was just a kid, wasn't there. It was during the 25th Anniversary celebration of the founding of the national park. Some man tried to set the bleachers on fire, and he burned to death right there in front of — I don't know — two hundred, three hundred people. It was the most awful thing any of them had ever seen. And there were little kids there."

"When would that have been ?"

Mrs. Sandusky looked thoughtful. The circulation manager said, "Well, the park was established in 1934. So the twenty-fifth anniversary would have been in 1959."

"That surely would have been in the paper, wouldn't it?" Rileigh asked.

"Uh huh, but if it was in 1959, there aren't any bound volumes. Remember, I told you that several years were destroyed by water leaking out of the roof."

Seeing the disappointment on Rileigh's face, she continued. "But if you're really interested, I'll see what I can find out about it for you."

Rileigh gratefully gave the woman her telephone number. In truth, she wouldn't have gone back upstairs to find the story even if it had been there. She had stood it as long as she could, and as soon as she got to her car, she called Chigger's phone. An electronic non-person informed her that the voicemail box for that number was full. Then it clicked off.

Rileigh drove to the hospital and reluctantly approached the Information Desk. Thankfully, the person operating it wasn't the same person who'd threatened to call security on her when she was here before.

"I'd like the room number for Mrs. Georgia, I mean, Gwenneth Stump, please."

The woman consulted a roster. "I'm sorry, but Mrs. Stump is in the ICU unit and only immediate family is allowed to visit."

"ICU!" Rileigh said the word airlessly. She'd taken it like a blow to the belly.

"The ICU is on the second floor and it has a designated waiting room. You can go there and maybe talk to family members."

Rileigh smiled her gratitude and headed for the elevator.

The ICU waiting room was jammed with people waiting for news of their loved ones. She recognized Georgia's aunt and uncle and two of her sisters in the crowd. Then she spotted Ian and went to him.

"How's Georgia?"

"They say she's doing good, stable. She's awake, but they're keeping her pretty drugged up. They've got a hyperbaric unit in there to help her breathe."

"Has she said anything about what happened?"

"I haven't been in to see her. They're just letting Chigger and Mama in for a few minutes every two hours. Chigger's in there now."

"You've got my number. Will you call me when you know something? Chigger's not answering his phone."

"Yeah, he's pretty shook. I'll tell you whatever I know as soon as I know it."

Rileigh hugged him tight, then hurried out before she broke down in tears.

Then she went to Frank Smothers' house. She had no reason to go there, but she couldn't stop herself. She couldn't go in, of course, all she could do was glare at the house from the road. She could hate it and him from here. She could swear a sacred oath that she would —

Wait.

There were two pickup trucks parked beside Smothers's pickup, and in the glow of the porch light and a mounted pole light, she caught a glimpse of several men standing around the steps leading to the porch and seated at the picnic table beside it, drinking beer. And there was Frank Smothers on the porch. Beside the grill. The son-of-a-bitch was having a cook-out!

He'd tried to kill her in the morning, and then he celebrated with his BFFs that night by grilling hot dogs and burgers— no, *steaks.* Definitely steaks!

She wanted to pull over, draw her Glock, walk up onto that porch and blow the worthless bastard's brains all over the barbecue grill.

But she didn't, she just kept driving.

You are going down, you son of a bitch. If it's the last thing I ever do, you are going down!

Chapter Thirty-Four

THAT NIGHT, the skies over the Smoky Mountains were clear and people descended on Clingman's Dome in droves to watch the Perseid Meteor Shower. This was Thursday night, August 10, the buildup to the great climax, which would occur from after midnight on Friday until dawn Saturday morning. Astronomers said that the display of meteorites would reach their zenith during that time, putting on a spectacular show.

The roads leading toward Clingman's Dome were crowded long before dark and hundreds of tourists got stranded in their cars, stalled in traffic, forced to watch the meteors in the sky above them instead from the great observation tower at the dome.

Roger Heywood had pulled over to the side of the Whippoorwill Lane, but it wasn't so he could look out his window at the meteor shower in the sky. Roger didn't even know there was a meteor shower and likely wouldn't have cared if he had.

No, Roger had pulled to the side of the road — and was grateful he'd been in a spot where there actually was a road shoulder— because the right front tire on his Mercedes had blown out. He called Triple A and they said they'd send somebody out as soon as they could. But they only had three trucks, and one of them was stuck in some kind of traffic jam around Clingman's Dome. The other two were out on other calls, but they'd send one of them as soon as possible.

Roger was fuming, furious. Not just at Triple A, though he was plenty pissed at them. This was a 2023 Mercedes-Benz, for crying out loud. An AMG EOS Sedan that had cost him a hundred and twenty-five thousand dollars and change. An electric car that he'd purchased in spite of his constant worry that the thing would run out of juice somewhere and he'd be stranded.

He'd had it for three months now, and this was the first road trip he'd taken in it. He'd driven it around Des Moines and had never had any problem with the battery going dead. But a road trip was the real test to determine if he'd spent a hundred and twenty-five grand on a lemon.

Roger hadn't bought the thing to "save the environment." He thought all that was total bullshit. Okay, right, he did believe in climate change. It was getting hotter — incontrovertible proof of that was everywhere you looked. Or where the media directed you to look, which wasn't the same thing as reality. But that was another story.

Roger could see with his own eyes that it was getting hotter. So what? News flash, folks, the climate of the world had been changing since the earth cooled off. There were glaciers that dug huge trenches in the earth, big giants of ice moving about an inch a year down from the polar ice caps. Because the earth was friggin cold then. It was called an Ice age. They moved down, and then they moved back up again. Why? Because the earth warmed up, moron. The earth got hotter all by itself the first couple of times without any assistance from helpful humans and their carbon emissions or cows and their farts. It was a cycle.

You could see that shit in the rocks in the geologic record. But in the past, there was no hysterical media or politicians out to advance an agenda or just looking for a good story to take the natural cyclic nature of global warming and claim it was all the fault of humans. We did it, they cry — like that hysteric little Swedish girl, what was her name, who yelled at the United Nations.

The climate nuts claimed cars had done it and cows farting and all manner of other things were at fault and so we had to stop doing that shit. Right. How are you going to keep cows from farting? The looney tunes probably planned to just get rid of cows altogether.

And along comes Elon Musk and he thinks, hmmmmm. Climate change + hysterical media + political agendas + stupid populus = electric cars. Stir the looney tunes up so they shut down all the US oil production, where, by the way, there are all kinds of regulations that keep the oil companies from polluting the environment. So we have to buy oil from other countries who don't regulate their refineries, while they're polluting the hell out of the atmosphere to make the gas we're burning.

Roger Heywood was way ahead of the morons who bought into the climate change myth — but that's not why he'd bought an electric car. He'd bought the damn thing just for show, for the same reason most people did. If you could afford the price tag on an electric car, you likely weren't the kind of person who turned out to march with a sign around some petroleum company's pipeline. If you had money, you did whatever you pleased. Roger had money, so he'd bought the priciest electric car he could find.

And what did he get? He got a car that the salesman

claimed could go up to six hundred miles on a single charge. Yet here he was sitting on the side of the road because his expensive electric car, the one that had every available bell and whistle, had lousy tires! They could make a car run on electricity and couldn't figure how to make a tire that didn't blow out?

When he got back to Nashville, he was going to march down to that car dealership and—

The vehicle approaching him from the other direction was slowing. Well, it was about damn time. He looked at his watch. He had called Triple A an hour ago and they were just now showing up. The vehicle pulled up in front of where Roger had pulled his car off on the shoulder of the road and left its lights on bright. Roger got out of the car and headed into the bright lights to give the Triple A driver a piece of his—

Gasoline? The driver walking toward him was holding a can of gasoline with the lid off! Dammit, couldn't anybody ever get anything right? He hadn't run out of gas in his *electric car*. He'd had a blow-out.

"I've got a flat tire, moron, not—"

Then the driver thrust the can at Roger and splashed gasoline all over him. Roger staggered back in surprise, looking down at his soaked clothing.

"What the—?"

The next splash was in his face. The fumes were so strong he couldn't breathe. It was in his eyes and he could barely see —. just well enough through squinted eyes to watch the Triple A driver strike some kind of flame and—

"Noooo!"

He tried to turn away, but it was too late. The *whumph* of the gasoline igniting sounded like an explosion and then his whole body did explode — *in agony*, excruciating pain worse than anything he'd ever experienced.

Roger screamed, screeched, fought the world made of flames, ran away.

Out into the road, on fire, shrieking, staggering, blinded. Couldn't breathe. Falling.

Then Roger Heywood, an architect who'd driven his brand-new electric car all the way to the Smoky Mountains from Des Moines, Iowa lay twitching in the middle of the road, his body and clothing engulfed in flames.

He was still smoldering a few minutes later when a car came around the corner and almost ran over him. The driver swerved to avoid the black thing lying in the road, and sideswiped a vehicle parked on the shoulder.

The driver of the Triple A truck saw the whole thing. He was behind the car that had swerved and knew if he veered off the road, too, he'd crash into the other two. So he didn't swerve, drove straight ahead. His truck bumped up over something in the road the other driver had swerved to miss. Maybe a dead deer.

The Triple A driver hit the brakes and stopped, got out of his truck as the driver of the car that had sideswiped the Mercedes-Benz got out of hers. The Triple A driver got to the thing in the road that he'd run over before the woman out of the other car.

When he saw what it was, realized what it really was, he turned aside and vomited. Backed away toward his truck, heaving and heaving.

The woman started to scream. She was still screaming when the Triple A driver dialed 911.

Chapter Thirty-Five

When Rileigh's mother greeted her at the door with an anxious "How's Georgia?" Rileigh lost it. She'd been pumped, flying high on the adrenaline high of pure rage when she drove away from Frank Smothers' house, and the concern on her mother's face drained that all away in a heartbeat. She was home, with her mother, and that provided the release she'd been fighting since the sheriff's voice had told her there'd been a fire at the *Y'all Come* cabin. She allowed herself to feel her fear. And guilt.

"Oh, Mama, it's all my fault," she cried, falling into her mother's embrace in tears. "She wasn't supposed to be there. I was."

She spewed out the rest amid strangled sobs. "I was signed up to work the shift this morning, but I had to go to Gatlinburg. So I asked Georgia." She heaved in a great sobbing breath. "No, I didn't. Asking implies that there's a question involved. There was no question. I needed her and she did it. I wouldn't let her refuse. Now, she's in intensive care—"

"Intensive care!"

The alarm in her mother's voice made her cry all the harder.

"Yes, intensive care. She breathed in a lot of smoke and that can, you know, cause permanent damage. And it's all my fault."

She couldn't talk anymore then, just cried. She sobbed until her ribs ached. Cried it all out while her mother stood with her arms around her, patting her back, crooning words that weren't words into her hair.

When the crying jag was over, Rileigh was exhausted but calm. She figured to go to bed, get a little sleep if she could, and then just go sit in the waiting room at the hospital. She knew Ian would call her if there was any change, but it would just feel better to be there.

Mama had made a pot of chili that had perfumed the whole house with its glorious aroma. It almost made Rileigh hungry. Almost. She went into the kitchen and ladled out a bowl, then sat down with some crackers to eat it. She hadn't had breakfast or lunch and the body needed fuel whether she was upset or not. You got to feed the machine.

She could hear her mother talking on the telephone as she ate, but couldn't hear what she was saying. At least she thought she was on the phone. Maybe she was talking to the mythical Rhett Butler about their cruise to—

No, couldn't go there. Landmine.

Mama appeared in the kitchen door and looked alarmed.

"What?"

"There's been another one. Another person got burned up. Gladys just called to tell me about it. She says there's a video of it posted online and it showed up on her Facebook page. She called Sally Mabry, and she said it was on her page, too."

Rileigh rushed into the front room and picked up her laptop. She didn't do Facebook, but her mother did. Going to her mother's page … there it was! How had somebody managed to get such a horrible video posted to so many Facebook accounts?

That was a question for someone a lot more computer savvy than she was.

"Mama, you probably don't want to see this. I'm sure it will be—"

"Of course, I don't want to see it. Now turn it on and we'll watch it together."

"It was as gruesome as the first two videos had been, though the lighting wasn't as good. It appeared to be out somewhere beside a road and as soon as the victim ran out into the road where car headlights weren't showing, all you could see was the flames in the darkness. Until he fell and lay there, burning."

"Oh."

That was all her mother could say. She turned to see her mother's face pale and her hands trembling. What had she been thinking? Why on earth had she allowed her mother to see such a thing? She slammed the laptop shut and directed her mother to the couch where she collapsed like her knees might have given way under her.

"I didn't know I never dreamed oh God. Dear God."

Her mother sat shaking her head, then turned to look at Rileigh.

"Don't you be fussing over me, child. I'm fine. I'll just sit here and get my breath." She nodded her chin toward the laptop on the table. "Go on now, I know you probably need to see that … that thing again. Just sit on the other side of the table where I can't see."

"Don't you want me to bring you—"

"Go on now, leave me be." She shooed Rileigh away, so

Rileigh went to the laptop, moving it to the other side of the table and opening the lid. Then she sat and watched the video again. She played it a third time and then a fourth.

Finally, she shut the lid and sat staring into space.

"God's Spark," who'd recorded the other murders, had recorded this one, too. The person operating the camera did the same thing in all three videos. Again and again the lens zoomed in on flames, just flames. You'd think they'd would want to record the person burning up, that they'd get their sick jollies watching the person writhe in agony and pain. But most of all three videos had concentrated on the fire rather than the victim.

That meant something, but Rileigh didn't speculate on what that was.

There was another thing that was the same in all three videos. Though you'd have to have all three of them for comparison, Rileigh was almost certain that the other two videos had the same element as this one. There was a mark, a scratch or something in the lower right corner of all three videos. Like maybe the camera lens had some dirt on it or had been scratched. If that was the case, it was possible that the killer could be identified by his cell phone alone.

Rileigh didn't even try to finish the bowl of chili she'd started in the kitchen. She went internet surfing, looking up different things. She Googled iPhone cameras and read about what they could and couldn't do. The iPhone 13 could zoom in. But other smart phones could, too. Someone who knew a whole lot more than she did about cell phone video cameras would have to examine the evidence and figure out what had left that mark on the videos.

As Rileigh worked, she heard her mother go into the

living room and turn on the television. She was probably trying to see if there was a story yet about the fire. Rileigh got up and went into the room.

"Turn it up, Mama."

Her mother turned up the volume that accompanied the picture of a scene on a roadside — the trailer said it was on Whippoorwill Lane — as a talking head described what had happened. But Rileigh didn't watch the talking head. In the background of the shot she could see Mitch — and His Eminence the Mayor of Yarmouth County talking.

Correction: the mayor was talking and Mitch was listening. Although what they were saying wasn't broadcast, you didn't need words to see what was happening.

The mayor was furious, yelling something at Mitch. Then he made a grand gesture —"Go!"

And Mitch turned and walked away out of the camera frame.

Holy shit, the mayor had just fired Mitch.

Chapter Thirty-Six

MITCH WAS STUNNED at the number of people who had shown up at the scene of the crime on Whippoorwill Lane. Of course, the roads all through the county had been jammed tonight with people either going to Clingman's Dome to watch the meteor shower or coming back from it. His deputies had had to block access to the road at the nearest intersections on both sides, because the road wasn't wide enough to divert traffic around, and other than this particular stretch of it, Whippoorwill Lane wasn't wide enough for somebody to turn their car around easily and go the other direction.

Whippoorwill intersected Kirkland Trace more than a mile away, and Turkey Feather Road about the same distance in the other direction. Blocking the road and diverting traffic at the intersections effectively trapped the cars that had passed before the roadblock, since there was nowhere to turn around. Mitch supposed all those people had just gotten out of their cars and walked here to see the show.

Mitch had been tempted not to allow the news vans

access when they showed up, but it wouldn't accomplish anything to bar them from the scene. And in truth, this was one story he wanted to get out, though doing so was very likely to come back and bite him in the ass.

He had talked to the two people who had come upon the body in the middle of the road. The woman who'd sideswiped Roger Heywood's car was so distraught she was almost incoherent.

But the Triple A driver had been lucid. He said he'd been directed to a call out on this road, a motorist stranded with a flat tire. He'd been on the other side of the county, getting a car unlocked for two high-on-dope teenagers who'd locked the keys inside. He told them to call someone to come and get them because neither of them was fit to drive, and if they didn't, he'd turn them over to the police for driving under the influence and for smoking weed, which was still a crime in Tennessee even if none of the law officers ever enforced it.

He said he'd seen the car in front of him swerve off the road and sideswipe the Mercedes, and that he had run over the body, although he hadn't known at that time that was what it was. Mitch emphasized what the man already knew — that the man lying in the road had been dead before the Triple A driver ran over him.

It was easy to put together what must have happened. The guy was waiting for Triple A, another car comes along and he thinks they've stopped to help. He gets out to greet them and is brutally murdered.

There was likely no forensic evidence, but the whole scene for fifty yards in both directions was marked with yellow and black police tape, and when the team came from—

Mitch saw Melissa Mendosa with WATE 6 News advancing on him like a bird dog that had spotted quail.

He steeled himself, wouldn't allow himself to think about squinting and sweating this time. He needed to be calm, concise, clear and assertive.

"Hello Sheriff—" her eyes flicked to his name tag for a fraction of a second but she covered well. "—Webster. Could we have a few minutes of your time for an interview?"

Mitch nodded assent and stood patiently waiting while she lined up the shot she wanted. He was sure she'd set it up so the background would show the pandemonium of first responders and vehicles, and the flashing red and blue lights reflecting off the rocks and trees.

She was just about to begin the interview when someone burst out of the crowd held back by the police tape and hurried forward. It was the mayor.

"Good evening Ms. Mendosa, we haven't been formally introduced," he said, ignoring Mitch like he didn't exist as he stuck out his hand. "I'm J.P. Rutherford, the Yarmouth County mayor. I will be your point of contact for information from now on."

As he said the words, he literally tried to edge Mitch out of his position in front of her.

Mendosa wasn't buying.

"It's good to meet you Mr. Mayor. But I came here to interview the sheriff. If you'll please excuse us—"

"You need to interview me," Rutherford said, and there was childish petulance in his voice, along with a certain desperation Mitch was sure the reporter picked up on. "I'll be handling all the press coverage of—"

"I will certainly want to talk to you, Mayor … what was it again?"

"Rutherford. J.P. Rutherford. But you can call me Joe."

Mitch managed not to roll his eyes.

"I will talk to you and get your official reaction to the

situation as soon as I'm finished interviewing the sheriff. Would you please—"

"I don't think you understand, Ms. Mendosa. I am in charge here. The sheriff works for me."

She paused and gave him an assessing look that Mitch was sure told her volumes.

"So are you telling me that you will not allow the sheriff to grant an interview to the press?"

"Well, no, I just mean—"

"Because if you are, I want to know why you're denying me direct access to information. Is there something you're trying to hide?"

"Of course not, it's just that the official version—"

He hadn't meant to say that, and his face immediately colored.

"I mean, the official description of events—"

"This smells like a coverup to me. And you are woefully mistaken if you don't think I can find out anything I want to know without ever talking to you. I will find out why you're staging a coverup and I'm sure my viewers—"

"No, no. It's not a coverup. I just thought you'd like to talk to the man in charge."

"I do want to talk to the man in charge. And the sheriff is in charge of this criminal investigation, isn't he?"

The mayor saw that he was beaten.

"Yes, he is."

"Then if you'll wait for me over there off-camera, I would like to talk to you when I'm finished."

The mayor shot a warning look at Mitch.

"You tell Ms. Mendosa what she needs to know." The look was full of fish hooks and rusty razor blades. "We need to keep the viewing public appraised of the actual situation, without any commentary on our part."

Mendosa probably read that whole script. She looked at her watch.

"I'm sorry, but I'm on a deadline. Please, sir, step aside."

The mayor went to the sidelines as she had directed, never taking his eyes off the sheriff.

"Are you ready to begin, Sheriff Webster?"

"Yes, ma'am."

Mendosa asked the expected question about what had happened, about how and when Mitch had been summoned to the scene and what he'd found when he got there. She asked about the victim, and Mitch said he was from Des Moines, Iowa, but couldn't release any more information to the press until the family had been notified.

"So that means the victim wasn't local, he was a tourist."

"Yes, ma'am."

"Would you please put this situation in context for our viewers? A tourist by the name of Earl Watson was burned to death in the parking lot of Quik Stop Convenience store on Monday, is that correct?"

"It is."

"And a second tourist, a woman named Veronica Langley from Oklahoma was killed in the same manner less than forty-eight hours hours later, in front the Beer Experience bar, is that correct?"

He nodded.

"Less than twenty-four hours after *that* murder, a *third* tourist has been targeted. And I use that term advisedly—targeted. Do you believe that's what's happening here?"

Mitch couldn't see the mayor's face from where he was standing in the lights, but he didn't have to see it to know what look that face wore.

"Yes, ma'am, I do believe that's what's happening here.

We have uncovered no evidence of any connection between the first two victims other than they both were visiting Yarmouth County from out of town. We have not had time to investigate a link between Mr. Heywood and the other victims, but I don't believe we will find anything except the fact that all three of them were tourists." He looked right into the camera. "I believe there is a serial killer out there who is targeting tourists, committing murder with fire as his weapon. I'd like to issue a warning to the tourists watching this broadcast to be extra careful in your interaction with strangers. Don't go out alone, stay in groups, and be suspicious. The bone-deep good manners your grandmother drilled into you when you were a child could get you killed."

"Thank you, Sheriff Webster." She held his look for a moment and he saw understanding and approval in her eyes. Then she turned to face the camera, and her assistant motioned for Mitch to step away, farther behind where Mendosa was speaking.

"You heard it here, first," Mendosa said. "The sheriff of Yarmouth County Tennessee is warning the public to beware of a serial killer he believes is targeting tourists."

Mitch felt a steel grip fasten itself around his upper arm and turned to see J.P. Rutherford beside him, clearly so angry that if he had been a cartoon, steam would have been coming out of his ears. The unadulterated rage on his face was a truly impressive sight.

"I warned you, Webster," he hissed between clenched teeth. "Obviously, you didn't listen. You best hear this. You're *fired*. Do I make myself clear? You. Are. Fired. I'll find somebody who understands authority and is capable of taking orders to replace Mum until he gets back." He made a sweeping pointing gesture. "Now get out of here!"

Mitch turned with dignity and walked away.

Chapter Thirty-Seven

RILEIGH HAD SERVED in Afghanistan with the son of the security guard at the courthouse, and the guard was glad to let Rileigh into the building after hours. She'd come rushing to town, hoping to catch Mitch in his office, and had breathed a sigh of relief when she saw his cruiser parked out back.

She walked down the darkened hallway, listening to the slapping of her shoes on the stone floor echo off the marble walls. She could see a light under the door that said Sheriff, Yarmouth County, Tenn.

She eased it open and stepped through and saw the dispatcher in her lighted office with headphones on. Stella. She'd been a hairdresser just out of hairdressing school before Rileigh went into the military and had cut both Mama's and Aunt Daisy's hair.

Stella saw her and started to get up, then realized Rileigh hadn't come to see her. She lifted the headphones off her ears.

"He's in his office," she said. She paused, obviously not one to spread gossip, but it was clear she liked Mitch. "The mayor fired him, did you know that? Went out to the crime scene he was working, where the tourist was murdered." She shook her head, reluctant to say more.

"That one hundred percent sucks," Rileigh said and watched agreement spread over Stella's face.

"Copy that." The dispatcher pulled her headphones back down over her ears and Rileigh looked down the short hallway where she could see Mitch in his office. He had a cardboard box and he was putting things into it. She walked quietly to his doorway, surprised that he didn't hear her, then cleared her throat and said:

"Want some company or is this a private wake?"

He looked up, startled, then just nodded

"Anybody's welcome. The more the merrier. We're going to be having a cake later, and be sure to stay for the fireworks."

She walked into his office and sat down in one of the chairs facing his desk.

"I saw you on the news tonight."

"You and every man, woman and child in Yarmouth County, it seems. The voice mail system here at the station had like fifty messages backed up on it."

"Did you listen to any of them?"

"A few. If the handful I listened to are representative of all the ones in the system, the citizens of Yarmouth County are equal parts scared and pissed off. One fella said he knew the locals were going to be blamed and that I should make it damned clear to the press that we were not a bunch of damned hillbillies, barefoot and missing teeth."

"That was a brave thing you did, saying the truth when you knew the mayor was going to land on you with both feet."

"I suppose part of me thought he was bluffing when he

threatened to fire me. Because I was surprised when he did it."

"You didn't look surprised on the screen."

"What do you mean? That Mendosa woman had ended the interview with me before he did it. Please tell me the camera crew didn't record the whole thing to broadcast on the nightly news."

"No, but I could see you in the background, talking to the mayor. You didn't need to be able to hear the words to know what he was saying, or that last gesture."

"The one where he points a bony finger toward the road? That one?"

"Yeah. You didn't have to know sign language too interpret what it meant."

They both fell silent. Mitch continued to load things into the box.

"You don't have a whole lot of stuff to move out of here because you never properly moved in."

Mitch glanced at the wall behind his desk, where a huge calendar hung beneath a man holding a spectacular trout. The date on the calendar was 2021.

"Mum left enough of his stuff around that I didn't think the place looked bare. Did you?"

"Yeah, it looked bare."

"Well, then, nobody will notice when I move out."

"People will notice when you leave. Trust me, they'll notice."

"I'm just another one of those Away From Here's high tailing it back to Away From Here. Or, no wait, what is it, I know — somebody from 'out there on the flat.' But Nashville's not flat. There are lots of hills. It's not Kansas."

He fell silent then, and they had used up just about every topic of small talk besides the weather and politics.

Rileigh suspected the two of them would agree on most political issues.

"It's rough," she finally said, launching the words out there in the silence that hung like a veil between them. "I know. Been there, done that. Bought the tee shirt and wore the sucker out and now I use it to polish my car."

He stopped loading the box.

"You saying you've been fired before?"

"It cuts a whole lot deeper than that. I'm saying I was a police officer who got fired for doing my job."

He stared at her for a moment.

"That pure D sucks," he said, and she smiled. "The moving shit out and boxing it up and the driving away. When you like the job. Love the job. And are damned good at it. And you do everything right and still get fired. Sucks."

He was studying her face. She didn't know how much further she should go by way of explanation and decided now wasn't the time or place to burden him with that story.

So instead, she asked, "You ever been fired before this?"

"Nope. Well, I haven't if you don't count juvenile offenses. They're supposed to expunge your record when you turn eighteen."

"Not a choir boy, huh?"

"That'd be a big N-O."

"Neither was I. Ask Georgia about it sometime. She and I–" It hit her then, stole her breath.

Mitch said, "I called right before the guano connected with the air conditioning and they're still just saying 'stable.'"

Mitch had called to check on Georgia, sounded like

more than once. Rileigh didn't have anywhere in her head to file that information.

"Do you know anything more than that?" he added

Rileigh shook her head. "That's what they were saying when I left."

And did a drive-by look-see at Frank Smothers' house. She ought to tell him that.

"I went by Frank Smothers's house on the way home."

"Doesn't he live——?"

"So it wasn't 'on my way.'" She clenched her jaw. "I'm not going to talk about what he did until I can prove it. And I *will* prove it. You can take that to the bank and open a checking account with it!" She shook her head. "But all that aside, he was home drinking beer with his homies, which means he's off the hook for setting this last fire, and that wasn't his M.O. anyway. He torched buildings, not people."

That brought the video to mind.

"Have you seen the last video?"

Mitch nodded. "After I got back to the office. It was just idle curiosity at that point."

"I noticed something about it. You'd have to have all three of them to make a comparison, but there was a mark in the bottom right corner of the video, and I swear I remember seeing that same mark on the other two. If it's a scratch or something on the lens, find the camera and you've got proof of all three." Mitch started to respond, but Rileigh plunged ahead with the remainder of her assessment. "And I also noticed that the videos zoomed in and out, but they didn't zoom in on the person burning, they zoomed in on the flames themselves. Like the fire itself was what the killer wanted to remember."

Mitch didn't bother to argue her fascination-with-fire theory this time, just let it go.

"There's one other thing worth mentioning. This afternoon, I went to the newspaper office to look at back issues to see if there'd ever been any other instances of somebody set on fire with gasoline and burned to death."

That got his attention. He stopped putting things in the box.

"What'd you find?"

"There was one case. I don't know the whole story on it — the old newspaper didn't exist anymore. But the receptionist told me about it. Some guy was trying to burn down the grandstands and caught himself on fire, burned to death in front of a crowd."

"Was it an accident or intentional?"

"Don't know that yet."

"What grandstands?"

"They built grandstands for the twenty-fifth anniversary of the founding of the national park."

"Twenty-fifth? That would have been–"

"In 1959."

Mitch made a humph sound in his throat. "That was more than *sixty years ago*. How could it possibly be related to these three murders?" He held his hand up before she could respond. "Just idle curiosity on my part, remember. It's not my problem anymore."

And Rileigh suddenly wondered whose problem it was going to be.

Chapter Thirty-Eight

THE FIRST THING Mitch did Friday morning was call the hospital and check on Georgia's condition. They would only give out the basic "stable," but the person he spoke to said they were allowing non-family-member visitors, so she must have improved from last night.

Then he went to the courthouse, because he wanted to talk to the deputies, tell them how much he had enjoyed working with them and what a good job he believed they'd done.

He went into his office and stood for a moment in front of the bare desk, feeling a wave of sadness wash over him. He had liked this job, liked the people. He would miss—

"Sheriff Webster," said a voice behind him and he turned to see Deputy Beau Mullins standing in the doorway.

"Not anymore," Mitch said. "Surely you've been informed by now that the mayor fired me last night. Hell, you were there, saw the whole thing up close and personal."

"I was informed alright. The mayor called me after I got home last night and offered me the job."

Mitch was surprised that he was surprised. Somebody had to take over the helm of this ship. It couldn't float rudderless in the storm that now raged in the sea around it. They needed leadership.

But he was still surprised.

"And I told him no thank you," Deputy Mullins continued.

This was Mitch's day to be surprised.

"Don't you want to be sheriff?"

"Well, yeah, maybe someday. But not right now."

It would be a monumental task for somebody to step up in the middle of all this and take charge.

"He said he'd fired you because of what you told that reporter last night, that tourists needed to be careful." Mullins took a breath. "And I told him I would have done the same thing."

Definitely his day to be surprised.

"I think Billy Crawford got offered the job, and he turned it down, too. I don't know about Jeb and Tony. The mayor was probably going down the roster of full-time deputies and they're the only two left. I figure he'll go to the part-times now, but I hope not. Some of them are hot shots, want to swagger around with a badge. All hat and no cattle, if you know what I mean." Beau appeared to consider for a moment. "But I guess that's probably who the mayor's looking for — a mile wide and an inch deep, some yay-hoo who'll be a puppet, do whatever the mayor tells him to do."

Mitch didn't know what to say and was saved from stammering when Jeb Rawlings and Tony Hadley came into the outer office, saw Beau, and came into the sheriff's office.

"Looks like we're a ship without a captain," Rawlings said. He looked at Mullins. "I hear you and Billy turned him down." Glancing back at Tony Hadley, he continued. "Me and Tony did too. That pretty much leaves the mayor high and dry."

"Somebody's got to do the job," Mitch blustered, still knocked off his game by how this was all playing out.

"You're the man to do it," said Rawlings. "If he doesn't want you, he's pretty much shit out of luck."

"This being a serial killer, can't you call in the FBI?" Mullins asked.

"It's not like on television. All these murders have been in the same jurisdiction, not all over the country. Appears to me the mayor had better be on the phone to the Tennessee State Police." Mitch spread his hands wide in front of him. "That's just what I think and the mayor probably isn't interested in my opinion right now."

He tried to shift gears and do what he'd come here this morning to do — thank the other officers. But before he could pick up the conversational ball and run with it, the receptionist interrupted.

"That file just came in from Knoxville, the one you kept calling them to complain about."

Mitch had sent off the footage from the CCTV cameras in the parking lot at the Quik Stop store. It was grainy and blurry, pretty much useless, but he knew the state forensics lab could clean up the images, so he'd sent it there. That had been Monday night. He'd called every day, as persistent as a little kid asking, *are we there yet?* He knew he'd been back-burnered because he was a county sheriff in the mountains and they had bigger fish to fry. He would bet they'd only gotten to it now because of all the publicity the case was getting.

Mitch wanted to see that video.

"I'll take a look at it." Not his problem, he warned himself, but he seldom listened to his own warnings.

The four deputies were reporting to work, so they left and Mitch sat down at the desk in what used to be his office and called up the file. The grainy footage had been transformed. It was still dark and shadowy, but the images were clear.

He'd asked Sundeep to get him the footage from the camera for an entire 24-hours — starting that morning, through the murder and all the way to dawn the next morning. He examined the cars in the parking lot, and on the street out front. Sundeep even had a camera angled to get images from the sides and back of the building — the area around the *women's* bathroom. It was dark and shadowy after sundown, but even then you could see the people going in and out of it. There was no camera on the other side of the building, a camera that would have recorded the murder itself and not just what happened in the front parking lot afterward.

After he'd watched a fast-forward view of the whole tape, he went to the receptionist out front.

"Stella, I don't work here and I don't have the authority to ask you to do–"

"What do you need–" The pause was brief, but it was enough to indicate that what she said next wasn't just a slip of the tongue. "—Sheriff Webster?"

"I need you to take down the license numbers of every vehicle in this video and run the plates."

"On it."

When Stella gave him the list of vehicle owners, he ran his finger down it, looking for anything, really. He didn't have any video footage from the murder scene in front of the bar. There was no camera that showed the parking lot, and the street camera six blocks away had not been working. He had nothing to cross reference, looking for a car that might have been at both—

He stopped with his finger on a name: Angus Park. Wasn't that one of the people Rileigh talked to, someone who'd had a structure fire within the past week?

Yes, it was.

He pulled up the enhanced CCTV footage and was impressed that Stella had been able to get the plate number off it. The vehicle was parked on a side street near the convenience store, from an hour before Earl was killed until a few minutes afterward. It was possible to see someone get out of the vehicle and then return to it later, a shapeless black form in the darkness. But when he checked the time stamps, he realized that, after the vehicle pulled away, there had been sufficient time for the driver to get to the Gatlinburg Public Library and post that first video.

Mitch got up from his desk and strode out of his office, snatching the car keys for "his cruiser" off the pegboard. He had no legal right to drive it. Shoot, in technical terms, he was stealing the damn thing. But somebody'd have to be willing to testify to that, and he had felt the others "closing ranks" around him this morning, figured there wasn't a soul in the office right now who'd admit to seeing anything at all.

He got into the cruiser and headed out to the address for Angus Park. No, this wasn't his problem anymore, but … yeah it was. This case would haunt Mitch forever if he didn't find the killer. No harm done chasing the only lead they had. Since the only connection was Rileigh, there was no guarantee the next sheriff, whoever that might be, would even be willing to investigate it.

Chapter Thirty-Nine

MITCH FIGURED he ought to leave a trail of little white rocks to find his way back out of the remote part of the mountains that his GPS indicated he would find the home of Angus Park. Park lived on the back side of Broomstick Mountain at the end of Pebble Road.

He might have decided he was lost if he hadn't had so many similar experiences trying to find remote places in the mountains. This was the worse one he'd ever seen.

Right now he ought to be out looking for a job instead of having a conversation with this man who amounted to the single lead he had in the baffling case of the serial killer targeting tourists.

He pulled up to a house, which sat on a bigger piece of reasonably-flat land than he'd expected to find this far back in the boonies. There was a garden beside the house, several outbuildings behind it, a meadow with livestock, and what appeared to be the blackened remains of some kind of building on the other side.

The driveway wrapped around the house to the back, and he followed it. Stopped near the back yard and looked around, but saw no other vehicles. It would appear Angus Park was not at home.

Instead of going to the house to find out, Mitch turned and headed out through the garden, where red tomatoes the size of his fist dangled from vines and the corn was taller than his head. He approached the building that had burned, and it appeared from its location and the access to it, that it had once been a barn.

A barn on Angus Park's farm had burned down and the arson investigator said it was arson.

Why would you burn down your own barn? Made a whole lot more sense that somebody who was pissed at you did the honors. Or stupid teenagers. Even in a place as remote as this, there had to be stupid teenagers. They were everywhere else on the planet, the delight of their overindulgent parents and the bane of anybody in authority — teacher or police officer— who came in contact with them.

Mitch poked around the blackened ruin but there was nothing to see, so he retraced his route through the garden, only barely resisting the urge to pick one of those juicy-looking ripe tomatoes and taking a bite, letting the juice drip down off his chin. Memories of childhood, when if you didn't steal food when you had the chance, you went hungry.

Mitch remembered the farm out in the country where he and his brother went every summer. They pleaded with their parents not to send them, begged and cried, and it never did any good because they had to go anyway, and when they got older, they realized that all that pleading not to go solidified their parents' determination to send them. Clearly they were undisciplined boys who needed to go to the farm, needed to work from sunup to sunset, needed to stand in the blistering heat hoeing weeds in the garden and sit on the floor in the dark, bare room where they could hear the rats in the walls at night.

He and his brother took turns standing watch, holding a boat oar they'd found in the garage as their only defense against the rodents who often came into where they slept, scurrying around in the dark, little claws clicking on the wood floor.

He resisted the urge to reach over his shoulder and touch the marks on his back, and shook his head to dislodge the memories. He had developed the skill to compartmentalize the portions of his mind where the images of growing up were stored. Just like his world had been compartmentalized.

One world was all sweetness and light, where he and his brother pretended to be normal kids just like everybody else, and then sneaked into the kitchen at night to steal food out of the cabinets. They had to fatten up during the wintertime, because there would be only work and sweat and hunger and pain all summer.

He got to the edge of the garden and veered to the right toward an outbuilding beyond the back yard. There was a path leading to it that suggested sometimes vehicles were driven down it. The building was large enough to hold a car, to hold several cars or tractors or pieces of farming equipment. The front bay doors were held shut with a hasp and padlock. There was a door on the side, but when he tried the knob, it was locked.

He went to the lone window and wiped dirt off a spot so he could look in. There was a car in the building. He couldn't tell anything about it through the dirty window.

He could have picked the lock, but he didn't. Instead, he walked slowly around the building and tried to get a better look through cracks between the slats of the wall.

But even the largest cracks only revealed inch-wide swaths of reality.

After a full circuit of that building, he went to a smaller one a short distance away. It looked like something of a tool shed, where maybe the lawn mower and yard equipment were stored. That building's door was also held shut with a heavy-duty hasp and a padlock.

That struck Mitch as odd. He hadn't been in Yarmouth County long enough to make such a judgement call, but it appeared to him that the locals were more welcoming than suspicious. This Angus Park lived way up here where nobody came by accidentally. Why would you feel the need to lock everything up? What could there possibly be in either of those buildings valuable enough to protect with a padlock? Unless he feared the car in there might be identified at one of the fire scenes.

Mitch went across the back yard and up onto the back porch. There was a trellis surrounding the porch on three sides, and it was so thick with honeysuckle vines and morning glories that it formed a dark tunnel where not a speck of sunlight got through. Mitch stepped into the darkness out of the bright sunlight and squinted to make out the door, a vague white shape a few feet in front of him.

He raised his fist to knock when something came down like a hammer on the back of his head. The blow knocked him to his knees, stunned, teetering on the brink of passing out, and he was shoved face forward onto the porch floor. He felt somebody take his gun out of his holster and he was powerless to prevent it, couldn't do anything more than hang on to consciousness with his fingernails.

Someone slapped something on his face, covering his mouth. It was a piece of duct tape. Something over his whole head, blocking out everything — burlap. It was a burlap sack. Then he felt himself sliding. He tried to hold on, gripped reality as tight as he could, but it was a lost cause. The darkness on the edges of his vision began to converge and he could do nothing but watch the light go out.

After that, he was in a place of quiet darkness where no light came.

Chapter Forty

RILEIGH WAS in the ICU waiting room early the next morning when Chigger came out through the "inner sanctum" door that lead to the patients' rooms, and his face was wreathed in a smile. He saw her, took two steps, picked her up and swung her in a circle.

"She's awake! She knows me! She's okay!" he said in what sounded like a tear-clotted voice.

"Put me down, Chigger Stump, before I smack you," Rileigh said, but it was tender, not caustic, and he eased her to the floor. She looked up into his face — circles under his bloodshot eyes, two days' stubble, breath that would seem to indicate a considerable amount of time had elapsed since he'd last brushed his teeth.

"You look like death on a cracker," she told him, and he just grinned stupidly at her.

She wasn't often wrong about people, could usually assess character pretty accurately. And everything she'd ever seen or heard, every interaction she'd ever had with Chigger had reinforced her assessment that he was a lowlife drug dealer who couldn't even do that well enough to make a decent living. She had always loathed him, angry that he'd managed to snatch up one of the most important people in her life and put her in a trailer house on the side of a mountain, chained there by five small children.

Well, maybe she'd been wrong. Somewhat wrong, anyway. She was still pretty sure he was totally morality-free, would do anything to make a buck, didn't know the meaning of honesty and decency and loyalty, but one thing was absolutely undeniable. Chigger did love Georgia. And for that Rileigh was profoundly grateful.

"Wait here a second, Rileigh," he said, turned and went back through the door where only the immediate family were allowed to enter. He came back a few minutes later.

"Okay, I talked Harriet into letting you see Georgia for a few minutes."

"Harriet?"

"The charge nurse."

Yeah, Chigger was definitely a charmer.

"She said only five minutes, and she is absolutely timing it." He turned and led Rileigh into the ICU where the most critical patients were attached to every medical device known to modern medicine. They all looked like they weren't likely to live another fifteen minutes. Georgia was in a bed near the windows. Her mother was with her, and looked up in surprise at Rileigh.

"Harriet said it was all right. Just for a couple of minutes. Let's go get a cup of coffee." Chigger led Pauline McGinnis back across the room and Rileigh sank down into the chair she'd just vacated. She took Georgia's hand and squeezed it and whispered, "Georgia, it's me."

Georgia's eyes popped open and shot to Rileigh. She had a mask over her face, IV lines and other tubes going in and out of her. But there were two pieces of equipment beside her bed that weren't hooked up, and Rileigh guessed that those might be the machines that'd been helping her breathe… and she didn't need them anymore.

"Rileigh…"

"Don't try to talk."

Georgia actually laughed, which set all kinds of dials and monitors to chirping and beeping, so she stifled it, reached up and moved her mask aside enough to whisper:

"That's so lame. Line out of a bad movie." She took a kind of rasping breath. "No points!"

Rileigh wanted to cry but she didn't. Georgia was back!

"Lean over, not much air."

Rileigh leaned closer.

"The door wouldn't open. Jammed."

What door? Then she knew. "The door of the *Y'all Come* cabin?"

Georgia nodded. "Couldn't get out. Had to break out the window."

White hot rage boiled through Rileigh, followed by a string of the most foul obscenities she'd ever heard, and she had heard them all. She said nothing out loud, though, just squeezed Georgia's hand.

"I got this."

"You have to go now," said a nurse who had come up soundlessly behind her. She had the demeanor of a drill sergeant, and Rileigh knew it was a great grace she'd been granted to be allowed to visit at all.

"I'll be back as soon as they'll let me."

She leaned over and pecked a kiss on Georgia's forehead, then followed the nurse out.

Rileigh avoided the hallway to the ICU waiting room, didn't want to see anybody, not now. She was in such a raging fury she couldn't have been civil right now to Jesus Christ.

She forced herself to calm down in her car, taking deep breaths. That son-of-a-bitch Frank Smothers really had tried to kill her. He had blocked the door so she couldn't get out. Rileigh had to talk to the sheriff—

Mitch had been fired. He wasn't the sheriff anymore. And she would be starting from scratch with whoever the moron mayor had appointed to replace him.

Her phone rang and she almost didn't take the call because she didn't recognize the number.

"Hello," she said, ready to eviscerate whatever telemarketer had the misfortune to draw her phone number this morning.

"Is this Rileigh? Hi, it's Mildred Sandusky here, from the Gazette."

Rileigh quickly backed up and recalibrated.

"Oh, Mrs. Sandusky. How are you?"

"I'm fine, dear. I told you I'd get you information about that man who died, the one who tried to burn the bleachers down."

"Yes. What can you tell me?"

"Well, I couldn't get any written accounts, but I know several women at The Pines, so I just went over there this morning and had coffee with them, asked what they knew."

The Pines was the senior adult living facility. Rileigh had visited a time or two with her mother. And Aunt Daisy.

"Anybody who'd been there had vivid memories of it, awful memories. Margaret Trace said she still had nightmares about it, more than half a century later."

Then Mildred Sandusky described in some detail the people she'd talked to and what they'd told her. All the stories were essentially the same. The twenty-fifth anniversary celebration of the founding of the park had been a big, big deal. Governors, politicians, everybody who was anybody was there, seated on a dias that'd been hauled there behind a truck, a big fancy metal thing. Bleachers had been build for "the commoners," and they'd been jammed full when the ceremony began, but suddenly a man appeared between the bleachers and the dais and started hollering.

"Thelma Bledsoe said he was yelling about the meteor shower being the fires of God raining down on the unrighteous, and that fire would rise up from the earth to join God's flames and consume all who had polluted God's beautiful creation. After that, the ladies weren't sure exactly what did happen. They said he stopped talking, looked around, like he was waiting for something to happen. But nothing did, and the police were converging on him for both sides to drag him out of there. And then–"

"Then what?"

"He burst into flames?"

"He what?"

"They said he burst into flames. Cleta Obenhaus said he was just suddenly a fireball, but Laverne Underwood — she has dementia, so you never know if what she says is real or not — but she said she was sitting near the bottom with her parents, and he had something in his hand, like a thermos of some kind. It must have been full of gasoline or lighter fluid or something like that. Cleta said that later they found rags soaked in gasoline under the bleachers, so he must have been trying to set the bleachers on fire. And apparently he tried to splash whatever was in that thermos on the bleachers or the people in the bleachers — nobody knows. But he musta spilled some on his own clothes, because when he struck a match, he was the one who got burned up, right there in front of three hundred people."

Rileigh thought of Earl Watson, Veronica Langley, and Roger Heywood who'd done the same thing — just without an audience.

"Who was the man who died?"

"His name was Abraham Park. The Park family who lives on the back side of Clear Creek Mountain, they're his descendants. I think Abraham Park's house is still there."

It is, Rileigh thought, and she'd met a man who was probably his grandson, the night of the meteor shower in June. And that man had tried to warn four-year-old Mason that God was going to destroy the world with fire.

God's going to rain fire down out of heaven, fire that will set the whole world ablaze.

Mitch needed to have a talk with—

Not Mitch.

Fine, then, she'd go talk to Angus Park herself.

Chapter Forty-One

RILEIGH LEFT the hospital parking lot and turned east, away from Black Bear Forge and into the mountains. She remembered Pebble Road, recalled that the last time she was on it, she'd been afraid she'd missed a turn and was lost. As she drove the winding mountain roads she thought about the sequences of events, trying to make connections.

She couldn't think of any reason Angus Park's craziness two months ago would make him decide to start killing people now. But his grandfather had predicted that God was going to destroy the earth with fire and he was the only other person in the county besides the tourists who'd ever burned to death. She didn't believe that was a coincidence.

When she got to Angus's house, there was no pickup truck parked behind the house. And it appeared nobody was home. Maybe he had taken his sister for some kind of medical treatment. This was a chance for Rileigh to take a look around, specifically, for cans of gasoline.

Before she got out of her car, she opened the console and removed her Glock 43X 9 mm pistol and slid it into the IWB, inside waist band, holster she wore. She was fully prepared to make a citizen's arrest if she had to, which was legal under Tennessee Code 40-07-09. According to that statute, she would have to see somebody breaking the law, or believe the person she was arresting had committed a felony.

Murder was definitely a felony.

She approached the house casually, but with her head on a swivel, looking all around to make sure Angus didn't surprise her. She stepped up on the front porch and knocked on the door. No one answered. She knocked again. Still no answer. The front windows on the house had drawn shades, but there were tall, narrow windows on both sides of the door.

She put her face to the glass and peered inside. When she'd been here the first time, Angus and his sister had been standing in the doorway, blocking her view. Now she could see the empty rooms clearly. What she saw was odd. The front door opened into an entryway, but she could see the front room to the left through an open door. She couldn't see the furniture, but she could see that the whole back wall appeared to be some kind of painting, a giant mural.

Before she thought about it, she tried the knob and the door opened easily. She wouldn't go in, just peek through the open door to see the painting on the wall. But as soon as she saw it, she had to get a closer look.

"Hello, anybody home?" she called out. You didn't just walk into somebody's house unannounced. Even if you suspected the person was a murderer, walking into their house uninvited was still B&E, breaking and entering. And that was a felony.

That you were looking for somebody was a lame excuse, but she'd had criminals use it on her before. *Hey, I just went in there because I was looking for Joe.* She didn't know how well they'd fared in court with that as a defense — probably not well at all— but she called out loudly anyway, certainly didn't want Angus to wander into his living room in his underwear and find her there.

"Knock! Knock!"

The house was as silent as a tomb.

Rileigh walked slowly into the front room where she'd seen the piece of art on the wall and literally sucked in a breath in surprise. And awe. There wasn't any furniture in the room, but there were lights along the floor that illuminated the walls above, and more along the ceiling that shined down on the walls below, uniformly illuminating all the walls and the painting on them. Because the painting wasn't just on the back wall. It was on all of them.

Turning slowly around in a circle, she saw that the mural went all the way around the room, from the floor up to the ten-foot ceiling, on all four walls. It continued unbroken *over* the front windows. She thought of the Sistine Chapel, how Michaelangelo had painted over the ceiling struts and other architectural features. The mural in Angus Park's front room continued unbroken over the door and window frames and across the shades on the windows. She'd walked in through one of two double doors into the room and when she looked back, she could see that the mural continued across the doors. Close the doors and you stood in the center of a three hundred sixty degree painting.

Rileigh was staggered. She had never seen anything like it in her life. It was an original piece of art, painted with either acrylic or oils, she couldn't tell which, a detailed rendering of the Smoky Mountains. As she studied it she realized it was the three hundred sixty degrees view from Clingman's Dome, the highest point in the mountain range

— though the viewing platform that had been built to offer visitors a clear view from there was not included in the painting.

Rileigh had seen that view hundreds of times, and she stepped closer to the mural and examined it. Totally accurate, as far as she could tell. It was as perfect as a digitalized photograph.

Who in the world could create such a thing? And how old was it? Had it always been here, painted when the house was built more than a hundred fifty years ago? If it had been, somebody had been retouching it over the years because the colors were so fresh and vibrant, it almost looked like wet paint. She stepped closer, reached out a finger to a spot that was shiny and the tip of her finger came back green. There were places on the mural that *had* recently been retouched.

Had the Park family lived in this house for generations with this mural painted on the walls of the largest room in the house?

Was this where they set up the tree at Christmas and— Rileigh reined in her imagination. Maybe the mural had been painted on the walls and it had just been a normal room with furniture and such. Or maybe it had been added long after the house was built. Maybe some of the residents of the house had moved all the furniture out of this room and turned it into ... what would you call it? A shrine, maybe, to the beauty of the mountains.

Rileigh walked slowly around the room, noticing the symbols. There were small red flames scattered through the mountains, red butterflies that most resembled little campfires. They looked a little like the symbols on the map of the Great Smoky Mountains National Park for the campsites where visitors were allowed to build campfires.

One thing was clear from the detail and magnitude of

the painting. Whoever had done it had loved the mountains, had preserved them here pristine, with no sign of civilization encroaching.

That thought stopped her. This rooms showed the mountains untouched by man. Maybe whoever painted it wanted this beautiful creation of God to *remain* untouched.

Clearly Abraham Park had hated the national park for bringing visitors to the mountains. He'd tried to destroy the ceremony celebrating the park. He wanted to keep the world out of his mountains because he feared the mountains would be destroyed by *tourists*.

244

Chapter Forty-Two

RILEIGH WAS oh so tempted to search the remainder of the house, but she resisted the urge. If she did find anything damning enough to indicate she needed to make a citizen's arrest right now, it would mightily screw up the case when it went to trial that the evidence had been procured illegally.

She went back out the front door, closed it behind her, walked around the house to the back. When she'd been here the first time, she'd seen the blackened ruins of the barn that had burned to the ground on the other side of a lush vegetable garden. She'd also seen a couple of outbuildings where she might be able to poke around, see what was in there.

She walked to the edge of the garden with a path beside it that led to the outbuildings. There might have been faint tire tracks on the path, indicating that a car had driven down it, but the path was so overgrown she couldn't be sure.

The first building she came to was large. It looked like

the kind of garage building you see at auto body shops. Like Frank Smothers'.

Nope, not going there. If she let herself think about that monster, she'd lose all her focus. Concentrate on the task at hand. There'd be plenty of time later to deal with that bastard.

The front bay doors were held shut with a hasp and a padlock, but there was a door on the side of the building and Rileigh tried the knob. It wasn't locked.

She stepped into the darkness of the building from of the bright sunlight and was momentarily blind. Just outside the puddle of light in front of the open door was the shape of a car. Rileigh reached into her pocket and took out her cell phone, tapped the flashlight app, and a surprisingly bright light stabbed out into the darkness.

There was at least one car in the building — perhaps two, but the light wasn't bright enough to tell if there was a second car. But at that moment Rileigh didn't care about the second car, because the first one had stopped her in her tracks. It was the Sheriff's Department cruiser that Mitch drove. Used to drive, before the mayor fired him.

How did a sheriff's department cruiser get locked up in a building on Angus Park's land?

She walked a few steps toward it, her mind spinning. This was the car that Mitch always drove and it had been parked in the lot behind the courthouse last night when she left after seeingMitch.

The new sheriff? Had Idiot Man picked somebody to replace Mitch already, and whoever it was had driven out here this morning before she got here and … what? Put his cruiser in this building and locked it up inside?

No, no, no. Nothing about this smelled right. All her gut-instinct alarm bells were clanging, loud as a forklift backing up at Home Depot. Because the really important question had yet to be asked. Where was the officer who'd driven the car and left it here?

She advanced on the vehicle slowly. Her cell phone flashlight produced pretty powerful illumination, but it was pinpointed, a beam of light that didn't provide enough light to see anything she didn't point the phone directly at. She went to the driver's side, tried the door. It wasn't locked. She opened it and looked inside. Everything was turned off, dead, but the shotgun fastened to the ceiling above the driver's seat was still there. The keys were in the ignition.

She looked in the back seat, nothing out of the ordinary there. She walked around the front of the car to the passenger side. She shined the light on the floor. Nothing.

She completed her circuit of the car, focusing her light on the vehicle and she almost missed it. Just outside the flashlight beam was something lying on the floor. She pointed the light at it.

It was a body! The body of a man in uniform, lying on his side. The hands and feet of the man were securely bound with duct tape, and there was a burlap bag over his head. She knelt and yanked the bag off.

Mitch!

Her heart took up the rhythm of a lunatic woodpecker in her chest.

He was unconscious. She didn't see any obvious injuries, so she shined the light up and down his body. There was a lump on the back of his head and a little blood, but no other injuries she could see. She rolled him over onto his back, shined the light into his face and slapped him gently on the cheek.

"Mitch!" She whispered the word, didn't shout it. Because while her concern for Mitch was taking up all the juice from most of the synapses firing in her mind, there were still a rebellious few asking pesky police officer questions.

Why had Angus Park knocked Mitch out and tied him up?

Better question: where was Angus Park now?

He could be in the building with them, somewhere out in the darkness her pitiful little flashlight didn't illuminate. That's why she was whispering.

She focused the light on Mitch's face and slapped him again, called his name.

"Mitch! Wake up! Mitch!"

He grunted softly and his eyelids fluttered briefly.

"Mitch!" She didn't say it louder, just leaned closer to his ear and whispered fiercely. "You gotta wake up."

Mitch was too big for her to toss up over her shoulder in a fireman carry and haul out. She glanced down at her phone. No bars. She wasn't surprised. Nobody got cell coverage back deep in the mountains like this. There was nobody to call for help. She was on the hook for this one.

"Mitch, dammit, open your eyes."

Mitch opened his eyes and there was no recognition of any kind in them. You could look into those eyes and right out the back of his head.

"Mitch, look at me," she averted the flashlight beam out of his face and shined it briefly on her own, so he could see it. His eyes moved toward her face and it appeared he tried to focus. A pleat of concentration stapled itself between his eyes.

"It's me, Rileigh, look at me. You have to wake up."

He blinked, squinted, blinked again, and she watched confusion replace the blankness in his eyes.

She shined the flashlight down onto where his hands were duct taped together. Looked like Park had used half a roll. She shined the light down at his feet. Park must've used the other half on Mitch's feet. She had nothing to cut the tape with, but she didn't think she could pull the tape loose either. And Angus could come back anytime.

Mitch mumbled something and she shined the light back on his face. He was looking at her, clearly not yet operating on all cylinders, but he was at least awake. She leaned close to his face and whispered in his ear.

"You're tied up and I have to get you out of here." She looked into his face and saw recognition there, but no understanding. It might take him awhile to come completely around, but he was at least awake and aware enough to help her get him out of here, because she'd never be able to carry him.

She grew still, weighed her options the way she'd have considered them if she were in a fire fight in Afghanistan.

The "enemy" was still out there, could be anywhere and could return at any time.

She had to get Mitch's feet free first, so he could walk, or stagger, with her holding his weight to—

To where? Should she try to get him upright and then walk all the way to her car?

Did she leave him here and go get her car?

Car.

There was a car right here with the keys in the ignition. If she could just get him into it, she could use it as a battering ram to open the bay doors. The back was facing the doors, and that was a good thing. From her vast store of images from demolition derbys at the county fair every year, she knew you did the ramming with the back of the car. If she used the vehicle to break through the door, she might have to hit it several times. It was possible she could damage the engine in the attempt, but she could crush the trunk and back bumper with no such fear.

Get his feet free, then.

She used the cell phone flashlight to examine the duct tape on his feet, looking for the end of it. When she found it, she put the phone on the ground with the light shining on what she was doing, and began to try to strip the tape away.

All the while, she was talking to Mitch in an urgent whisper.

"Mitch, stay with me. Don't close your eyes, stay with me."

He made another sound that was a little more articulated than a groan, a sound that might have been an attempt at a word.

"We'll talk later. Right now, concentrate on getting your marbles back together."

She had to keep him awake so he could stand and move on his own. No way could she drag his dead weight even ten feet to the car and get him into it. She couldn't have done that even if she'd had full use of both arms, but she didn't. Her left wrist was still held rigid by a black brace. Her thumb was stuck through one part of it, and her fingers extended out beyond it. But she could barely move her thumb, and her fingers didn't stick far enough out to be able to grasp anything.

The duct tape was stuck tight. She picked at it until she'd unfastened about six inches, then stood, put her foot on his leg to brace and put her back and right shoulder into it. It came free only a few inches. If she could have used both arms …

She ripped up as much as she could, using only her right hand, with the left steadying her grip. She pulled a piece free from the one below it, then grabbed the piece closer to where it was stuck down and tried to rip up a few more inches. It was slow going, and as she worked, her eyes darted out into the darkness all around, expecting an attack that didn't come.

By the time she got the last of the tape off his ankles, she was drenched in sweat and utterly exhausted, her right arm trembling from exertion. Mitch appeared to know who she was now and maybe even where they were, but he was groggy and confused.

Tossing the last of the duct tape away, she pulled his feet apart. Then she crawled up beside him.

"Mitch, you're going to sit up now. I'm going to lift your shoulders upward as much as I can, but you have to help me."

He seemed to mumble assent. Or not

On her knees above his head, she got her right hand on his upper arm beneath his shoulder, but could do nothing on the left side but shove with the braced hand.

"Help me out here, Mitch."

She shoved upward on his shoulder with all her strength and got it six or eight inches off the ground.

"That's your car out front, ain't it?"

The low rumble of the voice *behind her* startled Rileigh so profoundly that she almost squeaked out a scream.

Holding Mitch up with her right hand and arm, she was totally helpless to try to draw her gun from the holster beneath her tee shirt on her right side.

Had Park waited for this moment? Had he watched from the shadows until she had her hands full before he revealed himself?

He was standing behind the police cruiser holding a vicious-looking hunting knife. Two steps and he'd be on them, and they were totally defenseless.

Rileigh was hyper-aware that what she did in the next thirty seconds would determine whether she and Mitch lived or died. She began to lower Mitch back to the ground to free her right hand, babbling the first words that came to her.

"Yes, that's my car. I didn't think anybody was home, went and knocked on the door–"

Mitch suddenly tried to sit up, but all he could manage was to lunge upward before tumbling back down — on top of Rileigh, pinning both her arms to the ground.

"What are you doing here?" Park demanded, his eyes boring into hers.

"Just wanted to talk, that's all. Ask you a few questions. Then I found Mitch–"

"Shut up," Park barked the words, looking around, at the police cruiser and the two of them. Checking to see if they'd brought reinforcements. Maybe she could bluff, make him think—

She didn't have time to even form a plan, much less execute it, before he was on Mitch. He dropped to his knees and brought the knife down toward Mitch's chest.

Rileigh dragged her arms out from under his body, knowing she was too late, knowing Angus Park would plunge the blade into Mitch's heart or slit his throat before she could do anything to stop him.

Chapter Forty-Three

Angus Park reached out with the knife in his right hand, and used his left to lift up Mitch's duct-taped wrists. The blade was so sharp it cut almost through the whole restraint in one slice.

Rileigh was scrambling out from under Mitch, so she could lunge at Park, when he told her.

"Stop wiggling. This here blade's sharp, and if he don't hold still, I could cut him with it."

Rileigh froze in surprise. Didn't move or breathe, just watched Angus Park slice carefully at the remaining duct tape.

She had absolutely no idea what was going on, but she was not one to look a gift horse in the mouth. If Angus Park had changed his mind about whatever it was he'd tied Mitch up for, she was totally down with that. All she wanted was to escape. Then return with an invading army.

When Park had Mitch's hands free, he stood and held out his hand.

"Can you stand up?"

Mitch appeared to be about eighty percent back.

253

Clearly he knew what was happening and who it was happing to, but she wasn't sure he was making all the mental leaps, because it was certainly mental gymnastics to figure out what had possessed Park to take Mitch captive in the first place, and then what had changed his mind.

"Think so," Mitch mumbled and gripped Park's hand. The big man was as strong as a bull, and he almost lifted Mitch off the ground with no help from Mitch. Park draped Mitch's right arm around his shoulders and Rileigh draped his left arm around hers, with the threesome pointed at the open door when the light in the doorway was suddenly blotted out by a figure.

"What do you think you're doing, Angus?" said the voice of that dark shape. Backlighted like it was, there was no way to make out the features, but Rileigh thought she recognized the voice.

"You can't do this Sarah," Park said. But he didn't sound strong and assertive. It was more pleading than demanding and Rileigh absolutely didn't like the sound of it.

Then Sarah stepped through the doorway into the barn and some of the spill of light fell on her. Rileigh remembered her as tall and thin, but right now the woman looked like an Amazon, standing with a double-barrel shotgun pointed at the three of them.

"I can do and will do and you will as well," she said, her voice the firm don't-argue-with-me-anymore a mother used with a tantrum-throwing toddler. "Now get over here."

Suddenly, Rileigh was supporting all of Mitch's weight instead of only half of it, and it threw her so far sideways that she stumbled and they both fell to the floor. Rileigh rolled away from Mitch to—

"The gun," said Sarah, who'd stepped forward and

now held the barrel of the shotgun only inches from Rileigh's head. "You have a pistol. Take it out of the holster. I want it."

Rileigh had risen as far as her knees and her hand was already lifting her shirt to draw the weapon.

"Slowly. Can't shoot game with a shotgun, 'cause it blows the rabbit into so many pieces there's nothing left to eat."

That was the problem with facing a shotgun. At this range, Sarah would hit her target just by pointing the gun the right direction, didn't even have to aim.

Still, Rileigh was tempted to try. She and every officer in the world knew the principle. If somebody takes your gun away from you, there is a ninety percent chance they will use it to kill you.

Apparently, Sarah had sensed that second of hesitation and indecision.

"Don't. Just don't. You will die instantly if you so much as twitch."

Rileigh moved her hand and slowly lifted her tee shirt.

"Two fingers, now take it out of the holster in two fingers."

Rileigh did as she was instructed, grasped the handgrip of the Glock in two fingers and drew it out of the holster. She held it out in front of her that way, like you"d hold a dead mouse by its tail.

"Down on the floor. Easy. Don't even hiccup or you're dead."

Rileigh set the gun down carefully on the floor and lifted her hand away from it slowly. It was like she could feel the distance elongating, like the gun was a life raft and she was adrift in a stormy sea and the farther she got from it, the more likely she was to drown.

"Now sit down beside your friend."

Rileigh eased down off her knees to a sitting position beside Mitch on the floor.

"What do you think you're doing, Sarah?"

Again, it wasn't so much a question as a pleading whine.

Sarah ignored the question. She focused her attention instead on Rileigh and Mitch.

"It's fitting that you should be the first to face God's wrath."

The woman stepped to the side as she spoke, and now the light from the doorway illuminated her whole face. She was no longer wearing the head bandage that had covered part of her face. Clearly the bandage had not been to protect the incision of a recent brain surgery.

Rileigh didn't gasp in horror, but she barely caught herself. It was like looking at some horrible mask. The right side of Sarah Park's face was delicately beautiful. Fine features, high cheekbones, a wide, full mouth and feathered eyebrows that turned up on the end. Her hair was drawn back away from her face, held back with a golden barrette that had stones of some kind on it that twinkled in the light.

The left side of her face was a ruin. She had been horribly burned on that side. The charred skin of third-degree burns hung there blackened, and there were watery second-degree blisters so full they hung down her cheek by the weight of the liquid in them. Her left eye was completely gone, had been burned completely out of her face. She lacked most of her left ear as well, and her hair was burned away from that side, leaving nothing but torched, blackened skin and blisters.

Sarah seemed to be completely unaware of the horrible wounds. If she suffered pain, she didn't show it. She stood erect, holding the shotgun, and a small smile creased the corners of her mouth on the right and drew back charred lips on the left.

"Pick up the pistol Angus," she told her brother, and he stepped forward and lifted the pistol off the ground with his huge hand and just held it, not like somebody who intended to use the gun, but like he was holding a cigar box or a stuffed animal.

"Go into the kitchen and get the duct tape," Sarah told him. "The sack of groceries I just bought is on the table, and there's a fresh roll in it. I was leaving the grocery store and I stopped and thought perhaps I should get a fresh roll. Maybe we might need it."

Chapter Forty-Four

ANGUS PARK WENT out the side door of the building and left his sister guarding her captives.

Captives.

Rileigh's mind was making all sorts of connections and drawing all manner of conclusions, but the most pressing mystery right now was why they were being taken captive.

She could understand the woman killing them. After all, they were trying to expose her. Sarah Park was a serial killer who had burned to death three tourists in the past week. She certainly wasn't opposed to or squeamish about cold-blooded murder.

So why hadn't she killed them? Why was she letting them live? She had some purpose in mind.

"God delivered the two of you into my hands for a reason," Sarah said, her words eerily echoing what Rileigh had been thinking. "It's another sign from heaven."

Sarah fell silent, just stood there holding the shotgun on them.

"What do you want us for?" Rileigh asked, knowing it might not be a good idea to poke the tiger, but equally certain that she didn't have a whole lot to lose at this point.

"I was born in these mountains, in that house." Sarah gestured with her chin in the direction of the house. "I expected to die in them, maybe breathe my last breath in the same room where I drew the first one."

Angus Park was not an educated man, likely had dropped out of high school here. Maybe he had gone to work in the mines of Eastern Kentucky or West Virginia, though Rileigh was pretty sure she recalled the family owned a sawmill somewhere. Sarah might not be educated either, but it was clear she had more on the ball than her brother.

"But with all the long years between the birthing and the dying stretched out *behind* me, I was beginning to doubt, like my namesake in Scripture. I have known all my life God was calling me to a higher purpose. I knew I had a job to do. Some folks never do figure out what it was they were put on this earth to do. But I always knew. Oh, there were a lot of years in there where I pretended I didn't. For years, I acted like my life was my own, and I could do whatever I wanted to with it. You have that attitude long enough and God will slap you down into the mud, so you get a close look at the dirt he formed you out of."

She drew in a shaky breath and her voice momentarily took on a haunted quality.

"When God plants an evil seed inside your head and it begins to grow and grow, it's like a snake in there, squirming around, trying to get out. It like to drove me crazy."

"You painted the mural on the wall in the house, didn't you?" Rileigh asked.

Sarah Park didn't even look surprised that Rileigh knew it was there. Maybe she had been watching Rileigh from somewhere up in the trees from the moment she arrived, knew she'd gone into the house.

No, Sarah had been at the store.

Let me see. I take a sheriff prisoner. Oh maybe he wasn't officially one, but close enough. Knock him over the head, tape his hands and feet together, and put a burlap bag over his head. Then I hop in the car to run to the store for some milk and eggs and a cup of sugar.

It took a genuinely special kind of crazy to do a thing like that, to be so calm that nobody in the produce section would notice.

Actually, Sarah hadn't said grocery store. She'd just said store. She went to the store because she needed something badly, maybe something she didn't even realize she needed until she kidnapped Mitch.

Maybe something she needed because she'd kidnapped Mitch.

"Yes, I painted the mural, had all kinds of time after the gov-mint said everybody had to stay home. And I fixed where God burned it with the flaming finger of his right hand when he wrote my commission in fire on the wall."

Rileigh had been right. Some of the paint was fresh.

"The hardest part was the smoke. Couldn't make it look like real smoke, had to be mist rising up off the creeks and out of the hollows into the air like little baby clouds that didn't get formed all the way before they were born."

Angus came back into the building with a large roll of gray duct tape.

"You tape them up good and solid now," Sarah instructed him, gesturing at Mitch and Rileigh. "Don't want them and running off on us, not now that God has delivered them into our hands."

Angus said nothing, just went to Mitch, who was sitting up on the floor now, rather than lying on it.

"The two of you will have a great privilege tonight.

You will be the first to be visited by the fires of God to cleanse the world of the unrighteous."

As Angus continued to work on Mitch's hands, Sarah never lost the dreamy, otherworldly look in her eyes.

"I had to have linen, the finest white linen to drape around you, to purify you for the sacrifice."

Sacrifice.

Rileigh felt a knot of fear yank tight in her belly.

"Angus was the first to be marked by fire and he was only eight years old." Angus stopped wrapping tape around Mitch's ankles and sat very still. "Show them the marks, brother."

Rileigh looked at Angus Park and saw a man who was hopelessly trapped by a force of will stronger than his own. He set the tape down on the floor and unbuttoned the shirt cuffs on his left arm. Then he slowly rolled up the sleeve.

"Hold it out where they can see."

Angus did as his sister told him. He held his left arm out into the light where Rileigh and Mitch could see five wrinkled white scars down the inside of his forearm.

"He burned them with a white-hot poker out of the fireplace. Every night the fire fell from heaven, he burned his own arm so God would not pass over him. So when God came to judge the righteous and the unrighteous, he would see the marks on Angus's arms and know he was one of His own."

Angus rolled his sleeve back down and went to work on Mitch's hands, while his sister continued to talk.

"God spoke to me through fire, burned a message on my mountains."

Her mountains. The *painting* of her mountains. That would explain the spots of fresh paint, if she'd repaired her mountains after they received a fiery message from God.

"You will meet your maker tonight. You will know the

fiery wrath of God. We'll use the clothesline pole in the back hard. Angus can take the crossbars and the clothes lines down and leave just the pole. I have the right wood to make a pyre."

Rileigh made eye contact with Angus for a moment while he tied her hands. Then he made Mitch sit up, positioned Rileigh directly behind them, and bound the two of them together by winding duct tape around and around their upper bodies. It wasn't so tight they couldn't breathe, but they couldn't move at all.

He could read the pleading in her eyes. His eyes looked sad.

"Tonight, when the Lord God unleashes the mightiest of his fires in the heavens."

Yes, it was Saturday. The biggest show of the meteorite shower was supposed to be between midnight, August 11, until dawn on Sunday, the thirteenth.

"I will greet his fire, with fires from the earth. God has commissioned me to cleanse His creation of maggots."

She turned to Mitch and Rileigh and spoke to them directly, instead of pontificating at nobody in particular.

"I will tie you both to that pole, pile firewood around it, soak the whole thing in gasoline, and set the fire aflame." She ground out the next words through clenched teeth.

"And. You. Will. *Burn.*"

Chapter Forty-Five

Sarah Park saw the look of abject terror that took over that Bishop woman's face and it sent a thrill through her. God would reward Sarah's obedience, He would. If she did His bidding, He would take away the snake. And the pain.

Sarah feels the snake all the time, knows it is there in her head, but sometimes, like now, its wigging is an agony she can only barely stand. She reaches her hand out in the darkness, feels around on the table beside her bed, finds it, the piece of rawhide she bites down on to keep from screaming. She puts it between her teeth and clamps her jaw shut.

If the snake wasn't inside her head, with the bone of her skull in between, she would be able to see its movements the way a pregnant woman can look at the skin stretched tight over her belly and watch the lumps and bumps that appear there as her baby moves around.

But this is no sweet, pink-butt baby who will draw a breath when it is born and wail out its presence as another one of God's souls in the world. This snake will remain in Sarah's head until she has completed the work God assigned to her when she was a little girl.

The doctors call it a brain tumor. They have no idea they are dealing with a supernatural creature, created and controlled by Almighty God.

The pain ramps up and she sits up rigid in her bed in the midnight dark, biting down on the piece of rawhide, every muscle in her body clenched, determined not to scream. This is God-given pain and she cannot, she must not cry out, lest God decide she is unworthy of His gifts and takes them all away. Including the gift of life itself.

God gave her the pain, planted the snake in her head to bring her back to Him. In Scripture, Jesus tells the parable of the shepherd who leaves the ninety-nine sheep to seek out the one that was lost. She was lost, she was living life her own way, not paying attention to what God wanted, dismissing the purpose God had given her as a little girl.

The snake gives a mighty wiggle and Sarah screams, can't help it, the agony is too great. The snake has grown too big to fit inside her skull anymore. It is cramped tight in there and wants out, wants God to set it free. Sarah wishes God would release the snake, let it chew its way through her brain to her ears or her nose or her mouth, let it seek a way out of the cramped space inside her skull. Whatever its slicing teeth might feel like eating through her, it cannot be worse the than the snake as it is, trapped inside her skull.

It wiggles more, Sarah screams again, silently, tastes blood in her mouth from somewhere, and she staggers to her feet, holding the heels of her hands to her temples, trying to still the beast. She runs through the house in the dark, barefoot, runs from the pain she can't escape because it is inside her and will go where she goes.

She can't stand it, can't breathe, tries to scream but her voice is gone, her mouth sealed shut, the world swirls around her getting darker and darker and then she sees nothing, hears and feels nothing. She is in a dark, black place that must surely be hell.

When Sarah opens her eyes, she can't make out where she is. She is confused, lying on boards, not in her bed, lying with her face pressed against boards, the feel of them cool against her cheek.

And the snake is still. It is asleep. She didn't dare move for fear of waking it, setting it free to crawl around inside her skull. But she must move. She must get up, open the kitchen drawer, get out the knife so she can use it when the snake returns.

She stands slowly on trembling legs, holds onto the counter to pull herself erect. She moves slowly, trying not to move her head at all, thinks of it as a fishbowl balanced on her shoulders and she must move so slowly the water in it does not slosh around. Her fingers feel along the counter for the drawer, unable to lower her head to look for it.

She pulls the drawer open and her fingers slip inside, find the handle of the knife, the big butcher knife that Angus sharpened just the other day. She pulls it slowly out of the drawer and lifts it to her breast, where she embraces it as she would a loved one.

The snake awakens with a powerful movement that sends agony through her skull and down the sides of her head, through her temple into her jaw, agony so profound she can't move, can barely keep hold of the knife. She staggers, has to get away from the pain that hurts so bad she can't think. The knife in her hand is her escape, but the pain in her skull is so intense she can't summon the strength to use it. The agony consumes her, and then the darkness comes again.

When she awakens this time, the snake is awake, too. She can feel it in her head, breathing. But it is not moving. It remains perfectly still. She is lying on her face on the floor of the living room and she slowly rises up onto her knees, shecan feel that the front of her night-gown is wet.

She sits back on her knees slowly, and kneels like that, as if in prayer, but she isn't praying because the sound will rouse the snake. She tastes blood, opens her eyes and lowers them to look at her night-gown. It is soaked in blood. The blood is still gushing out of her nose, down her upper lip and pouring off her chin. Sarah has never had a *nosebleed before, but she is certain this is no ordinary nosebleed. It is blood from the wounds the snake is making in her head.*

She still holds the knife in her hand. She must do it now while there is no pain, slit her throat before the snake has time to stop her. She lifts her hand slowly. She will die looking at her beautiful mountains that—

There is a small light on the wall, on the mountains on the wall. It looks like it is a tiny flame. She watches the flame grow, but it doesn't get bigger, doesn't grow into a fire, it moves. The flame makes a line of fire across her mountains and she watches it in fascinated horror.

The line of fire moves in a curve, then turned and curved another way. Suddenly there were tiny bits of flame all across the center of the mural on the back wall. They all move, make lines of fire that twist and—

The flame she saw first stops moving, and she looks at the flaming trail it has left behind. The line has formed the letter S. She watches in fascinated horror as the other lines moves and changed, forming other letters. P appears next to the S. Then the letter A appeares beside the P. When the letter R begins to emerge she realizes that her name is being written on the wall in flames.

God's flaming finger is writing her name across the mountains!

The knife drops out of her suddenly numb fingers and clunks on the hardwood floo,r but the sound is so muffled Sarah can barely hear it.

When the writing is complete, the flaming letters glow, casting a flickering light all around the room. S. Park. Sarah Park. But no. That's not it. The letters are all capitals and they form a single word: SPARK.

Sarah hears the command of God in her head. The snake becomes the command and she hears it voiced inside her skull.

You are to be my SPARK, the spark that lights the fire to cleanse the mountains of unrighteousness.

It is the same command she received all those years ago as a child, a command she had not obeyed. She and Angus had had a job to do the day Grampa died, and neither of them did what they'd been commanded to do. Grampa told them that it was the will of Almighty God that the maggots swarming all over his creation should die, be burned alive for their wickedness.

But she and Angus have failed. She wanted to obey, but Angus wouldn't let her, and at that time he'd been bigger than she was. Not anymore. She has whittled Angus's soul down smaller and smaller every day until she is the strong one, and he will obey her. Because God has been displeased with their disobedience, and he has waited all these years to give them both one final chance at redemption, one shot to get it right this time.

God will send His fire from Heaven. She is to sacrifice the unholy, burn them alive as an offering to appease God so he will not visit his wrath upon the earth. But the offering does not appease God, and now Sarah has been commanded to burn the mountains themselves, set fire to the earth that will rise up and meet God's fire in the sky.

Sarah continued to kneel in awe, staring at the letters burned in her mural. The snake remains perfectly still, but she can feel it breathing. The pressure inside her skull as it breathes in and out is a pulsing pain, bearable, an ever-present reminder of her obligation to God.

After a long time, she gets slowly to her feet, carrying the unmoving snake in her head carefully. She goes to the wall and touches the marks left by the fire. She has received God's message. Now she must make the mountains perfect again, so she goes to the storage room and takes out her paints, uses shades of green, burnt umber, brown and black, and slowly, meticulously repairs the mural until the only indication that the lines of fire were ever there is the shininess of the fresh paint.

Then she dips her brush into the red paint and begins to put flames in the mountains. Tiny flames at strategic points where she will set incendiary devices. She knows every inch of her mountains and knows just where to start the fires so that they will converge and become one mighty blaze that will destroy forever the Great Smoky Mountain National Park.

Chapter Forty-Six

RILEIGH SAT with her back against Mitch on the floor of the building where Sarah hid Mitch's cruiser. Their hands were tied in front, so they could have used them, but the rest of their bodies were bound by duct tape so securely that there was no hope of escape. Outside they could hear Angus and Sarah working, tearing off the cross bars of the clothesline and taking down the wires. Maybe hauling wood to use on the pyre.

Then there was only silence. They must have completed the job. They had left the two prisoners locked in the building, Rileigh supposed, to wait until dark for the fires from heaven to begin to fall. The building was no longer dark.

Sarah turned on an overhead light when Angus was finishing up the duct taping on Rileigh. It was a fluorescent, the old-fashioned kind, dangling from the ceiling at the back of the building where there was a workbench of sorts. Rileigh had examined everything she could see from her position on the floor, looking for anything they could possibly use to cut through the duct tape. It was maddening to sit here and be able to see her own gun lying on the worktable where Angus set it down. Sarah probably hadn't intended to leave it behind, but it didn't really matter, because Rileigh couldn't use the weapon with her hands and feet duct taped together.

"Can you feel your hands?" Mitch asked her.

She wiggled her fingers. "Yes. Can you?"

"Yes."

Which meant that the bonds were not so tight that they had cut off circulation. That was one advantage of using duct tape to bind a prisoner, she supposed. It would hold tight without cutting off circulation. How humane of the Parks.

"She's serious, you know," Mitch said. "She really means to kill us."

"Angus mentioned when I was here before that she has a brain tumor. The tumor's at least part of what's going on. Brain tumors can change people's personalities, could make them suicidal or violent or–"

"Murderous?"

"Yeah, murderous. But I don't think that's all that's going on. Those scars on Angus's arms. There was some serious mental disfunction going on in that family long before anything began growing in Sarah's skull. I told you about the guy who tried to burn down the bandstands at the twenty-fifth anniversary celebration for the park? It was their grandfather, Abraham Park."

And Mitch had blown her off like something that long ago couldn't possibly be relevant today. She'd been pissed at him for it, but her anger was gone now. There wasn't room in her chest for any other emotion but fear.

"Mildred talked to some people who had been there at the celebration. They said it was awful. That the man was trying to set the bleachers full people on fire. But he must have spilled some gasoline on his own clothes because when he lit a match, *he* burst into flames. I'm sure his grandchildren were there, saw him do it."

Rileigh was thinking about the mural on the wall in the living room, about the flame symbols all over it.

"I think she intends to set fire to the woods, too."

"The woods, what woods?"

"All of them."

"What makes you think that?"

"You didn't see the mural she painted on the walls of the living room. It's the most amazing mural I ever saw. The Smoky Mountains." She conjured up in her head the beauty of the art. And it was art. "The paint on it was fresh in some places, shiny like it hadn't been on there as long as the original paint. She's painted over something recently, maybe repaired something. But she also added red dots all over the painting, little red flames. I've been thinking about those, picturing the locations, and if those flames mark the spots she intends to start fires, the way she's positioned them all — fire at the base of mountains, spreading up the slopes — if she lit every one of those fires, she could catch the whole national park on fire."

Rileigh cared about that, would do anything to stop the woman from torching the trees, but right now she couldn't think about that part either. Couldn't jam any other thoughts into her mind, because fear had swollen so big inside there there was no room for anything else.

Burn to death.

Set on fire.

She shuddered at the thoughts, but she couldn't drag her mind away from them. The videos of the three people Sarah had killed. Running, screaming, dying. And Dogpatch. The image of him jumping out of the Humvee and running away, a fireball, screaming and screaming ...

The horror of that defied description. How could she countenance dying like that herself? She wanted to scream at the thought, had to stifle the scream that was at that moment crawling on hairy black legs up the back of her throat. If she started screaming now, she might not be able to stop.

"I can't even think about … about burning," she couldn't force the words out.

"I don't know any worse way to die." The stark honesty in Mitch's words stole her breath. "I've wanted to die to escape pain. I know what that's like. Nothing like fire, though. There isn't anything like fire."

Rileigh thought of the scars on Mitch's back she had seen the day he came running out of the woods when she found Tina Montgomery's body. Was that what he meant, that he'd wanted to die from the pain of whatever had caused those scars?

Rileigh had wanted to die a few times in her life, too, but not to escape physical pain. She'd wanted to die because the pain of losing friends, watching them die terrible deaths. She didn't want to live in a world where things like that happened. Didn't want to go on waking up every morning carrying that load of grief and guilt. Survivor's guilt. She had made it home. She had survived.

But she wouldn't survive this. There was no escape. She would not live to see another sunrise.

Suddenly, her heart began to hammer, faster and faster. She was going to hyperventilate, have a panic attack, and there was nothing she could do about it, nothing—

"Hold your breath."

Mitch said the words from behind her.

"You can't breathe into a sack, so hold your breath. It will stop the panic attack."

She couldn't.

"Do it," he commanded. Rileigh made herself stop breathing, had no idea how hard it would be, it was the hardest thing she'd ever done because her whole body was screaming with need. She gritted her teeth, tears seeped out of her eyes and down her cheeks. She squinted her eyes shut and concentrated.

Gradually the urge to gasp for breath subsided and she dared take a little sip of air. Then another little sip. Her heart was still pounding and she couldn't seem to do anything about that. But her breathing stabilized. She wasn't going to panic, get hysterical, lose her shit.

"Thanks," she whispered.

"You owe me."

"What?"

"When I start losing my shit, it'll be your turn to talk me off the ledge."

Chapter Forty-Seven

TIME DRAGGED BY.

The terror still gnawed at Rileigh's insides like a lazy rat, but it was impossible to remain in the state of almost-hysteria for hours. Her nerves eventually calmed. Nothing about reality had changed, and she certainly hadn't "come to terms" or whatever some shrink would say with the reality that she was going to die, or the manner of her death. But what Sarah had planned for the two of them, their death sentence, couldn't be carried out until after dark, and that was hours away.

Rileigh knew nobody would miss either one of them yet. She had gone by to see Georgia, but after that she could have been anywhere. Oh, eventually, her mother would begin to wonder. But not for hours. When Rileigh didn't come home for supper, when it got late and Rileigh didn't call, then Mama would start to worry.

Well, maybe she would. But Rileigh had to admit it was entirely possible her mother wouldn't know she wasn't there. Her mother might get so wrapped up in Rhett

Butler and the fantasy world he occupied, that she didn't even realize her daughter was missing.

Even if she did, there wasn't anything she could do about it. She'd worry, call friends, try to locate her, maybe, but the bottom line was that Mama wasn't going to be sending the mounties out looking for her.

Nobody was going to come to Rileigh's rescue.

And Mitch?

Mitch wasn't even the sheriff anymore. There was nowhere he was officially supposed to be. Now the cruiser, yeah, after awhile there would be questions about where it was. When the mayor showed up at the police station, and surely he would show up, if not to run the show himself, to introduce whoever he'd selected to take Mitch's place.

And when he did, the people who knew Mitch had taken the cruiser would have to admit where it had gone. Maybe they'd search for it then, search for Mitch. Probably not, but again, even if they did, Mitch had told nobody where he was going.

Nobody was going to come to Mitch's rescue, either.

They were on their own.

"I hate to be Captain Obvious here," she said, "but we're going to have to figure some way out of this."

"Yup. Got any ideas?"

"Nope."

"Neither do I."

"Well, we have all afternoon to think of something. We'll have to jump them, find an opening somehow."

"Uh, the jumping them thing. I'm still so dizzy, I'm not sure I can stand up."

"Concussion."

"Yeah, probably. In the movies, they always make it seem like you can knock people unconscious and they'll come to and be able to grab a guitar and play the riff at the beginning of Johnny B Goode behind their heads."

"Can you do that? I mean, without a concussion, can you do that?"

Mitch looked a little embarrassed. "Yes, but if you handed me a guitar right now, I'm not sure if I would be able to play a simple chord."

Well, it looked like Rileigh was going to be on the hook for saving the day.

"Surely they're not going to keep us here all day without anything to drink or a potty break. Won't burden you with TMI, but I had three cups of coffee this morning and if she doesn't—"

"Thanks for that, I don't need a visual."

In spite of everything, Rileigh smiled.

And Sarah Park did not abandon them completely. About mid-afternoon, when Rileigh was wondering if it really was possible to die of a burst bladder, the brother and sister came back into the building, Sarah held the shotgun trained it on them when she spoke.

"Here's how this is going to go," Sarah said. "Gonna cut you apart and untie your feet. Then I'm gonna take you out to do your private business one at a time." She looked at Rileigh. "You first."

Angus knelt beside her feet and pulled out the knife he'd used to sever Mitch's bonds. As he quickly sawed the restraint away, Sarah grabbed Rileigh's gaze and held it.

"You need to understand that I don't bluff. If I say I will do a thing, I will do it. I don't make threats. When Angus takes you out of here — just around the corner of the building. You can get your pants down and up with your hands tied and you can do your bidness in the weeds. I am going to stand with this gun here." She shoved the barrel of the shotgun against Mitch's temple. "No way you're going to jump Angus and get away before he can call out. If I hear a sound, a squeak, a scuffed rock, anything that don't sound right, I'm going to pull the trigger and blast the sheriff's brains all over the floor. Are we clear?"

"We're clear."

Angus took Rileigh out and everything happened exactly as Sarah had ordered. Then he brought her back in and told her to sit beside Mitch. Then Angus produced some plastic zip ties.

"Duct tape's too much trouble."

Obviously the two of them were building this kidnapping-and-murder plane as they flew it. They hadn't intended to take prisoners and they were figuring out how you did a thing like that on the fly. Which meant eventually they'd screw something up. Rileigh had to be ready when they did. If there were any small opening, she had to go for it.

Then Angus sat Rileigh down next to the work bench at the back of the garage and used the leg of the bench to secure Rileigh in place — setting the leg between her feet and securing her ankles together with the pole between them.

Angus helped Mitch upright, he staggered sideways and almost fell. Sarah rammed the barrel of the gun into the side of Rileigh's head. "You best not trip and fall, cause if I hear any commotion at all out there, I'm gonna pull this trigger."

Mitch made it out and back without incident and the duct tape around his ankles was replaced with a zip tie as well. He was zip-locked to the other leg of the workbench. Then Angus cut the duct tape off their wrists and pulled their hands behind their backs this time and replaced the bonds with a zip tie.

"You folks ain't going to need your hands for anything else," Sarah said. She brought each them a glass of water, held it while they drank, then the brother and sister left the building.

Rileigh heard the hasp clunk shut and the snap of the padlock. Then silence.

Rileigh scooted, hopped on her butt around the work-table leg until her back was against the trashcan, so she could lean back against it. Mitch had been positioned so he could lean back against the wall. They sat facing each other now. It had been more comfortable being taped to Mitch. And the feel of his body had been comforting, too.

Still, it was good to be able to see his face.

"How's your head?"

"Pounding."

"Still dizzy?"

"It's getting better."

"You know we have to go for it the next time we're untied."

"Yeah, I'll be ready."

Then they both were silent. The seconds dragged into minutes and the minutes dragged into hours. They had no idea what time it was, how long they'd been tied up. They were alone in the room, but after awhile, they weren't. The black, hairy-legged spider of death was there, too, in the shadows waiting for them.

Was Rileigh ready to die? Hell no, she wasn't ready. She was ready to live. She was almost healed from Aunt Daisy's attack. She felt reasonably healthy and strong. When she stood up in the canoe of her life, she saw bright shining water ahead.

How do you get your head around the knowledge that you don't have a future? That there's nothing out there in front of you but a few hours before an agonizing death.

Suddenly, Rileigh ached to be tied up again to Mitch, to feel the warmth of his body behind her. She looked at him and his eyes were closed, but he wasn't sleeping.

He was doing what she was doing. He was trying to prepare himself to die.

Chapter Forty-Eight

VOICES DRIFTED into the building from outside and the two of them were instantly alert, straining to catch the words. They could hear the voices because they're raised. The brother and sister were arguing.

"Can you hear what they—"

"Shhh. Let me concentrate."

Mitch was tied to the workbench leg closest to door. Rileigh was tied to the leg on the other side. Mitch leaned out toward the door as far as he could, straining to listen.

Rileigh could only hear random phrases, words here and there.

" … we failed…"

"…you wouldn't let me…"

"…we couldn't do that…"

"… were just kids…"

"…God's command…"

"…Grandpa said…"

What she could tell and didn't like, was the fact that Angus' tone was defensive. His words sounded conciliatory. He whined. He was weak. If either of the Park siblings was likely to rethink their plan, clearly it was Angus. But his sister was very definitely running the show.

The voices moved so far away from the door that Rileigh could hear nothing anymore. Mitch appeared to still be listening.

Then he stopped leaning uncomfortably toward the door and rested his back against the wall behind him.

"I didn't get it all, but I got some of it. I think I know what they were fighting about. When they were children, maybe ten or twelve, they were supposed to do something. I'm not sure what it was, Angus was saying that their Grandfather was wrong, that he shouldn't have recruited two little kids to help him. That whatever happened, it wasn't their fault. Sarah said the two of them were, too, at fault. That it wasn't their grandfather who wanted them to do whatever it was. They had been commanded by God to do it. They hadn't defied their grandfather, they'd defied God."

"Any idea what it was they were supposed to do but didn't?"

"Couldn't catch that. But I don't believe Angus had any idea that Sarah was killing tourists. I think she got that burn on her face when their barn burned down. Maybe she set the fire and it got away from her. Or maybe she was practicing using gasoline to start a fire. Sarah wouldn't go to the doctor about it, made Angus bandage it himself, just to hide the wound from people. She wasn't concerned about the burn because the end of the world was coming. So what difference did it make? Like rearranging the deck chairs on the Titanic. She believes it's *all* going to be over soon."

"It *is* going to be over for us." Rileigh said the words quietly so he wouldn't hear.

And it wasn't just Rileigh and Mitch who were in

danger. If Sarah got away with killing them, and then went out and set off whatever devices she'd placed on the spots designated by the flames on the mural, who knew how many people might be killed.

Rileigh couldn't let it happen, couldn't let Sarah set the woods on fire. Somehow, she had to think of something! She slammed back against the trash can in disgust — and the can wiggled.

Was it possible she could keep banging into the thing until she turned it over? Maybe, but what would be the point in that?

There might be something in the trash can they could use, something to help them get away, a weapon maybe.

Rileigh rammed her body into the trash can again and it wiggled more.

"What are you—"

"Maybe I can knock it over. And maybe there's something in it."

Yeah, long shot. But it wasn't like Rileigh had anything better to do with her time. She banged the can again and again. It scooted almost out of reach, so she had to change position, hit it from the front to knock it back where it had been. Then she banged some more, finally realizing that she had to do it in a kind of rhythm, get the can rocking and make it keep rocking, going farther and farther over with each blow. She lost all track of time, didn't know if she'd been at it for an hour or ten minutes, but the aching pain in her back from the impacts against the can told her she'd done it dozens, maybe hundreds of times. She'd get a rhythm going, then hit the can too hard and knock it away, or not hard enough, and lose the momentum.

Then it worked. Like she'd been rehearsing a dance step, trying to learn it for weeks, and suddenly she just did it. She hit it, the can tilted backwards. She hit it again before it could come fully back to rest on the floor, and it tilted farther. Hit it again and it alllllmost went over. Hit it again—crash. The trash can fell over on its side, scattering its contents on the floor.

And Rileigh could see nothing they could use.

Mitch couldn't see what had fallen out of the can.

"Did you find anything?"

"Not yet."

She was reluctant to give up hope, her eyes scanning the wadded up paper, newspapers, pieces of cardboard boxes, a broken ax handle, half a dozen beer cans and — then she saw it, the lid off some kind of can, sardines, maybe. It wasn't attached to the can anymore and it was upside down so she couldn't read any label that might have been on it. But she didn't care what it had been. Right now, it was an old, slightly rusty can lid. And it was *sharp*.

Rileigh hopped on her butt as far away from the workbench table leg as she could get, then leaned back, tried to stretch out her hands bound behind her, but she could only move them a few inches. Craning her neck to look over her shoulder— she was almost there. She wiggled the fingers of her right hand and they brushed against the can lid. Then she forced herself to calm down, she needed her hands to be steady. She strained outward with her tied-together hands, leaning forward at the waist to grant them even a little more reach.

Her fingers brushed the can lid, then she grasped it between two of the fingers on her right hand and moved it slowly closer and closer to her body, until she was no longer straining to touch it. She scooted the can lid gently up against her butt. Then she began examining it, and—

Ouch!

She didn't cry out, but the sharp edge of the can had cut her finger, sliced right into it. Which meant the lid was sharp. But was it sharp enough to cut through the thick plastic of a zip tie? Carefully, she maneuvered the lid so she could grasp the side of it with two fingers on her left hand, and could—

Ouch!

She almost cried out in pain this time. The piece of sharp metal had cut deep into her finger, and she could feel the warm blood coursing out of the cut onto her hand and fingers. But she didn't drop it, held on with now bloody fingers and began to carefully saw the piece of plastic tie on her hand back and forth across it. She cut another finger, then the one she'd cut the first time. She held on, using her blood-smeared fingers to force the piece of plastic on her wrist back and forth across the edge of the lid.

When the plastic tie let go, she was so surprised she dropped the lid and had to dig around with her hands, strain to reach out, so she could grasp it to slice through the remaining strand of plastic. Then her hands were free.

And her gun was lying on the worktable bench right above where she was sitting.

Chapter Forty-Nine

THE DOOR suddenly opened wide and Rileigh could see with horror that it was dark outside. And there was a bright, flickering light outside, outlining Sarah in the doorway. A fire.

Sarah held the shotgun at the ready and Angus lumbered along behind her.

Rileigh quickly put her hands behind her back and pretended she was still tied up. She could see the shiny red spots around her where blood dripped from her bleeding fingers, so she scooted around, tried to smear them with her butt.

"It's time," Sarah announced.

"Take me first," Mitch said boldly. He knew that Rileigh was free and was trying to give her time to reach her gun.

"If you like," said Sarah, and she nodded at her older brother.

He didn't move.

"Angus, we've talked about this. We've decided."

Angus remained where he was for a few seconds, then took the few steps from the doorway to where Mitch was tied to the leg of the worktable next to the door, knelt, and with one quick motion of his sharp hunting knife, sliced through the zip ties around Mitch's ankles.

"Think about what you're doing, man," Mitch said to him.

"Shut your mouth," Sarah said, but Mitch didn't bother to obey. What was she going to do, shoot him?

"Your sister has murdered three innocent people, poured gasoline on them and set them on fire."

As Mitch spoke, Angus pushed his body to the side so he could get to the tie that bound his hands around the table leg. "Can you do a thing like that?"

Angus paid him no mind, just sliced through the tie and Mitch's arms fell free. He groaned as he moved them around his body and rubbed his wrists.

"Get him up, time's a'wastin," Sarah said.

Angus grabbed Mitch's upper arm and lifted him up off the floor as if he were a small child. Mitch stumbled sideways.

"Stand up," Sarah commanded

"Giving it my best shot," Mitch mumbled and tried to right himself, but he was leaning heavily on Angus's grip on his arm, and it was obvious he genuinely couldn't stand on his own.

Angus turned and led the parade, holding Mitch upright, and half-carried him out the door into the night. Sara gave Rileigh a look and smiled, with the half of her horror face she could move. It was an ordinary smile, the kind you'd give a server who provided good service, or the teller in the bank who puts the money envelope in the little plastic missile and shoots it through the vacuum tube. But on Sarah's face, the one-sided grimace was a horrible parody of a smile, a monster's grimace.

"I'll be right back," she said, and it flashed through Rileigh's head that it must be painful to talk, to move the burned lips and cheek muscles. Painful to smile.

But Sarah gave no indication she felt anything at all, just turned and followed her brother and Mitch out the door. As soon as she was out of sight, Rileigh stopped the pretense of being affixed to the leg of the table, put her palms on the floor on both sides of her and scooted on her butt out from under the workbench. There was no time to release the plastic tie on her feet and she had no intention of picking up the bloody can lid again to use as a knife.

She grabbed hold of the leg of the table, instantly slick from the blood on her hands, then got to her knees and rose, standing with both feet tied together. The gun was lying about halfway down the workbench, a couple of steps away and she held onto the edge of the table and hopped toward it. She lost her balance, but she grabbed the edge of the table to stop her fall. She hopped again and grasped the gun with the bloody fingers of her right hand.

"Put the gun down," Sarah said from the doorway, backlit by flickering light, pointing the shotgun at her.

In one motion, Rileigh picked up the gun and threw her body sideways, lifting the gun toward Sarah, trying to steady it with the fingers sticking out of the brace on her left wrist.

Her slick fingers found the trigger and she fired, pulled the trigger a second time before her shoulder slammed into the floor and the gun flew out of her hand, slid and bounced off the wall. Sarah held onto the shotgun as she staggered back against the doorframe. A bloom of red blossomed on her right upper arm and another one on her thigh.

She grunted, but made no other sound.

Rileigh crawled as fast as she could with both feet tied together, reaching out toward the pistol. If Sarah shot her, it would be an easier way to die than burning to death.

She managed to get to the gun, but it was lying with the barrel pointed toward her and before she could turn it around, Sarah's foot came down on her hand, pinning it to the floor.

Rileigh used the brace on her left wrist as a club and slammed it into Sarah's shin, knocking her off balance. When her foot came up off Rileigh's hand, Rileigh grabbed the woman's ankle, threw her own body backward and yanked as hard as she could.

Sarah fell backward as Rileigh pulled her foot out from under her and landed on her side, with the shotgun still clutched in her hands. The scuffle had knocked Rileigh's gun out of reach again, so she lunged at Sarah, trying to throw her body on top of the other woman as she reached out and managed to grab the barrel of the shotgun. She pulled as hard as she could with her right hand as she pounded Sarah with her braced left hand.

Then the two of them were wrestling for control of the shotgun.

The world shifted down into slow motion. Rileigh fought like a woman possessed. She had bled all over the shotgun and it was slick, it took every ounce of her strength to hold on. She bared her teeth and bit down as hard as she could on Sarah's hand on the gun, caught her thumb and clenched her teeth on it, felt the bone snap. She would bite it off if she could.

Then something grabbed her hair and lifted her upper body into the air.

"Get off her," Angus snarled and Rileigh lost her grip on Sarah's thumb, but she held onto the shotgun, slugging away with her brace, writhing in Angus's hands, struggling to free herself from his grip.

But he had her hair firmly in the great paw of his hand and he slapped her hard with the other hand, the blow catching her on the cheekbone and nose, snapping her head to the side. Blood flew out of her nose. She lost her grip on the shotgun as Angus lifted her relentlessly upward, and with her feet still tied together, she could get no leverage to pull away. She twisted her head from side to side, slinging blood in both directions, and tried to grab his arm with her good hand as she hammered at him with her left.

There was a scuffling sound and Angus grunted, let go of her. Rileigh fell back down on top of Sarah's body, and caught sight of Mitch with a piece of wood, swinging it at Angus's face. Angus dodged and Mitch staggered then, off balance. Angus grabbed the piece of wood, yanked it out of Mitch's hand and used it to hit Mitch in the side as he fell.

Rileigh's body was lying on top of Sarah, pinning the shotgun between them. Her face was only inches from Sarah's monster face, where the burned skin had been torn in the struggle and a piece of it hung down, revealing her upper teeth. Rileigh reached up and clawed at Sarah's lone good eye, tried to punch it out, but Sarah twisted her face and Rileigh's hand slid across it to the burned side where her clawing fingers raked the flesh and eye away.

Then something hit her on the back of her head. She felt all the strength in her body leave it as she collapsed on top of Sarah. She fought to remain conscious and managed it, but the world was gray all around, sound was muted, and she had no control over her body. She was only a spectator to what was going on around her. She felt

Angus lift her by the arm off Sarah. Then he flung her aside like a rag doll.

Rileigh landed on her side beside Sarah and the momentum carried her tumbling body over. She came to rest on her belly, her cheek pressed to the dirty concrete.

The back of her head pounded in rhythm with her heartbeat and she struggled with all her will to fully remain conscious panting on her belly as Angus punched Mitch in the face and he flew backward against the wall. Angus grabbed Mitch as he bounced off the wall and dragged him over to the workbench. He stood for a moment fumbling around with something, then he pulled Mitch's arm up against the leg of the workbench and affixed it there with a zip tie.

Rileigh could see her pistol only a few feet away, and she struggled to make herself move toward it. She couldn't seem to lift her head up, so she commando -crawled, dragging herself forward like a slug across the ground. Big feet appeared in front of her face and Angus grabbed her right arm, dragged her back on her belly to the workbench and dropped her there.

From her viewpoint, she could see the bloody can lid she'd used to cut the zip tie off her hands. It lay in the shadows beneath the workbench where she'd left it. Then Angus yanked her right hand up. Pain shot through her elbow as he twisted her arm around and affixed her arm at the wrist to the workbench leg with a zip tie.

Then he stepped back. You could hear the bellows of him panting.

He said one word, gasped it — "Sarah" — and then she heard his footsteps cross the room. Her face was turned toward the wall, and she couldn't manage to lift her head to turn it the other way so she could see. She could hear though, as Angus cooed to Sarah as if she was a baby.

"... be all right ... get you out of here ... bandage ..."

Angus grunted with effort, must have picked his sister up off the floor. Heavy steps clunked out the door. He didn't close it behind him, and Rileigh could see the flickering light of the campfire outside dancing on the wall in front of her face.

Chapter Fifty

THE ONLY SOUND in the world was the sound of Rileigh and Mitch panting, trying to get their breath back. Mitch said something, but Rileigh didn't catch it at first. As soon as Angus left, she had slumped down on her belly, closed her eyes and tried to let unconsciousness take her.

But after fighting to remain alert for so long, unconsciousness refused to do as requested. She thought of what Aunt Daisy always said: "Flies on a screen door. The ones on the inside want to get out and the ones on the outside want to get in."

She tried to take a mental inventory of all the places she hurt. Her right arm was killing her, twisted as it was and attached vertically to the leg of the workbench. As soon as she was able to, she'd get to her knees and then sit down beside the table leg, so her arm wouldn't be twisted. But right now, moving seemed pretty much out of the question. The top of her head was screaming where Angus had grabbed a handful of her hair, but she didn't think he had pulled any of it out. And from the stuffed up feeling in her nose, and the swelling of her left eye, she figured Angus had broken her nose and blackened her eye. She stuck her tongue out and felt around with it. He'd split her lip too.

Those appeared to be her only injuries, other than the growing lump at the base of her skull where Angus had hit her. It had knocked her to the brink of unconsciousness, but she didn't think he had hit her with anything. With the force he put behind it, some piece of wood or pipe or anything like that would have broken the skin. He'd likely linked his fingers together and slammed his combined fists in a hammer blow to the back of her neck.

Besides the obvious traumas, she hurt in various places all over from the battle with Sarah. And all the twisting and pulling of her legs, bound together at the ankles, had gouged the plastic ties into the skin there. She could feel blood on her feet.

She let out a breath and continued to lie on her face in that not-yet-fully-conscious world of gray and shadows. She thought of Sarah then and her heart leapt in her chest. She had done some serious damage to that bitch. She'd shot her twice. All things considered, gun held in slick fingers and falling sideways, landing two rounds on target was pretty impressive.

Of course, where they'd landed on target was not impressive. She thought of the drilled-into-her-adage of her instructor in the police academy in Memphis. "It is seriously difficult to deliver a fatal wound to a moving target."

As if she needed to hear that after four tours in the Middle East. This time, her target hadn't been the one moving, she had been, but her intent to land two body shots to the torso had been knocked aside. It didn't appear that the shoulder wound was anything but a graze. But the wound in the thigh was nothing to sneeze at. It all depended where on the thigh the bullet had caught.

Clearly it either passed through or lodged in her leg without shattering her femur, which would have been nice. Ideal would be ripping out the femoral artery that ran down through the leg, but clearly she hadn't hit that, or Sarah would have bled out in a matter of minutes. So the bullet had apparently missed the important parts. Dammit!

Oh, sure, it had done some damage — couldn't take a nine millimeter slug in the thigh and go out later for a game of tennis. But it was obvious that the damage had not been, and likely would not be fatal. And fatal is what she'd been aiming for. She'd wanted to kill the bitch!

But she had broken her thumb, bit into it, through the bone. And that sucker would bleed, too.

She suddenly realized that some of the blood in her mouth might not be her own and she spit, trying to clean it out.

Other than that, she'd tried to blind Sarah, poke out her one good eye, but she'd missed, merely scraped burned skin off—

That image. Rileigh didn't want that image in her head. Refused to know what was under the fingernails of her right hand.

"Rileigh!"

She heard it this time, Mitch's voice, and she realized that color had returned to the world, and it was again in sharp focus.

Clumsily using her braced left hand, she pushed herself upward off the floor so she could turn her head, and the pressure and pain in her right hand lessened immediately. She began a complicated, scooting maneuver that eventually placed her body in a sitting position next to the workbench leg that her right arm was affixed to, with her feet out in front of her. She was facing Mitch, who was leaning against the bench leg nearer the door, held there by a zip tie on his upper left arm.

"Are you all right?" he asked.

She thought of Georgia, lying in Intensive Care, making fun of her own, trite "Don't try to talk," and the ghost of a smile crossed her mangled lips.

"You get no points for that," she told him, knowing he wouldn't understand her and Georgia's private joke. "I'm not dead, I'm functional."

"You look like shit."

Another of their private jokes flashed through her head: their retort to any kind of critical statement. *Well, you're ugly and your mama dresses you funny.* But she didn't say that one out loud. She wasn't in the mood for humor.

"Superficial damage." She brushed the conversation aside. "Your right hand is free. See if you can pick at that zip tie on your arm and get it open."

"Been trying." She realized then that his words were coming slow. He'd already had a concussion when Angus punched him in the face. His injuries were worse than the black eye he'd have by tomorrow.

By tomorrow.

Neither of them would see tomorrow if they didn't do a better job of escaping from captivity than they'd just done.

"How are you — serious question, where are you hurt?"

He slowly raised his hand to his head.

"Headache. Confused and dizzy. Angus heard the gunshots and just dropped me and came running in here. If I'd been able to stand up—" She could hear the anger and frustration in his voice. "—I could have stopped him."

He ran his hand over the lump on the back of his head, where Sarah had hit him ... how long ago? Hours. It was good dark outside. And the meteors were falling from the sky.

"Can you get the zip tie off? My left hand's just about useless."

He reached up and began to tug and pull at the plastic tie, but there was no strength in his arm or hands. Rileigh turned and tried to use the poking-out-of-the-brace fingers of her left hand to loosen the tie. But without an opposable thumb to grasp with, it was useless.

Well, there was always the can lid again. She would have to get to it, could probably reach it with her foot if she stretched —

Angus appeared in the doorway. He said nothing, just went to Mitch and used his hunting knife to slice through the zip tie. Mitch slumped backward once he was no longer held upright by the tie.

"Come on, get up." Angus pulled Mitch's upper arm upward and Mitch staggered to his feet, tried with a feeble effort to pull free, but Angus was able to drag him out of the room as he resisted feebly.

Rileigh was alone and terror yanked such a knot in her belly that she couldn't breathe for a moment. Were they going to go through with it now? Maybe, Angus was taking Mitch out to—

Stop it, no time for wishful thinking. Angus was taking Mitch out to tie him to that clothesline pole. Rileigh had only a couple of minutes to get free. She turned her attention on the can lid. Stretched out her foot until her heel was resting on top of it. Then she began to slowly drag it back toward—

"Your turn," Angus said and she jumped. She'd been so intent on getting the can lid that she hadn't heard him come in. No, her heart had been hammering so hard in her chest she could barely hear anything at all.

"No, Angus, don't. Don't do this," she begged.

He used the knife to slice through the plastic tie binding her feet together, then used it to sever the tie that held her arm to the leg of the workbench. Then he lifted her in a single motion up onto her feet.

"Listen to me, Angus. Your grandfather was insane. God isn't raining fire down upon the earth. It's a meteor shower! Your sister's crazy, surely you can see that. The brain tumor has made her insane."

He had his head turned away so she couldn't see his face, but she felt him tense when she said that.

"It's not her fault. She's sick. She needs help, needs a doctor. Don't let her insanity control you."

Angus stood for a moment very still beside her.

Chapter Fifty-One

Angus holds tight to the arm of his wiggling sister, who is thrashing around, trying to get out of his grip, kicking at him, pulling away. But Angus won't let go. He absolutely will not allow her to run back under the bleachers, find the Bic lighter she dropped and set fire to the oily rags Grandpa placed under the bleachers.

Angus figured out why Grandpa had placed the rags where he had, and why he'd smelled gasoline there. The pile Angus was supposed to set aflame at one end of the bleachers and the pile Sarah was supposed to light at the other end. Those are where the steps lead up into the bleachers. And Grandpa had soaked the wood of the steps in something that'd burn, probably gasoline. Those are the only two ways out. Grandpa intended to trap the people in the bleachers— men, women and little kids— with fires on both ends.

Grandpa wanted to burn up as many people as he could.

Angus and Sarah can hear Grandpa talking now, and Angus drags Sarah out far enough beyond the end of the bleachers that they can see him too. He is haranguing the crowd, telling them that God is raining fire down from heaven because of their unrighteousness, and that the national park is an abomination, that it is like a fly breeding

298

maggots, drawing more and more people to the mountains to soil and defile them.

The crowds on both sides watch Grandpa in wonder and surprise, the crowd in the bleachers and the much smaller group of dignitaries that occupy the dais facing the bleachers. Angus doesn't know why his Grandfather didn't start the fires under the dais, but from his position across from it he can see the reason. Workmen built the bleachers to hold the crowd. Carpenters spent weeks erecting them.

The dais, on the other hand, was some sort of wagon. It had probably been attached to a truck or a tractor to haul it here. It has a skirt all the way around it to hide the wheels. The skirt is red, white and blue, and is gathered up in folds every three feet or so where there's an American flag. It's probably some mobile platform politicians haul around when they're campaigning.

But Grandpa has been talking for long enough that the police officers stationed around the area had started moving this way. They will grab Grandpa and haul him away, and then the ceremony will go on as planned, and nobody will ever know how close the crowd had come to being incinerated.

Grampa glances at the advancing police officers and begins to talk louder and faster.

"a festering wound on God's creation, an abomination in his sight. And he will not allow the unrighteous to continue to defile what he created for man, his most beloved creation."

Angus thinks about what Grandpa had said when he positioned them behind the bleachers, how he'd grabbed Angus's arm and spoke right into his face, the foul smell of his rotting teeth making Angus gag.

"You have been commanded by Almighty God to avenge the evil that has been brought to this place," Grandpa tells him. "If you fail to do what the Lord has commissioned you to do, he will bring down upon your heads all manner of suffering. You will never marry, will go to your graves barren and childless because God will not allow the disobedient to reproduce others like them."

When Sarah asked what would be the signal for her and Angus to set the rags aflame. Grampa said they were to flick their BICs when he calls on God to rain fire down on the unbelieving.

Grandpa glances again at the approaching police officers and pauses, then gathers himself. He looks toward the sky and cries out in a loud voice, "I now call on Almighty God, creator off all things, to rain down upon you the fires of heaven."

He stands for a beat or two with his arms raised, then looks expectantly toward the end of the bleachers where Angus was supposed to be at that moment setting on fire. He stares at it for a moment, then turns his eyes toward the other end of the bleachers. And when he does, he can see Angus and Sarah standing there, looking back at him.

If looks could kill, the evil eye their grandfather casts on them would have struck both of them stone dead. The officers are converging on him from both sides, will lay hands on him and —

Grandpa suddenly pops the lid off the stupid little thermos bottle he'd been holding.

And he pours the contents over his own head!

Sarah cries out and Angus gasps. Then their Grandfather looks both of them in the eyes … and flicks his Bic.

There is a horrible whump and Grandpa is suddenly engulfed in flames. He doesn't cry out in agony at first. He stands upright for a moment, then falls to the ground and writhes on the ground, screaming the most horrible scream Angus has ever heard. He has never heard a human being make such a sound in his whole life.

Grandpa screams and burns. The police run toward him, but there is nothing they can do. He is a ball of fire and there is no possible way to save him.

The grandstands erupt in anguish, women screaming, men crying out, a rumble of horror and disbelief.

Angus turns his face to Sarah and she is smiling. Sarah stands completely still beside him, her arms at her sides, watching Grandpa burn to death in front of her. And she is smiling. Then he hears her whisper.

"It's so beautiful."

Chapter Fifty-Two

ANGUS STOOD mute for a few seconds beside Rileigh, as if maybe he was considering what she'd said. But then he yanked her forward and began to drag her along beside him.

She yanked sideways, struggled to pull away, but he had ten inches and a hundred and fifty pounds on her and nothing she could do made any difference in his forward progress.

He dragged her out of the building into the night air and she staggered when she got a look at what waited for her there.

They had indeed removed the cross beam from the clothesline pole at the edge of the yard. Mitch was tied to it with some kind of rope wrapped around and around him, binding him upright. At his feet was a pile of wood, some dry limbs, but most chopped pieces that looked like they'd been cut to put into a fireplace. And beside the fence, sitting on the huge tree stump, was Sarah.

She was a ruin. The burned portion of her face that Rileigh had savaged with her fingernails hung in tattered pieces off the bone and dangled there. Her teeth were visible through the hole in her face and her right eye was completely gone. She had a white bandage of some kind around the top of her right arm and a bit of blood was seeping through. Her right leg had a bandage around the thigh, wrapped around and around it, but there was a blossom of red on that bandage, too. Beside her was a small bonfire, and Rileigh could see what appeared to be a torch in it, with the unburned end lying out across the grass.

"Noooo!" Rileigh screamed. She used the brace on her left arm to swing in around her body, striking out at Angus, but it hit harmlessly on his massive chest and fell away. "Don't do this. God is not telling you to do this, she is. And she's crazy, just like your grandfather was."

She felt Angus tense at the words, but no other reaction was visible.

"You are wrong," Sarah said. Her voice was a rasp, and the words were slurred and hard to understand, because she was forcing them out through burned lips, and some of the air was coming out the hole in her cheek. "Grandpa told us God would punish us for our disobedience. He said we would never marry, that we would go to our graves barren. Now, God is preparing to destroy the world, and if we are disobedient again, he will send us to hell with all the unbelievers."

Angus dragged Rileigh forward and shoved her at the pyre. She tripped and fell over the wood stacked at the bottom of it, and had to grab hold of Mitch's body to keep from falling.

Then Angus lifted the can of gasoline.

Inside her head she screamed, a cry of terror and horror so loud it would have ripped through the very throne room of God himself — but fear had stolen her voice and her breath, and she could not make a sound. When flames started eating her flesh, she'd scream then.

Those videos, flaming figures writhing in pain.

Dogpatch as he ran across the sand.

Wally shaking is head. "What an awful way to die!"

Rileigh was about to be burned to death.

She tensed, cringed away from the feel of the gasoline Angus was about to splash on her body.

But Angus didn't splash the gasoline on her. He didn't pour it on the wood at the base of the pole where Mitch was tied.

Angus turned the can up and dumped the contents over his own head. His sister screamed, "No, you can't–"

Angus took two giant steps and dragged his sister off the stump and into his arms. She didn't struggle to get free, just stared at her brother in silence.

"Don't do it, Angus," Mitch said. "Don't–"

Angus leaned over, picked up the end of the torch that was lying in the grass with one end in the bonfire. He lifted the torch high into the air, held it there, like the statue of Liberty. Then with his hand still raised, he turned his wrist and lowered the flaming end of the torch toward the top of his head.

"Nooo!" Rileigh screamed. And then the gasoline caught.

As his hair and clothing burst into flames, he flung himself and his sister into the bonfire, crashing down on the burning wood, sending pieces of it out in all directions.

Angus didn't make a sound. Sarah was silent, too, though she struggled to get away when the bonfire flames caught her hair on fire. Angus held her tight, his grip never faltered.

Rileigh turned her head away from the fire and held onto Mitch, burying her face in his shoulder. She shook as tears streamed down her cheek, but she didn't make a sound. Just stood in silence, trying not to breath in the noxious smell of the two bodies burning in the bonfire.

"Cut me loose," Mitch said into her hair. "Do it quick before the fire spreads."

Rileigh was instantly alert, tried to scramble to her feet but just fell down on the pile of wood. The fire was dangerously close, and the gasoline had spilled on the ground.

The knife, the knife… where had Angus dropped it?

Then she spotted it lying in the dirt. She ran to it on wobbly legs, picked it up with her bleeding right hand, and ran to where Mitch was still tied to the pole. The fire was spreading along the trail of spilled gasoline, catching the grass on fire.

Rileigh couldn't even glance at the bodies. She concentrated on getting a grip on the knife hilt with her slick fingers, became aware of the pain of the deep cuts then. She had forgotten that they hurt.

She sawed at the rope wrapped around and around Mitch's chest, finally made it through one strand of it, and then began to unwind the rest.

The fire moving along the trail of gasoline got to the edge of the pyre, which had been soaked in gasoline. There was an instant blaze, just inches from Rileigh's feet. She grabbed Mitch by the shoulder and shoved him away from the flames as she wrestled with the rope that was binding him. It was coming loose, but not fast enough.

Then Mitch was holding onto her with freed hands, pulling her along with him as he staggered away from the flames. They fell to the ground just beyond the pile of burning wood and crawled desperately, dragged each other away from the fire.

The rest of the woodpile caught and the fire instantly

leapt out in all directions, licking dangerously close to them as they scrambled away. They kept crawling even after they were far enough not to get burned. Neither had the strength to stand, so they just crawled along in the dirt together, out across the driveway to the other side, then collapsed in the grass.

"You need a doctor," Mitch said, holding her bleeding hand up into the flickering firelight.

"Pot calling the kettle black," she mumbled, and now she couldn't take her eyes away from the burning pyre. The bonfire and the fire in the wood around the post had joined, becoming a huge conflagration that sent flames ten feet into the air. Sparks sailed away on the breeze.

She followed the progression of the sparks upward and then she was looking at the sky. It was filled with falling stars, the most brilliant display she had ever seen.

She stared up at it and cried.

Chapter Fifty-Three

RILEIGH WORE a tight glove over the fingers of her right hand. The physical therapist had recommended it after the stitches were taken out, to protect her hand but also to make sure the wounds didn't open up when she used her fingers.

Which she tried not to do, because it *hurt*. Though it wasn't so hard, now that the brace was off her left wrist and she had full use of that arm and hand again.

Mitch told her he was going to get her a pair of boxing gloves, or maybe two catcher's mitts to wear on her hands for protection.

She told him she would get him a football helmet to protect his head.

He'd suffered a severe concussion, and didn't even bother to protest when the emergency room doctor told him he'd have to remain in the hospital for several days.

That was fine with Rileigh. His room was two floors down and at the other end of the hall from the room where Georgia was recuperating from smoke inhalation, and Rileigh liked having them both together like that. Convenient.

Safe, but she didn't say that part out loud.

Mitch was released from the hospital a day after they let Georgia go, and Rileigh insisted on driving him home, where he would have to recuperate for another two weeks before he returned to work.

To work as the Sheriff of Yarmouth County. The mayor had been totally backed into a corner when Rileigh got in touch with Melissa Mendosa of WATE 6 News and told her what'd happened to Mitch, how he'd been fired for warning the tourists. And how he had found and stopped the serial killer — was severely injured doing it — even after his badge had been stripped away. That he'd even saved the Great Smoky Mountains National Park itself by uncovering the locations of incendiary devices that would have burned it to the ground.

The mayor had actually come to Mitch's hospital room to offer him his job back, to apologize for losing his temper, saying it was all a terrible misunderstanding. Why, he'd never really *fired* Mitch, would never do such a thing. Mitch took what he said all wrong, that's all, blew it all out of proportion.

Mitch said that watching Sundeep Singh announce he would be running against Rutherford for mayor next fall was worth getting bonked on the head.

Rileigh said that nothing was worth having her fingers sliced open to the bone, but she had to admit it had been gloriously fulfilling to see Deputy Mullins slap handcuffs on Frank Smothers and throw him in the back of a cruiser.

Beau had allowed her to come and watch the arrest. The charge was attempted murder for trapping Georgia in the building and then setting fire to it. He should have been charged with Felony Stupid, too, for leaving a gasoline can covered with his fingerprints in the woods behind the building.

Rileigh lifted her gloved hand to her eyes and shaded them from the sun as she carried the small bucket of chicken feed out into the chicken yard. She had been enjoying the sunshine, enjoying the air scented with pine and cedar, until it was scented with chicken shit instead.

"Here chick, chick, chick," she said as she tossed the feed out to the birds. "Here chick, chick–"

She heard the distinctive ring of her cell phone — far off— and realized she had left it on the kitchen table. She'd never get to it before whoever was calling hung up, so she hoped they'd leave a message.

Then she heard the ring cut off in the middle, heard her mother's voice. Mama had picked the phone up off the table and answered it. It was probably Georgia, asking Rileigh to stop by the grocery store on her way home from work tomorrow to pick up some bananas.

Mama stepped out onto the porch, her face wreathed in a glowing smile. She held the phone out toward where Rileigh stood just inside the chicken yard and called out:

"Rileigh, it's for you, dear. It's Jillian."

The End

What To Read Next:

Elderly women are disappearing from inside a locked ward at a psychiatric hospital.

Ex-police officer Rileigh Bishop thought she was done with her aunt after the old woman was committed to a psychiatric hospital for attacking Rileigh with a chainsaw.

She was wrong.

Pick up your copy of Closer By The Hour today.

About The Author

Lauren Street has always loved a mystery. As a kid growing up in bible belt country she devoured every whodunit book she could get her sticky little hands on and secretly investigated all of her (seemingly) normal boring neighbors. Sometimes their pets and farm animals too. All grown up now and living in the UK with her thoroughly unsuspicious (and often unsuspecting) husband, she writes domestic psychological thrillers about families torn apart by secrets and lies. And she sometimes still peers over garden walls to check up on the neighbors.

Also By Lauren Street

The Bishop Smoky Mountain Thrillers

Hide Me Away

Fuel To The Flame

Closer By The Hour

A Gamble Either Way

www.ingramcontent.com/pod-product-compliance
Lightning Source LLC
Chambersburg PA
CBHW010533100726
47903CB00011B/2992